WELL SORTED

The London Short Story Collection 2

WELL SORTED

The London Short Story Collection 2

EDITED BY THE
LONDON ARTS BOARD

Library of Congress Catalog Card Number: 95-69751

A catalogue record for this book can be obtained from the British Library on request

These stories are works of fiction. Any resemblance to actual persons or events is purely coincidental

First published in 1995 by
Serpent's Tail, 4 Blackstock Mews, London N4, and
180 Varick Street, 10th floor, New York, NY 10014

Phototypeset in Sabon by Intype Limited, London
Printed in Great Britain by Cox & Wyman Ltd, Reading, Berks.

Contents

Preface vii

London Underground *Tim Connery* 1

A Mackintosh Sky *Sheena Joughin* 14

The Enigma of Fur *Deborah Levy* 26

Trigger *Crispin Green* 35

The Scent of Strawberries *Alison Love* 62

Mates 4 Life *John Riethmüller* 74

Some Londoners *Lauretta Ngcobo* 82

The Mongoose Factor *Simon Miles* 98

The Bracelets *Marion Molteno* 107

Strange Attractors *Hari Kunzru* 115

Changes *Francis King* 127

Hearts and Flowers *Deirdre Shanahan* 141

The Traffic is at a Standstill at the Hangar Lane Gyratory System *Elspeth Edwards* 150

The Choice is Yours *Mark Walder* 161

Millennium *Atima Srivastava* 175

Lost Maps of London *Geoff Nicholson* 194

Rosa's Ritmo *Alix Edwards* 204

Coming Down South *Alan Day* 216

The Apotheosis of Lea Bridge Road *Iain Sinclair* 223

Ice *Kirsty Seymour-Ure* 237

Lost and Found *Alan Tuppen* 248

About the Authors 255

Preface

The inaugural London Short Story Competition in 1992 resulted in the anthology *Smoke Signals*, an eloquent testimony to the vitality of writing in London in the early 1990s. Two years on, the second Competition attracted more than 450 stories, which revealed both a passion for writing in the capital and an extraordinary wealth of imagination. The main Competition was judged, with exemplary diligence and good humour, by Esther Freud, Blake Morrison and Marina Warner. This year, for the first time, there is an additional award, the Jack Trevor Story Memorial Prize for the best funny story, which was both sponsored and judged by Michael Moorcock.

Five writers – Francis King, Deborah Levy, Lauretta Ngcobo, Iain Sinclair and Atima Srivastava – were spared months of anxiety over whether their work would be included, as their stories were specially commissioned for the anthology. To these writers, the four judges and all others involved in making the Competition such a success, many thanks.

Literary culture in London comprises many diverse elements. The London Short Story Competition is rare in bringing together so many of them in a common enterprise. Its continuing success means that it will be a pleasure for the London Arts Board to launch the third Competition, in the summer of 1996.

John Hampson
Principal Literature Officer
London Arts Board
May 1995

WELL SORTED

The London Short Story Collection 2

London Underground

TIM CONNERY

It's not easy being a ghost. Most of the time it is dead boring. There is nothing to do but watch and listen to living people and, take it from me, when your haunt is the London Underground system one hour's aimless drifting around the tube tunnels listening to the complaints of the living can seem like several dull lifetimes.

Once I was alive. Now *that* was exciting, especially on the night I mugged the old lady only to find out that she wasn't an old lady but a WPC in disguise who kneed me in the groin and punched me in the face and made the mistake of thinking I was finished. She paused to take her handcuffs out while her two colleagues were running over, and I made the most of the opportunity to stab her with the blade I had taped to my boot. I took off as the two burly PCs hesitated, undecided as to whether to help their fallen comrade or batter me into oblivion. In the end they split it; one stayed and one chased me across Tottenham Court Road into the entrance to Warren Street tube, over the barriers, down the escalator and on to the Northern Line southbound platform, where my momentum carried me forward on to the rails and right into the path of a train. A quick flash of a terrified driver's face under the word Kennington, the sound of people screaming and then blackness. It was as quick as that.

You'll have heard of near death experiences and people walking along tunnels towards a bright light; well, that happened to me, only when I emerged from the tunnel I found myself on the platform at Warren Street where I had so daringly tested the tube driver's reflexes. I knew I was dead and I knew I was a ghost; I had started my tedious afterlife. The rules soon became clear: I could not be seen or heard, nor could I touch anything. I could only haunt that part of the Underground which was underground; if I tried to ride one of the trains which went above ground at some point I never would make it: as soon as the train started to leave the underground tunnel I would suddenly find myself back on another train pulling into Warren Street, the Northern Line southbound. Always Warren Street. I hate it.

The boredom was chronic from the start. Hour after hour, day after day, month after month I listlessly dragged my ethereal body around, wondering how long this tedious part of existence would last. And then, on the first anniversary of my death, something weird happened. It was late, and I was on the last Victoria Line tube to Brixton. There was only one passenger on the train, a youngish bloke reading a book. Suddenly he shivered, and looked around. His eyes fell on the spot where I would have been if I had a body and I swear I actually saw his hair stand on end. His eyes bulged, he stood up, his jaw fell open and he pointed at me and screamed.

'Oh my God! No! Oh my God!'

I looked around, bewildered, and then I saw it. In the reflection in the window I saw this being, this hideous thing. It had half a face, the other half was missing, had been ripped off. Its one eye was hanging out of its socket. Its flesh was white and marbled with dried blood. It was dressed in rags. I raised my arm in horror, and the creature raised its arm. It was me.

'Oh my God! No! Oh my God!' I screamed in unison with the young bloke. He looked like a cartoonist's vision of a man who had just seen a ghost, and I knew how he felt. I had never seen one before either, and the fact that it was me didn't make it any easier. We screamed at each other for ages, then he fainted. I must have passed out too, because the next thing I know I'm at bastard Warren Street again. Since then, on my deathday, I make sure I am nowhere near anything reflective.

I can leave out the next fifty years because they were all the same to me. Even though I have no real body and consequently no eyes, I swear my eyes have watered constantly with boredom. Then, one day, I read the headline on someone's paper: LONDON UNDERGROUND TO BE FRANCHISED. That was the end of it. Non-profit making stations were closed down, leading to a shoddy service that eventually collapsed. The underground system was dead. No one had the capital to restart it. The miles of empty tunnels became a haven for the homeless; those who were mad or desperate enough to have to live on the streets moved in and colonised. They formed groups and little tribes of their own at the various stops on all the different lines. There were fights and disputes over territories, but most of the time it was peaceful. Five years of this, and then another change. I don't know what had been happening up on the surface, but someone somewhere must've made the decision to get rid of the homeless problem once and for all: they sealed them underground.

Tunnels were bricked up, station entrances filled with concrete. The homeless were sealed in catacombs that corresponded exactly to my own haunting ground. Perhaps on the surface there was some sort of outcry, but it was never heard down here. For about a year food, water, clothing and medical supplies were sent down the lift shaft at Russell Square, but then the lifts stopped coming.

The next ten years were dreadful. Disease and hunger spread. I thought they would all die. Most of them did, but some adapted. I saw evolution in action. Survival of the fittest? Depends how you define fittest. If 'fittest' means the ability to live off rats, to drink filthy water that trickles through the curved walls of the oldest stations, being able to breathe stale, stagnant air and being able to mate with your fellow grey, shrivelled mutants, then yes, the fittest did survive.

And I move among them now, marvelling at their ability at having survived down here for over forty years.

Billy sits at the bottom of a curved tiled wall, watching the rat on the rail. It is gloomy here; the only light comes from the flickering candle on the wall. The candle is actually made from the fat of Billy's dead mother. He doesn't know that her adipose tissue has been put to such use, but it wouldn't bother him if he did, for his is a society where recycling is a way of life, and he never knew his mother anyway. He watches the rat and removes a catapult from inside the rags he wears. He loads a sharp stone and takes careful aim, his ill-educated brain making complicated ballistic calculations. He fires and misses; the rat scurries off. No food for Billy now. He picks irately at the scab on his scalp, chucking away the clump of matted hair that comes off with it. He gets to his feet and shuffles off back to the main platform where Max gives him the standard greeting, holding his hand out with the palm upwards in the universal begging fashion.

'Hungry and homeless,' says Max.

'Hungry and homeless,' says Billy, returning the greeting.

'She's worse,' says Max. 'You've got to come.'

They walk towards the tube train rusting at the side of the platform. Each compartment of the train has been turned into a home, with plastic sheeting covering the doorways like tent flaps. Someone is roasting a rat over an open fire outside one of the doorways. Naked toddlers cavort around the flame, chased by hideous in-bred dogs. Although I have no real sense organs I find the smell is overpowering. The platform smells like a toilet (but not as bad as their toilets – their smell you wouldn't believe). Max and Billy duck through the plastic sheeting of the last compartment.

Inside it is relatively tidy, except for the plastic crates, bits of metal, rubbish and dirty clothing strewn all over the place. Mary, Max's little girl, sits on the floor trying to trap a cockroach in a tin. She looks up at Billy and smiles, holding out her hand with the palm upwards.

'Hungry and homeless,' she says.

Billy nods in reply. Like most teenagers he is a moody bastard.

Max takes Billy over to a filthy bed where a young woman, whose name I have never been able to get, lies sweating in a fever. Max pulls the covers off her, revealing her gangrenous legs. Billy leaps back, his hand over his nose. The smell must be bad for him to notice it, so I loiter at a safe distance.

'Ugh! What's that smell?'

'Her legs,' sighs Max. 'See? They've gone bad. Rotten. They're just not healing.'

'They've gone off,' concurs Dr Billy. 'I expect you want me to go Northbound now?'

'It's her only hope. That tribe at Russell Square have got the stuff to cure her. You must go for me, Billy.'

'They won't give it out unless you have got something of

real value to trade. And they're religious nutters. It's hard to guess what they would want.'

Max replaces the covers over the young woman. 'I have got something they'll want,' he says. 'But you'll have to guard it with your life.

Max turns and passes through me, walking towards the back of the train. He kneels and pulls up a section of the floor, removing something covered in sacking. He handles it gingerly.

'This is valuable. And easily breakable. You mustn't unwrap it, Billy. It mustn't get damaged. It's been in my family for years.'

Billy stares in awe.

'Is it a holyrelicantique? From the surface?' he asks.

'Yeah. A real holyrelicantique.'

'It better be real,' says Billy. 'They kill fakers.'

Billy takes the wrapped parcel, a cylinder about a foot long and seven inches wide, and puts it in the bag he has slung over his shoulder.

'Okay,' he says. 'I'll do it. But remember our deal. I get all my meat from you for free.'

'Yeah. And just to show you I mean it – Mary!'

Mary looks up from her cockroach. 'What?' she whines.

'Get Billy his meat.'

Mary tuts and goes over to a chest. She rummages about inside it and pulls out three dead black rats with their tails knotted together. Billy licks his lips.

I move past them to go outside and they all shudder.

'It's cold in here,' says Billy.

'It's not usually,' says Max. 'I wonder where that draught is coming from?'

I had forgotten that this evening is the hundredth anniversary of my death. I had better be careful.

I am following Billy along a dark tunnel. We have been walking for hours in the dark. I know Billy has the sensation that he is being followed because he keeps turning and looking back. He won't see anything, even with his blazing torch held high, for I won't become visible for a few hours more, so it gives me a kick to spook him a little now, just to keep him on his toes. We emerge from the tunnel and Billy hops on to the graffiti-covered platform. He scrapes the dirt off the London Underground sign and I see we are at the Embankment. Billy suddenly jerks back, every muscle tense, his nostrils twitching. Three figures appear at the other end of the platform.

'You're dead!' shouts one, and for a minute I think they're talking to me, but then they run at Billy.

I am jealous of Billy. I used to love fighting, that rush of adrenalin, the high of hearing your opponent cry out, the whacking, slapping, punching, kicking, cracking . . . The urge to turn bone to jelly. Even now, with no hormones and no circulatory system, I can feel that exciting chill flowing through my non-existent veins. Billy, you lucky bastard . . .

Lucky bastard Billy tugs at his waist, pulling out a chain with a spiked ball at the end. He whirls it above his head and leaps at his attackers. He is extraordinary. He reminds me of me when I was alive; he can take it and he can give it out. His opponents don't stand a chance because Billy doesn't care about being hurt or maimed or killed, he concentrates on the *now* of the fight, not what might happen to him.

Billy kills one of them and leaves the other two dying. I watch, wondering if I might see another ghost rise from the body of the dead one, but nothing happens. (It never does. In my one hundred years down here I have seen many deaths but not one other single dead soul.) I follow Billy, battered and bleeding but triumphant, as he limps along the platform. We move on.

Several hours later, thanks to Billy's complete lack of a sense of direction, we arrive at Russell Square.

The old Piccadilly Line tunnel is knee deep in water, and Billy wades cautiously through it as we approach the station. Russell Square is full of the robed maniacs that live there: men, women and children all dressed in white (or as close to white as you'll get down here) sheets and all staring down at Billy as he sloshes along the track. Billy stops and stretches his arm out, palm upwards.

'Hungry and homeless,' he says.

One of the robed men raises his arms and lifts his face towards the ceiling.

'Mind the gap!' he yells.

'Mind the doors!' the others yell back, raising their arms.

'Will passengers please mind the gap and stand clear of the doors!' the first man rejoins.

It is their holy greeting. A weird lot, this bunch, whose conversations can sometimes consist entirely of catechisms of old tube train announcements or advertising slogans off the long-faded posters on the walls. It doesn't seem to bother Billy, though; he has the same gormless expression as usual.

A tinny banging sound comes from nearby, and as Billy hoists himself off the track on to the platform the crowd parts and a small procession comes forward. Leading the procession is a small boy banging an ancient empty paint pot. Behind him is a slightly bigger boy carrying a large bound book, and following him is the man who I recognise as their priest. The priest wears his traditional flame-coloured robes, has his hair in dreadlocks and his beard long and matted. He looks like Rasputin on LSD.

'What,' he says, eyes riveted on Billy, 'do you want?'

'I have brought you a holyrelicantique.'

The crowd all gasp and start blessing themselves with the sign of the cross, calling out as they do so:

'Spectacles! Testicles! Wallet! And Watch!'

'Silence, my flock!' roars the priest, and he addresses Billy again. 'Many come bearing holyrelicantiques. Few are genuine. Would you like to see the last man to bring a fake?'

From inside his robes the priest produces a skull.

'Alas, poor relic. His death was hell.' He smiles amiably at the skull and then tosses it casually over his shoulder and grins at Billy. 'I've shown you mine. Now you show me yours.'

Slowly, his eyes never leaving the priest's face, Billy reaches into his bag and pulls out the parcel and gives it to the priest, who carefully unwraps it. The priest's face changes from spiteful (but insane) to astonished (but insane).

'I . . . don't believe it!'

He holds up a dusty brown bottle. I move closer as the priest blows dust off the label, and the writing there takes me back a century. In his hands the priest is reverently holding a Woodpecker cider bottle.

'A chalice!' the priest cries. 'A genuine holy chalice!' He shows the bottle to the crowd, pointing at the picture of the woodpecker. 'See the emblem of the Holy Dove, symbolising the Holy Spirits!'

'Spectacles! Testicles! Wallet! And watch!' The crowd bless themselves.

'May the Holy Spirits come among you!' says the priest.

'Whisky! Vodka! Gin! Meths!' cry his people.

The priest turns moist-eyed to Billy. 'Oh Angel of the Holy Chalice, how can we thank you?'

Billy seems more sure of himself now. 'There is someone

sick back where I come from. She needs something to cure her. Her legs have gone off.'

'Fetch the Holy Panacea! Fetch the Universal Cure-All!'

The small boy bangs the pot. A weak-sounding trumpet (more like a kazoo) rasps from nearby. People start rejoicing. The priest turns to Billy.

'You must stay for tea,' he says politely. 'But first, a quick mass in your honour.'

His people gather around him. Billy stands uncertainly while all the others kneel. The boy with the large book hands it to the priest, who opens it to reveal a front cover of *The Big Issue*.

'In the name of the Big Issue,' he says, turning the page to reveal a front page of *The Sun*. 'And of the Sun.' He picks up the empty bottle of Woodpecker. 'And of the Holy Spirits.'

'Amen,' the congregation reply.

The priest opens the book at a *Sun* editorial. I can read it quite clearly: in large letters it says BURY THE HOMELESS SCUM. He lifts his eyes to heaven and prays.

'And the Big Issue said to His Sun: Put my children underground out of harm's way. And His Sun did and, yea, His children went forth and multiplied, on the Northern, the Central, the District, the Bakerloo, the Jubilee. And verily did He give unto them a Travelcard for zones One, Two and Three.'

'Valid after 9.30am weekdays,' the others respond.

'And at Russell Square He did send down manna from heaven, and when His children fell ill, He sent the Cure-All, the Holy Panacea.'

The boy bangs the paint pot, and a woman solemnly approaches the priest bearing a small, tatty green and yellow box. The priest takes it and looks at Billy.

'Billy, bringer of the Holy Chalice, take this back with our blessing.'

He motions for Billy to hold out his hand. Billy does, and I see the box clearly: it is an old Anadin box. The priest shakes it so that a single tablet falls into Billy's hand. The crowd start chanting.

'Nothing. Acts faster. Than Anadin.'

'And now – ' the priest stops, and stares oddly in my direction. 'What is . . . that?'

All eyes turn towards me. I feel funny, faint. A mist seems to be gathering around me. People start backing away. The mist glows, becomes luminous.

'What is it?' asks Billy, staring fascinated at me.

'I don't know', says the priest.

The horror that is my ghostly apparition is starting to become more defined.

'I don't think I want to hang about to find out!' says the priest, and he takes off.

I am totally visible now. A horror from beyond the grave. People start screaming and running in all directions. I shuffle towards Billy.

'Billy,' I try to say, but all that comes out of my half jaw is an unearthly groan, one that scares the life out of me and sends Billy scrambling off after the priest.

I follow them. For some reason I feel an affinity for Billy. In this moment I have when I will be able to contact a human being after a hundred years of silence I feel I must talk to Billy. For the first time in my life – if life is the right word – I feel like offering help to someone. I want to tell him about gangrene, how to stop its spread. I want to tell him about life after death, warn him about its horrors. I drag my twisted body through snaking corridors, always managing to keep Billy and the priest in sight. The priest scrabbles madly at rubble obscuring a doorway and screams as I approach. Billy pushes past him, diving through a small hole in the rubble and I follow. We are in a dank, dark lift shaft.

'Wait, Billy!' I mean to say, but what comes out is 'Ugh! Igghy!'

Billy panics and scratches at the walls of the shaft. The bricks are loose and crumbly; he easily makes handholds and starts climbing the walls. I pursue him, my scary hands also finding purchase, and we climb quickly. His path is blocked by the old lift at the top, but fear gives him strength and he punches his way through the weak rusted flooring. I follow him into the lift. The doors are open and he runs out into the ticket hall of Russell Square station, rushing about looking for a way out, but the entrance is bricked up. And then I see it.

There, in the bottom corner of the blocked doorway, a circular hole, about the size of my hand. A rat is emerging from it, and, as it plops on to the floor, daylight – the first daylight I have seen for a century – streams in after it. I lunge at the hole, pushing what is left of my face at it, sucking in . . . *Fresh air!* Sweet, glorious fresh air! My head spins, and I claw wildly at the hole, widening it in minutes, just enough for me to squeeze my twisted head and shoulders through. I drag the rest of my body out into the open.

The sunlight hurts my eyes, and it takes a while for my vision to clear. I am surprised to find I am standing on grass. The huge hotels around Russell Square are mossy ruins. The sky is blue. Birds are singing, and that is the only noise. A warm breeze blows across me. I look down at my hands; they look normal. My clothes are no longer rags. I feel my face, and realise it is whole again. A whimpering behind me makes me look around: it is Billy, staring out of the hole in the wall. He looks petrified, but it is not of me, it is of the huge expanse of the blue sky. It is blowing his mind. I realise now how inhuman he looks, with his wolf-like ears and huge spider-monkey eyes. His eyes are watering with pain as they try to take in the daylight, and then he pulls himself away, back into his dark world, as I rise up, up into the blue, noting the ruined city beneath me and marvelling at its tranquil beauty.

As I rise into the sky I notice a tunnel with a light at the end of it, and I will myself towards it.

A Mackintosh Sky

SHEENA JOUGHIN

He was kissing me, very badly. He obviously had to think to do it, so while his hands were sticking to bits of my trunk, trying to find something to pull up, or down, or off, his tongue was resting. It rested on mine, thick and filling, like a spare lip in my mouth. I felt like biting it. Eventually he found a way through to one of my breasts and moved his mouth to that. We heard my breathing change.

'Take your jumper off,' he said, and rolled on top of me. 'I can smell you,' he said, for some reason.

I could smell him. The top of his head was a twisted mix of Silk Cut and scent and Blue Stilton. Stilton soup had been soup of the day, again. I'd scratched it on to the downstairs blackboard myself, and nearly broken my leg when the chair I was stretching from had collapsed. They often did that. Nick used to keep a camping chair behind the bar, and take it out to sit on if he came in for a night-cap. The customers were too fat.

'I want you,' said Dusty, and moved his legs apart so I was trapped between them. I felt rather sick. The collar of his shirt was poking my nose. I could barely breathe, with his wardrobe-weight pressed against me.

'I think I'm going to throw up,' I said. 'Could you get off?' I opened my eyes to see the tassels of my standard lamp making tiny jerks above my head. I belched some cheesy red wine.

'I feel sick,' I said.

'You're gorgeous,' he said. 'Take your jumper off.'

He explained that he'd been wanting to take my jumper off all night, which seemed unauthentic, since he'd been flirting with Alison since the place opened. They'd been leaning into each other, drinking Buck's Fizz as I arrived for my seven-thirty start. There were no ashtrays on the tables and there was no water in the fridge. She'd been sheathed in her usual black elastic. He'd only walked me home because I'd said I needed more drink and taken two bottles from behind the bar. Pilfering, we called it, rather than stealing. We were very badly paid.

I usually tried to get drunk before I went to bed that summer, because Nick had left me. Well I'd left him, but he'd been seeing someone else, so I had to everyone said. Every other customer who came in told me about the Spanish girl he was with in the Dome. I told them he was teaching her Gaelic, which was what he told me, but in the end I started not sleeping and I left a bitter note one morning and moved back to Sterndale Road. I hadn't seen him since, although everyone said he was in a state and she'd gone back to wherever she came from. Perhaps I should see him. I still couldn't sleep. I told Dusty the mean details and the measure of my unhappiness as we chain-smoked, back at my place.

'Sex,' he'd said. 'You need some good sex, to clear your head. He's a mummy's boy. You were wasted on him.' Then he blew in my ear and we lay on the couch and my feet ached and I felt drunk. Nick always said it was best to be sick.

'Get off,' I said to Dusty's stubble, and he did this time. He lay on his back, and trailed his right hand around my crotch.

'I'm going to the bathroom,' I told him.

'I'll be waiting for you,' he smiled. He had tiny teeth.

'You're gorgeous,' he called to my back.

'Shut up,' I said, and I held the door handle for a swaying moment before I attempted the stairs.

When I got back, after swilling out the bath, I felt much better. Dusty was snoring, on his back with his arms by his side, like a fallen boulder on the couch. I needed a cigarette to clear my mouth but all the packets were empty or stuffed with wrinkled stubs. I lit the longest butt I could find, which tasted disgusting. I must get to a Seven–Eleven.

'I'm going to find some cigarettes,' I said to the lump on my couch. It snored evenly on.

'I'll buy you some too.' I unfolded his jacket from the back of a chair and took a fiver from the inside pocket. Then I spread it on top of him to keep him warm and hoped he wouldn't mind the money. I'd get Silk Cut – he liked those. You couldn't call it stealing. I pulled my bra straps right and tucked everything in and looked at myself in the mirror. I was very flushed. I was twenty-six. I smoothed my hair down and put on some lipstick and laced my shoes and found my bag and left the room. The Seven–Eleven was about a twenty-minute trip, one way. Dusty might wake up and go home. I left the light on. I checked that I had my key before I pulled the front door behind me and moved into the warm wet outside air. I noticed that I couldn't walk in a straight line and that the streetlamps were blue. A cyclist passed, spinning light rain from his glossy tyres.

'Hi,' I said to him.

'Hi,' he said.

Outside Au Temps Perdu, the black bags of empties that I'd dragged up to the dustbins a couple of hours before were waterlogged and leaning. I kicked one to hear the bottles ring. I locked my hands over my head to block the steady rain as I loped on through pooled leaves and litter, singing 'Every Time We Say Goodbye'. We'd had it on that night a lot. Alison liked it best.

Across Brook Green I slowly sang and down the Shepherd's Bush Road. Too much movement there. People with beer cans and bare limbs and lorries and unstuck posters. Cars, with headlamp rain and steam-train smoke. Too wide and noisy, with sirens. So back into a side-street with festoon blinds and coloured doors and narrow pavements. Low houses with families and gates. Occasional skips, half-blocking my way, and floorboards, and a narrow mattress, and a car alarm. And then a pair of legs, with cowboy boots on the end of them, sticking out of a blanket. A snoring man on his back at three-thirty in the morning, halfway down Luxemburg Gardens, where in Paris of course there are always men asleep. They sleep on their backs there too. Flat-out. Unafraid of what might fall from the sky, or of passers-by trying to kill them. I couldn't sleep like that if you paid me, but men don't seem to mind. This one was clearly very drunk. He didn't stir when I patted him with my foot, so I bent down to check he was not hurt, and I realised that it was Jasper, Suzanne's man. One of our most regular punters. And not a blanket on top of him, but a coat. Suzanne's blue cotton coat, that I'd helped her to find on the coat rack as she left. She'd left with Jasper, after-hours as usual, banging into collapsing chairs and holding one another through the door. Jasper had kissed me tenderly goodbye, and said see you very soon, and what a nice dress I was wearing and, 'Enjoy it, you're a long time dead, remember', which was what he often said when he was drunk. I was fond of him. He helped with the rubbish, and had a high forehead I liked, like Nick. It was lolling back now on to a tumbled wall, so I felt it to check the temperature, like you do with sick children. It was cool and solid. He seemed at rest. I was tempted to lie down beside him, but I could see that it would be putting things off. I tucked his coat covering firmly round him and pulled the collar up over his chin, and then I felt the brooch there, which Suzanne wore on most of her clothes. Her Art Nouveau tulip head, upturned for the taking. I mustn't leave it there. I must take it to her, before I did anything else. It was silver. And I must ask her why Jasper was asleep in the street. Perhaps she would come to collect him. She lived nearby, off the Fulham Palace Road. It would be nice to see her. She would probably have cigarettes and anyway, she liked me. She'd held my hand as I'd served her banana meringue thing that night, and asked if I'd been in touch with Nick. She knew all about everything because I always asked her. She wore strappy sandals, like mothers in old photographs, and red lipstick, and laughed a lot, and held court on emotional matters. 'See what Suzanne says when she comes in,' we'd say to each other: it was the best advice to give. But I think we thought she lived with Jasper. Maybe they'd had a row. She'd know what to do about Dusty on my couch, anyway, and feeling so drunk. She might let me stay with her. I unpinned the brooch and fastened it to my jumper, and set off. At the bend in the road I turned to shout goodbye to Jasper. Perhaps he would wake up and go home, wherever that was.

Something thudded against the basement window, from the inside where the light was, as I negotiated the steps down to Suzanne's front door.

'Stuff Jasper's farm in France,' a male voice shouted. 'Stuff the marinated peaches.'

A woman made a noise, and then I rang the doorbell, pleased that its green square button that shone seemed to be staying still. I noticed that I was still humming 'Every Time We Say Goodbye'. It sounded rather nice. I ran my hand over the tulip brooch. They would be glad to see me.

I rang the bell again until a man was standing in front of me, with a hallway behind him. He was wearing a Fair-isle jumper that confused me because it was like the ones my mother used to knit. It seemed like Nick's, that I wear. He stared at me, so I stared back.

'Suzanne's in bed,' he said.

'I am not in bed,' Suzanne shouted, and walked out of a door frame with no door, which she then leaned back onto. She had a glass in her hand.

'Chrissie, darling,' she smiled out, so I walked in past the jumper and she slid towards me to hold my arm through the shapes of the paintings on the wall.

'I found your brooch, on your coat,' I explained. 'On Jasper, in Luxemburg Gardens. He was asleep.'

'Passed out, more like,' said the man.

'Did he seem okay?' Suzanne asked, frowning into my face. 'I've never seen him so wrecked before. He's lost his keys. He's hopeless. Did he seem okay?'

'I'd say he's very comfortable,' I nodded as she pulled me into a kitchen, by my fingers, like a child.

'This is Oliver,' she told me. 'We're divorced. His cigarette lighter has just broken.'

'I've got one', I said, 'But nothing to light.'

'Perfect,' she smiled and lifted a pack from a half-finished crossword puzzle, lying across the table. We smoked. I didn't sit down, but Suzanne did, crossing her legs up on to the chair next to hers.

'This is Chrissie, Ol,' she exhaled, as she crushed her filter into a saucer. 'She works at Temps Perdu.' Then she said 'My mother's dying.'

Oliver took a peach from a box of them, on the floor, and a knife from the table clutter. He started finely slicing the fruit, and said Suzanne was being hysterical.

'Ring the hospital, stupid,' he partly shouted. I was surprised Suzanne let someone call her stupid, and surprised that she had a mother to die. My mother was dead already. I sat down.

'Just ring them up, for Christ's sake. No one said anything about death, to me. They just said she's had a mild stroke, that's all.'

'Are you sure? They didn't say she might die?' Suzanne seemed to be still holding my fingers.

'Of course not. Why should she die? She's tucked up in a nice white bed, being taken care of. And even if she was, they wouldn't have told me. They don't say things like that on the phone. I'm just a man taking a message. A message my wife is ignoring.' He glared at me. 'Although I've been waiting for her for three hours. I don't even like her mother.'

'Oh that's nice.' Suzanne turned to stare at me too. 'My mother knitted the jumper he's wearing. She gave us her car.'

'The car that you wrote off six weeks later.' Oliver poured himself a drink from one of three half bottles of our House Red, open on the tabletop. I wondered how they'd got there, as Oliver ate peach. Suzanne watched him, carefully, and then:

'How did you get in here, anyway? How come you were here when they rang. The house isn't a wine-bar, you know, that you just call into. And stop drinking my wine.' Oliver put his glass down.

'I got in by using my door-key. My key to my house

where my son lives, remember? The one you asked me to call in and say hullo to, remember?'

'The one who always stays with my sister on Fridays, remember?'

'Look, ring the hospital. Have a drink. Or don't have a drink, in fact. You're drunk. Just make the phone-call, then we can all go to bed. It's four o'clock in the morning.'

We all looked at the would-be station clock, above the door. It was four-eighteen, in fact. Suzanne poured herself another drink.

'Stop bossing me about. I'll ring when I'm ready.' She stood up then sat down again.

'When did they call, anyway? Was it ages ago? How long does it take, when they have a stroke?'

'How long does what take?'

Suzanne put her head on her arms. I took a peach and started to peel it. I asked where her mother was but no one answered. Suzanne had started to cry, noisily, with a lot of gulping in of air. It sounded like my own crying in the mornings then, when I would wake up and feel the terrible gap of the day. It was tiring to cry like that. Like being sick, but in reverse.

'Don't cry, Suzanne,' said her husband, like men do, watching. Then he walked around the table to her and stroked her hair, which was red and had been tied up but was now half-down. He lifted odd strands from around her face, to tuck them into something. He was surprisingly good at it. It looked quite neat when she lifted her head.

'I can't,' she sniffed, rubbing her nose with her hand. She bit into a finger. 'I can't ask them. What if she's dead already?' She pushed her face into the zig-zags of his jumper. She squeezed the folds of his corduroy legs. Her chin was in his groin.

'You do it Ollie,' she whimpered. 'Ring for me, please. Just this once.' She took his hand and kissed it.

'Please,' she said, then looked at me.

I felt I should do it if he wouldn't, but he said he would, after a while of silence, so I started peeling my peach again and tried to remember which of my sisters had told me about my mother that night. We used to take it in turns to be with her. It was always too hot in the hospital. Then too cold at home. Nick was away. I went to the wine-bar and rang him from there, when I found out, so I wouldn't be lonely when he said goodbye. I talked to Dusty, I think, late on. I seem to remember he was helpful. I suppose he was still married then.

It was a long time ago.

Oliver was still collecting Suzanne's hair up on to the top of her head. I thought I should leave, but didn't want to disturb them.

'Have a cigarette,' I said to the room, and felt foolish.

'I'll ring,' Oliver decided. 'I'll do it now. Have a cigarette.'

He went into the hall to the phone and we heard him saying 'my wife' and 'I see' and 'fine' and 'thank you' as we smoked together.

'Your hair looks lovely,' I said, 'like that.' And then Oliver was in the room again saying it was all okay but Suzanne should go up there, and looking in his pockets for a wallet and telling her to take something to read. He said he'd wait home for word. He explained that I would walk her down to the tube, so I stood up and went to the door, while they kissed I supposed, and then Suzanne and I were out in the rain, under a mackintosh sky, saying nothing. I hummed 'Every Time We Say Goodbye' for a few yards, then stopped, but carried it on in my head.

At the tube station Suzanne remembered Jasper. I said I'd ring Oliver for her and ask him to go and check up on him, if she liked. Or we could ring the police and tell them he was there.

'What would you do?' she asked, very pale in her black plastic, and I said I wouldn't do anything if I was her, with everything else to do.

'He'll manage,' I said. 'Have you got change for a ticket?'

She hadn't, and neither had I. I only had Dusty's five pound note. She had a twenty, from Oliver. We walked through the swimming pool light of the ticket hall, with the opening flower-stall and the mirror on the photobooth, and the fluorescent-strip clock that said 5.31, and stared at the neat buttons of the wall of machines. Apparently they took notes. I smoothed the twenty into a slot.

'Press King's Cross,' Suzanne told me. 'We can walk from there. She's in UCH. Will you come too?' She watched the flower-stall man's dog. 'Please come with me, Chrissie.'

I bought two adult singles to King's Cross. I hoped the chocolate machine on the platform was working.

The tube was pleasingly empty; more suitcases on it than people. Great leather cases with airline labels sprawled around a dozing man with a moustache and no lips. Not a good kisser, I decided and wondered what had happened to Dusty. He'd be okay. Two girls talked and yawned to each other with their legs side by side and their feet up on the faded plaid seats. They too had bags. They were all from Heathrow, of course, at this time in the morning.

'Nice to be getting back to London on Saturday morning, all brown and sea-sidey,' I said to Suzanne at Baron's Court, where she had her head on my shoulder. She didn't answer. She was falling woozily asleep in the fluid movement of the train. Her hand was limp on my leg. I moved it on to her bag and watched the strip lights rush past the windows. We rocked in and out of more or less empty stations.

Earls Court.

A woman with a pleated skirt and the newspaper sat far away from us. I hoped we didn't smell of our trailing night. I felt filthy.

Gloucester Road.

'Sting A Burglar Today', I read above the No Smoking sign, next to a poem by Elizabeth Bishop about losing a watch and houses and a person. I stared at a picture of a giant wasp, and ate my last piece of fruit and nut. Strange that Jasper had lost his key. He had a Filofax and a mobile phone. He had a child, he'd told me once, drinking sweet strong white wine in a snowy late-night. Suzanne had fallen asleep that time too. She must be one of those people who sleeps when there's nothing to be done. I don't do that. I can't sleep until I've done everything I can.

South Kensington.

Knightsbridge.

The man with no mouth struggled his luggage out just in time. He would be staying in a hotel there. There were plenty.

Hyde Park Corner, with its brown and cream tiles, like a Jersey cow, and its arrows and its Way Out.

Suzanne started to softly snore, and re-crossed her legs. It would be Green Park next.

Green Park with its deckchairs, by the Rolls-Royce shops, where Nick and I spent our summer holiday once, and had a party on my birthday. There were no more buses by the time we left so we walked back through the park to the Palace gates and I was sick so we got a taxi. It cost £4.80 I remember, and we had to use all our change and had no money for the gas meter back at his house. Back at our house.

Suzanne's head lolled on to my breasts. I rolled it to rest

on her own seat-back, and hoped she would wake up before King's Cross.

I'd never met her mother.

At Green Park I stood up and I minded the gap and I gulped the dust. I liked the slam of the doors and the lurching away and I smiled into a poster of a beach in Greece, because I was going to Nick's. I would hail the pale light of a taxi, against the sweep of Piccadilly and the milky pool of the park, and I would pay with Dusty's five pound note. Suzanne couldn't blame me. She'd see that. I'd known Nick since I was seventeen. I had a key to his house. He still had one to mine. I didn't want to go to a hospital. I wanted to see a man I knew in his own bed, on his back.

The Enigma of Fur

DEBORAH LEVY

They call me Milkpaw on account of the white fur on my hand. I am a loser, an egoist and a would-be guru with a stash of aspirins in my bathroom cabinet. Small but perfectly formed, I proudly display my lovebites at every opportunity. My girlfriend Eddie calls me a London slut, but it's she who cruises for kicks and hustles for money while I do the Hoovering. Today she's gone off to swap coats with her pal – something suede for something leather, always on the look out for clothes that will kill her. I feel the same about music. I want to be killed by music.

I was offered eternal life via cryogenics but turned it down because I like there to be an end to things, even myself. It's true my false breasts and fur hand, both achieved via cosmetic intervention, make me happy, but artificial intelligence enhancements I cannot afford, and anyway Eddie likes her men thick. She says don't worry darling, you have a heart, a mind, and a conscience, what more could a man ask for?

Look, sometimes I yearn to live on a palm-lined drive in Florida, sunning myself at the edge of one of California's blue pools, singing testosterone-charged moody tunes out into the American sunset to accompany the surfers making their way home across the highways of blond sand, the Pacific rolling and moaning and everything in a petroleum haze. Don't think I have not dreamed of cruising America's tremendous steaming tarmac in a chrome machine, waving my milkpaw out of the window at bronzed brunettes in bikinis and neon baseball caps. But this is London with its caffs full of bacon fat and women with fleshy arms serving great plates of liver and potato to single blokes stuffing their pale faces, and deliquent suburban kids like myself, one time leader of a teenage motorcycle gang – factory fodder they called us in my dad's time, eating great fry-ups and doing the crossword puzzle. Yep. I, Milkpaw, am just a mess of biological drives: eating sleeping shitting shivering sweating, and sometimes, if Eddie's up for it, making love after midnight when the tubes have stopped running, and the late buses with their bad-tempered drivers heave and creak past shops selling sofas and wardrobes made from the trees of Norway. Gosh my sentences are getting longer: that's what narcissism does to language, you stuff it with yourself and it swells like cotton wool soaked in vodka. There's a mad woman who lives next door and every time I walk past her house she shouts, 'You're a sick man!' An ambulance came for her the other day, and two men carried her out on a stretcher. Something came over me and I haven't even been able to tell Eddie. I knelt down and kissed her, and stroked her forehead like she was some loony sleeping beauty and I a city prince. Except I did not want to wake her, I wanted to kiss her into sleep. Poor woman did not get to ride off with her prince on his horse, but in the last ambulance in London left for poor folk, rolling past the Asian corner shops and the large bank with its tinted windows and perfumed girls behind perspex. Has it always been like this? If I press H on my personal computer and then S for search it comes to History and it's blank. A blank file for me to fill in. So that is what I am doing now. Writing the history of Milkpaw into my personal computer.

Look, I am going to hang twenty plastic budgies made in Hong Kong on the little bay tree in the garden and marry Eddie. I'm going to wear a goatee beard for the occasion. I could wear a moustache, or a heavy metal kid wig but the goatee seems right and proper to take the vows. We're going to throw a summer party in our garden, despite the cat shit. There's two tulips out and four daffs and where we sowed some grass, rye seed from Woolworth's, there's a bit of green – drunk from April city rain that stings the eyes but makes plants grow. We dug the soil to plant the grass and now the cats have paws soaked with mud and everywhere inside the house, on carpets and chairs, are catpaw prints like fossils you find on rocky beaches.

We have lived through the ecstasy of catastrophe me and my girl. We press our toxic bodies against each other and make shopping lists, staring into mall windows like we stare at TV. We just get so much pleasure gazing into the windows, girl stroking my white fur, murmuring 'I love you tom cat.' She asks me what race nation colour and creed I belong to and I say I will have to look it up on my PC when we get home. But there are other things to do when we get home, which is why I write this at dawn when Eddie's out hustling or staying over at her mum's – she says her mother is her dearest thing after me. Her mum makes her little snacks when she's hungry or wired up: prawn mayonnaise on a bagel, cheese and homemade pickle, little jellies with fruit in them – sweet small things she dreams up to make for Eddie whom she adores and calls 'my youngest bottle blonde'.

My girl and I love to laze on the old kelim rug from somewhere in Persia. I inherited it from my grandpa who was something in oil in the old days. Our bodies are hesitant and love-soaked. The moon is oily, the trees swollen with black blossom against the flamingo chemical pink of the sky: a sight of awesome beauty, of decadence, of nature corrupted and thrilling. We order a takeaway from Pizza Express to soak up our hunger and celebrate living in the metropolis where everything is instant, coffee and pasta, joy and grief, where everything is volatile and moods swing between violence and tender makings up. Although our interior worlds are volcanic, exotic, troubled, the every day is beautifully predictable. Eddie and I eat eggs on Sundays, read the world press, smile at our playful cats and make phone calls to friends. We say things like you're looking lovely today, or do you want another cup of coffee, and lots of do you remember when we did such and such? We endlessly discuss what we were feeling at the time, the mood and colour of it, a passing comment that meant something, a row that had us both in tears – we both cry easily and never carry handkerchiefs. After breakfast we get dressed and browse in bookshops or go tadpoling in the river near the council estates. Best of all we sit in small parks on benches dead people have donated to the human public. Our favourite inscription reads 'This bench was donated by George "titch" Daniels and his beloved wife Joan 1959–1998.' You might think this is small fry to record for the future and only of interest to the sentimental and senile, or to those who find life frightening and buy cards with puppy dogs on them and eat sweets on train journeys, but they are the moments that I treasure beyond all others. Sometimes when I'm feeling morose and tanked up on too much gin I say to Eddie, 'What have I done with my life?' and she replies, 'You have kissed me beautifully, Milkpaw, that's what.'

Look, we made the date for our wedding and even cut the grass that had by now grown a couple of inches in the garden, a grandiose and triumphant gesture because there isn't much of it but it made us feel like we had a lawn like rich folks do. I hung the plastic budgies on the sickly branches of our bay tree like I said I would and Eddie whitewashed the wall at the back. Her mum came round and said it looked like a postcard she once saw of a fisherman's cottage in Greece. She rolled up her sleeves and baked two hundred potatoes and Eddie put on a CD of early fifties rock'n'roll because that's what her mother loves to cook to, dancing her way to the mounds of butter she mashed with garlic and parsley, using the peppermill as a microphone to mouth the words while she ground her pelvis into the cupboard under the sink. We made pitcherfuls of margaritas and Eddie barbequed chicken over an old oil drum sawed in half. When all the neighbourhood cats came round and circled the drum we threw them the giblets and felt it was only right that the local beasts joined in to send us off. I ran a hot bath perfumed with the rose oil we save for special occasions and idled in the water like a chief, flexing my ankles and marvelling in a general sort of way on the wonders of the skeleton. Relishing a bit of introspection and vanity, dizzy from the balm of rose and steam from which I finally dragged in a vision for an outfit, I made my way into my dressing room. Despite the goatee beard, I finally decided to reject the exuberant and baroque, and go for something more democratic. Denim is not hysterical. It is not pompous or flash. It speaks a language everyone understands, from London to Poland, from the gambling casinos of Vegas where cocktails are ninety-nine cents, to the golden spires of Istanbul. A denim trouser suit will sheath my body. For I, Milkpaw, despite my exotic hand, am Everyman, giving life a go like the rest of us, trying not to be too sad.

When we presented ourselves to each other in the garden to the rapturous applause of all our friends, we looked familiar to each other and that was comforting. Not strange or enigmatic. Eddie wore her silver mesh dress, lime sandals, and yards of eyelashes. Her breath smelt of Colgate, her hair of chemicals, her skin of violets. Smoke from the chicken made my eyes water, coursing down my cheeks, making rats' tails of my beard, and of course I didn't have a handkerchief. Eddie held on to my milkpaw while the vicar said words like honour and cherish. A car alarm went off. A starling twittered, a cat hissed, a helicopter hovered low in the the cardboard-coloured sky. The next-door neighbours flicked channels on their TV. A football exploded in an advertisement. A baby searched for its mother's nipple. A portable phone rang and no one answered it. An electronic watch bleeped. Someone told a terrible joke. Our ansamachine uttered the voices of friends who couldn't come, declaring their apologies. The fax spewed congratulations on to the carpet and John cried because Clare said she was leaving him for good. In my mind's eye I doused the world in paraffin and set fire to all those years of evolution and elephants. Then I recreated the world and brought back the elephants. I made national holidays: wildlife week, children week, a lot of beer week. Out of the corner of my fevered eye I saw my best man whip a piece of paper out of his anorak pocket. It was exciting and powerful, that gesture, and I was simmering with adrenalin when his tender tough city voice wafted through the smoke to my ears. 'I have known Milkpaw since he was seven years old and crazed with the need for pink chews wrapped in little squares of wax paper. Even then he was a hedonist amazed at how the humble sweetmeat turned his urine pink. The twilit age of twelve saw him chasing pigeons and growing cabbages in my dad's allotment. Fourteen and he was preening himself for adolescence in jackets with sharp lapels, pioneering noon time liasions with local girls at the

Odeon instead of going to school. At sixteen he told me he wanted to retire. Now in the year 2000 he has found his love companion, his beard is milky white like the ancient philosophers and he is writing a history of the Every Day. Milkpaw is a little sinner and a microbe but I love him all the same. Good luck. I love you boy.'

Someone threw rice over me. Gnats hovered. Leaves trembled. Pete and Mike exchanged a look. A cat pounced on a piece of chicken, a soap opera star announced she was pregnant and burst into BBC tears, a greenfly flew into Bob's mouth. Someone finished the last paragraph of their novel in their head. Lynette told Bart she loved him for the first time and Sue confessed she had let Jesus into her heart. Ice cubes were crushed for another jug of margaritas and then it was time for Eddie's best woman to read her speech. Tanya, with her perfect silicone cheekbones, stepped forward in black riding boots with lizard-skin toe caps and put her arm around my glowing bride.

'We grew up together Ed and I. This gal could have married into money and brains but she's married into fur instead, all right? The one thing I know about Ed is she's on the case all right. A case of wine that is! No, Ed's in the real world all right. She knows the price of butter and beer and she knows the price of a cab ride. She knows not to believe the newspapers and she knows to keep her body out of the sun. All right! Ladies and Gentleman, put your hands together for this great gal, All right!'

I am deeply moved. That was a speech blown like glass from a boiling heart. A masterwork that will one day be studied in schools by sophisticated teenagers in Wonderbras who are interested in the strobe and pulse of panic. Tanya repeats all right! all right! all right! because she is scared and doesn't know what to do with the gap between all right and not all right. I admire her for it despite the fact she tried to humiliate me on my big day with a fur joke. In fact I would like to put my arms around her and say everything is going to be okay, like a father might do when his daughter is inconsolable and he doesn't know why. Is she hungry? Is she cold? Is she lonely?

Look, Tanya is queen of psychic terror, all right?

All right!

Eddie and I, the last two smokers on earth, sit under the bay tree, limp with love and too many margaritas. Her pale face rests on my shoulder and when the wind jitters the Hong Kong budgies, it is as if they alone can express all that we feel and are too weary to voice.

'Tomcat,' she whispers.

'Hmmmmm?'

'Catch those birds, we don't know where our next meal is coming from.'

They call me Milkpaw on account of the white fur on my hand. I am a loser, an egoist, a would-be guru and a small time historian. Now that I have downloaded the contents of my tiny mind on to a computer disk, tanked up on Holsten Export, sneezing and shivering like I do, I am probably immortal. One day a robot boy will be able to read this, and count my spelling mistakes with his blue metal fingers. But even without the help of my PC, with its shift edit return delete quit merge print paste rulers and clipboard, I've survived for twenty-six years. My body is stuffed with the gauze of information and the soul has gone out of fashion. Yep. Despite the small semis and dodgy drains in my street, no London rat has ever given me the plague. All right! All right! I'm a box of quantum energy in denim. An angel boy dancing on the head of a pin, in loafers from Shelley's. I told you I wanted to be killed by music. For music to send healing rays through my body and awaken another version of myself that I have packed in my mind's eye in ice.

For the future.

Trigger

A cat's life and times in a city block of flats

CRISPIN GREEN

It's a good thing you dont have a bus fare
It would fall through the hole in your pocket
And you'd lose it in the snow on the ground

Yesterday I met a man upon the stairs who was not there
He was there again today – I wish the Hell he'd go away

The other day the little boy who is the neighbours son living just along the balcony in the flat at the end, said to his runny-nosed sister 'WOTS THIS THEN?', and so saying he extended his hand and splayed his fingers skywards in all directions implying some kind of beast or animal. His sister sniffed up her nose and replied 'GIRAAFF?' 'NAHH', came the reply. She considered again. 'N'ORSE?', 'NAHH' 'HALSATION DOG?' 'DOBERMON DOG?' 'NAHH' 'ROTWHILER DOG?' 'NAHH' 'A CAT!' 'NAHH' Here the sister paused for a sniff and then said flatly, 'I DUNNO.' Her brother simply turned his extended hand earthwards so that all finger-tips pointed down giving the appearance of an animal on its feet and in doing so he said dryly, 'IT'S A DEAD ONE O THESE.'

Now my being a cat has nothing to do with my low

opinion of the boys amusement which often involves him chasing me at any opportunity he gets when I have the bad luck to meet him on the stairs. I know simple things please simple minds and he probably gets it from his mother who also passed it on to his runny-nosed sister. I would say that they get it from their father except they don't even know what a father is so far away is the father, and the farther the father is the more further they are from knowing farthers from fathers. But that is enough of them because it is taking me further from what I want to say about the world I find under my nose.

My name is Trigger and this is my story. I've lived all my ten years of life which in human terms is equivalent to seventy years so you could say I've packed a lot of living into my ten which is as much or even more than he will ever do even if he completes his four score years and ten as alloted to men and women.

I've lived all my alloted time with a man who feeds me from tins. Periodically he changes the cat litter in my tray which he euphamistically disguises by placing a cloth-covered box over it, leaving entrance for me to do my business. The printed fabric and potted plants which adorn my box don't fool anyone who visits because if he is lazy and doesn't change my litter or 'DO THE CAT'S TRAY' as he calls it, no amount of odour from a spray-can will stop the cat's litter from humming its malodouress melody just as the guests are savouring some exotic candle-lit dishes my man has painstaking spent all day preparing (probably accounting for the memory-lapse which resulted in him not cleaning my box) for which he attempts to cover embarrassment by digression. He will say something like; 'THERE'S A NEW FAMILY OF REFUGEE BOAT PEOPLE MOVED IN DOWNSTAIRS WHOSE COOKING SMELLS JUST LIKE MR WONGS

IN GERRAD STREET IN SOHO Y'KNOW THERES TEN OF 'EM INCLUDING THE GRANDPARENTS AND THEY'VE JUST HAD 'N INDUSTRIAL EXTRACTOR FAN FITTED IN THEIR KITCHEN WHICH BLOWS HOT AIR UP THE STAIRS WAFTING WITH VISIONS OF RICKSHAWS IN DOWNTOWN SAIGON AND HOT BACK-YARDS IN SHANTY-TOWN TEEMING WITH SCRATCHING CHICKENS AND FILTHY SWINE AND ROTTING UNSEAWORTHY BOATS OVERLADEN WITH HUMANITY ALL BONE AND SKIN CONTINUALLY BAILING OUT THE REMORSLESS SHARK-INFESTED CHINA SEA – O DO HAVE SOME OF THE CHICKEN IN THE POT CYNTHIA AND DO HELP YOURSELF JUSTIN; WHAT?! YOU'RE BOTH VEGETARIAN!' and so he blunders from one faux-pas to the next. Anyway, let him carry on – simple things for simple minds, because I have to pass on to other matters here and time is pressing – As the wise man said – 'SMALL IS THE CORNER OF THE WORLD IN WHICH WE LIVE AND SHORT IS OUR TIME IN IT' (this is particularly true if you're stuck in a small boat in the middle of the shark-infested China sea or if you're a cat in inner-city SW2 who crosses the road once for the first time and finds that all of nine lives but one have been used up in a flash!)

Now, how my man came to be to be my tray cleaner and provider of tinned food are important matters to consider; and how I came to live, and how I came to live where I did are matters inextricably bound together.

My custodian at 101 FALORN HOUSE, PLACHAM PARK ESTATE, SW2, an estate not disimilar in its appearance and compactness to the nearby remand prison, Brickstone, a stones throw down the road, – an estate known to be one of the largest in the capital distinguished in its own right, known to taxi drivers to be a place to avoid taking fares to after darkness and equally well known to those in the law enforcement business as well as the local fire brigade, ambulance and social services to a degree which has made it a focus for government reports with a topicality which has appealed to social studies students who are ever keen to use it as material with which they furnish their seminars and dissertations on urban deprivation, pet abuse, child abuse, the cycle of theft, the theft of cycles, one parent families and families with no parents . . . as I was saying, my custodian of 101 FALORN HOUSE, PLACKHAM PARK ESTATE, SW2 was visited by the twin sisters GEM and NYE one day. They had been sent out by their parents and told not to return home (under pain of a good drubbing) until they had fulfilled the duty given to them which was to dispose, disperse, or dump the unwanted litter of kittens that had issued from their cat. And so they knocked at No. 101 FALORN HOUSE bearing me, one of the said litter, a fluffy ball of fur, soft as cotton and no older than seven days. New to the world and everything in it my eyes looked equally at all things. My ears quivered delicately at the sound of a leaf being picked up by a sudden breeze or contorted in all possible directions at the shrill of a car alarm in the courtyard. They held me out to the man at No. 101 saying that if I was not taken in soon by someone they'd have to drown me in the bath and put me in the black refuse sack provided by the council and drop me down the rubbish shoot to save me from being homeless and unwanted, 'TO SAVE ME FROM BEING HOMELESS AND UNWANTED!' How humane! It still brings tears to my eyes to think of the humanity in the local community.

We should not fool ourselves that the old spirit of care and mutual welfare which is traditionally engendered and fostered in the local community is dead. NO! Like a seed which finds a crack in the concrete of a three lane moterway it sends up a green shoot and flowers in the hundreds and thousands of similar estates up and down the country.

My custodian was touched to the core of his heart by the 'humane' dilemna as it was put to him on his doorstep that day by the twins GEM and NYE. He was so taken by my plight that he took me in and from that day forth I've shared my life with him at No.101 FALORN HOUSE, PLACHAM PARK ESTATE, SW2. Saved from the ignomous and anonymous fate of bath drowning and black bag chute burial as awaits those who are homeless and unloved I suddenly found my status in life as a TENANT of a LOCAL AUTHORITY PROPERTY and as such I needed an identity to go with it – in short I needed a name, because everybody who breathes on this planet from LOCAL AUTHORITY TENANTS to floating new-borns becalmed in the shark infested CHINA SEAS has the right to a personal name.

My custodian pondered on this for some time until he hit on his first idea. His train of thought ran like this: Because of my 'ASSYRIAN' markings I was to be called 'TIGGER' who is found in the pages of the story of CHRISTOPHER ROBIN AND WINNIE THE POOH. (Personally I cannot see any connection between ASSYRIA and MR MILNE'S story, but there you go. I had as much say in the matter as I did when my life hovered in the balance between a chute burial and life at No.101 FALORN HOUSE); anyway it was not to be because no sooner had these 'associations' crossed the mind of my man when his brow furrowed and his hand went to his chin and as he thoughtfully fingered his jaw bone he slowly murmered to himself placing each word delicately as if it were a fragile object being stood on a shelf lest it should fall and be dashed to pieces before a careful inspection could take place . . . 'WHAT ABOUT THE NEIGHBOURS LIVING OPPOSITE?' and at once his thoughtful voice faded to a whisper as the various degrees and aspects of his neighbours who lived opposite him floated across his minds eye like an unwanted vision, So! What the fuss? You may well ask.

NOW THIS MAY take some explaining. Neighbours always do take a lot of explaining as socio-economico-urban studies students will tell you and to explain your Neighbours can take longer than the time spent living next to them. The general layout of the neighbours and his relationship to them is like this. Those who lived on his side of the block he was to say the most, on nodding-head terms. He'd given up trying to greet people with a cheery 'HULLO! GOOD MORNING! FINE DAY TO BE ALIVE AND KICKING – WHAT YOU SAY!' because this was too much for some people who'd either turn and flee the other way or else scowl suspiciously as if he were a dipper intent on picking their pockets. There were some who were more generous though and they would give a quick nod followed by a quick 'ALRIGHT,' to which the appropiate answer was a quick nod followed by a quick 'ALRIGHT.' Depending on how this was done, the vigour of the nod and the crispness of the 'ALRIGHT' it could be deduced how everything was with that person on that particular morning. And to greater or lesser degrees it implied how miserable the person was feeling on a scale from one to ten: like so:

1. Not so bad

2. So – So
3. Could be worse
4. Could be better
5. Under the weather
6. Stressed
7. Under pressure
8. Who are you lookin at?
9. Sod off ponce
10. (See footnote)

Now the relationships thickened between my man and those neighbours who lived either side of him or directly beneath him. There was no one living above him because he himself lived on the top floor and it would be a pretty foolish thing for someone to live on top of the roof although this should not be dismissed as idle speculation because it has been known to happen. After all if you are homeless and unloved living on top of the roof is better than being drowned in the bath and black-bagged in a council refuse sac before being dumped down the chute or finding yourself in a rotting wooden hulk becalmed in the middle of the China Sea surrounded by shark fins and teeth! No! The special relationship with these neighbours whose periphary of living space touched on my mans space seperated only by walls and floorboards

FOOTNOTE:
10 – This number is not a verbal expression of well-being or otherwise. Here one has to learn by experience in the field how to recognize subtle inflexions of voice and the varying manner in the delivery of the nodding and alrighting to be able to anticipate the number 10 on the scale of misery and how to take quick evasive action/retaliation from the trajectory arc of a bunch of knuckled fingers aimed at ones chin. END OF FOOTNOTE.

came from the deeper understanding of one anothers problems, hopes, joys and disappointments as it came through the walls and out of the fire place in the form of sounds, cries, ecstacies, anger and at times, profound silences that had one wondering if your neighbour was taking up a new religion or conspiring to murder. These sounds and meaningful silences would place all who shared them in a sphere of intimacy in which they still all nodded and said 'ALRIGHT' to one another, but among them the unspoken scale of misery from one to ten would take on new dimensions of colour and texture adding to its meaning in a way it would be complicated to draw or represent here – it would probably be impossible. It might be possible to do it with a hologram in which a three dimensional image can be projected onto thin air enabling a viewer to walk around the immaterial representation appreciating all its varying aspects at a leisurly pace rather like the way SATURN, JUPITER, MARS and VENUS can be seen and understood along with our EARTH, MOON and SUN at a planetarium, but no one has done that yet and it would probably take a life times work to do so because neighbours take a lot of explaining.

To return to 'THE NEIGHBOURS OPPOSITE' there was none of this nodding and alrighting with them – No Siree! If you so much as looked in their general direction they were liable to demand what you were 'starin' at and if you didn't have a quick and satisfactory answer it could turn pretty ugly for you so it was best to pretend that they were not there by avoiding eye-ball contact. However, pretending as much as one might try did not stop them from being there and about to drop on you like a ton of bricks from a great height should you be unfortunate enough to come under their shadow.

There was one family who originated from 'GLAZ-GEE' and who never stopped quarral or fighting. They would fight over anything from football to love or money or anything just for the crack of it on their way back from the local 'THE DIRK AND DAGGER.' It was difficult to know exactly what they fought about because they always shouted at the tops of their lungs no matter whether they were saying 'AI WI HAVE PRORIDGE'ND CHUPS FER BREAKFAST' or 'SPILL ME PINT O HEAVY ONCE MORE AND I'LL PUSH YER TEETH THREW THE OTHER SIDE OF YER FACE' – it all sounded equally loud and rasping. BUT if shouting was their natural way of talking when they wanted to SHOUT they could SHOUT loud enough to wake their ansestrol spirits whose remains lay strewn around the valleys and mountains of GLEN GOE. They were GREAT SHOUTERS with WHOOOOOOOO's and YEEEEEEEEEEE's and AAAHHHGGGGGGG's and OOOOOOOO II IIIII E E E E EEE's when they really got going. They had an Alsatian dog called SABRE who would add to their shouts his fearsome rasping barks which could turn the post man's legs to mince meat as he crossed over the courtyard. Next to barking and rasping SABRE liked nothing more than mucking in with a good punch-up and getting an indiscriminate bite of anything going. The most appetising times for SABRE were when his own kith and kin were really getting stuck in and mixing it with great WHOOPS and SHOUTS along with flaying arms and legs, punches and kicks, the spilling of blood and splintering of teeth and ripping out of tufts of hair in the courtyard outside FALORN HOUSE after a good binge in the pub up the road spent boozing whooping and watching CELTIC thrash RANGERS live on afternoon sport Tee-Vee. SABRE would join in and run amok among them nipping an ankle here an elbow there and sinking his teeth into a succulent fleshy thigh or backside rump until they'd decided they'd all had had enough. Thoroughly exhausted, they'd pick themselves up and return indoors leaving a large crowd of onlookers agog. These onlookers consisted mainly of nere-do-wells and excitable children with demented pet dogs straining at their leashes for a chance to act out SABRE'S blood-lusty behaviour. When at last the POLICE arrived (they'd always arrive after the event) all they found of the reported 'domestic disturbance' was an animated gathering of young people re-enacting the mêlée in a playful way while others stood around speculating as to whose and how many teeth were scattered around their feet and questioning each other if it was human hair or dogs fur that lay in clumps in the BLOOD SPATTERED areana outside FALORN HOUSE.

Upon sighting the arrival of the POLICE, this volatile group, still keen for excitement and drama would imitate the WHOOPS and SHOUTS of the GLAZ-GEE folk and DANCE in front of the blaring POLICE vans swooping in to the courtyard before scrambling helter-skelter in all directions through the warren of bye-ways and yards around PLACKHAM PARK ESTATE SW2 followed in quick pursuit by the men in blue who thought they were chasing the trouble they'd been diverted to sort out!

While police gave chase to the riotous mob of youths, calling for reinforcements by shouting into their two way radios which hissed and crackled into every nook and cranny of the estate the GLAZ-GEE slumbered oblivious to the sequential consequences set in motion by their rough and tumble on their way back from THE DIRK AND DAGGER. Flushed with there excesses they returned to their flat and were in a state of stupor and collapse, heaped and sprawled in their front room, being lulled by the flickering light soporific voice of a sports commentator debating the finer points of a county cricket match being played out on some distant green where the only thing that might threaten the tranquility of English country life might be a lone cloud set in the corner of an otherwise rippleless expanse of clear blue. Those of the GLAZ-GEE folk who wern't already sleeping where they had spread themselves like exhausted combat troops, passed around cigaretts and a party-size can of larger and nursed their wounds.

At times like these the SCOWLER PROWLERS who lived opposite would make themselves scarce to avoid the encircling police net being trawled around Falorn House and the surrounding buildings. The SCOWLER-PROWLERS were a group of fourteen to twenty-year-olds who'd hang out along the top balcony outside their front door scowling from this vantage of height at anything which moved below. If somebody happened to pass nearby or approach the communal entrance to the flats the scowling grew greater and would be accompanied by a hiss, like a sibilant serpent darting a forked tongue at the approaching footfall of a stranger. They lived parentless. Abandoned to fend for themselves by a mother who spawned them and then found herself eaten out of house and home as they increased in years, size and number. She moved to other accomadation nearby from where she'd make a weekly visit to her sons to make sure their beds were made and that they had clean clothes. This was the extent of her maternal duty and people could say what they liked about her boys but to her mind as long as they had clean sheets and clothes which she washed and hung out to dry every Monday morning then it would automatically follow that her boys were good and clean too. She worked hard enough as it was stocking shelves at SUPERSAVERS up the road without having to see them on their way to school. Besides they had an older brother, CHEIF SCOWLER PROWLER. When he wasn't being detained for stretches of time on 'business' he lorded over his younger siblings with his own personal brand of education. Like Ghandi, he knew that if he set an example by his behaviour his brethren would be sure to follow.

After an absent STRETCH he made sure to announce his return in style. Driving up in a showy car, stepping out with the latest and most costly trainers from America, flashing gold bracelets and finger rings he'd limber up with a burst of rapid shadow boxing manouvers to shouts of sibling approval from the top balcony to which he'd ascend three steps at a time for a serious session of 'business discussions' behind closed doors.

Following on from such happenings outside FALORN HOUSE there would occur a series of BREAKIN'S AND ENTERIN'S AND TAKIN'S particularly from the top floor properties which shared the roof access with the SCOWLER PROWLERS flat; except that theirs would never seem to get broken, entered and depleted. Other residents would return from a hard days work to find gaping holes where their upstairs windows had been tightly shut previously that morning before they left for work. Silently, mysteriously, nimbly their cheque books and cheque cards along with video, telly and hi-fi not to mention the cheap jewellry with extreme sentimental value had been spirited accross the roof tops into a dispersal network whose branches spread far and wide as later attested by the bank statements sent to the residents who'd 'lost' their cheque books and cheque cards in this way – hitting them with a second shock wave just as they were beginning to feel the full meaning of POST TRAUMA

Experience. Residents who'd never been to the likes of places like DOTTINGHAM, BLOTTINGHAM, or BRISTOL and who wouldn't know how to get there without studying a road map or coach time-table would learn that their credit cards were freely being used in those places at boutiques, sports shops, and Chinese restaurants.

As fraught exchanges took place between distraught tenants of FALORN HOUSE and their bank managers to negotiate the liability factor for the wanton and autonomous way their credit cards and cheque books were splashing out in places they'd never even been to the SCOWLER PROWLERS would be conspicuous by their absence. Collectively they'd transmorgified into a beast, satiated after feasting on its prey and content to retreat to the corner of its lair to sleep it off.

It was out of consideration of neighbours opposite like the SCOWLER PROWLERS and the GLAZ GEE folk which made my custodian reconsider his original choice of name for me. You see, how could he in all respect to his street credability step out of his front door in full view of the likes of the GLAZ GEE folk and the SCOWLER PROWLERS who cussed and hissed at everything in sight – how could he in all seriousness brazenly step out in front of the neighbours opposite rattling my box of Kitty Kat buscuits calling out the name he had first chosen from the story of CHRISTOPHER ROBIN and WINNIE the POOH? Imagine it might go like this:

'Tiger! Tiger dahlink! Where are yoouuu? Come Tiger pusums. It's time for your tea. Tiger! Tiiggeer!

At which point in calling for me he might give a dainty rattle and shake of my box of buscuits in front of him trying to attract my attention, and certainly succeeding in attracting the attention from the balcony opposite where the clan of the GLAZ GEE folk stood momenterily transfixed as one eye balling head erect and swivelled with its total attention fixed on the sight of my man shaking my box of Kitty Kat like a bunch of poseies with his light words ruffling up their brains the wrong way. Would he do this knowing that he might be inviting a torrent of their invective which might go like this:

> 'TIGGER'??? 'TIGGER'??? Wha kinda ugin stewpid name fer a cat is tha?! Only some kinda Nancy couldee thunk o a name like 'TIGGER' fer eees cat. HAR HAR HAR OOOCH SEEE YO OOU JUMMIE! 'TIGGER DAHLIN! YER Frig gin TAE is in the Box!' HAR HAR HAR!!!

This might bring out the SCOWLER PROWLERS who in turn could let loose their own brand of ribaldry at my man's expense which might go:

> 'TEEGAH? TEEGAH??' IM A NO GO CALL DE CAT SENSIBLE NAME LIKE LION OF ZION, STA! LOOK IM CHASE IM PUSSY CALL TEE-GAH! YES STA! IM A BIG PUSSY GO SHAKEY-SHAKEY-SHAKEY DE BOX FOR IM LICKLE TING A LING PUSSY IM A GO CALL TEEGAH, STA! HAR!

Transfixed by this vision of persecution in which he foresaw himself bowed under the weight of a cruxifiction of his own making while being mocked by the people, my custodian was forced to reconsider his original choice of name for me. The result was more of a modification rather than a complete overhaul of name.

And so it came about that my name was to become 'TRIGGER' after the horse by the same name who was the ever-trustworthy steed of ROY ROGERS, the cowboy who used to ride onto our Tee-Vee screens each week to uphold the good against the evil, defending the weak and meek against the tyranny of brutish greed and ignorance. Hardly a week would go by without the hero losing his scalp or being shot full of holes and good ole Trigger would always be there in the nick of time to save his skin whether it be pulling him out of the quick sand from the end of a rope gripped between vice like teeth to kicking in the doors of a burning barn where our hero had been bound and gagged and left to an infernal fate after being bushwhacked by a bunch o two bit cattle rustlers he'd been trying to bring to justice; Yes Siree! Give ROY ROGERS and TRIGGER one episode at Falorn House and he'd have the whole place sorted out in a week from rehabilitating the SCOWLER PROWLERS and socialising the GAZ GEE folk to doing charity work for the local Rotary Club to getting the courtyard swept and the roof tiles mended to fixing the leak from the overflow at number nine which has been dripping for years and spreading moss green dampness accross yards of surrounding bricks and mortar.

If anything, my modified name counterbalanced the cries and calls from other pet owners on the estate who'd command their dumb familiars with shouts of:

'C'MERE BLADE!!'
or
'SIC 'IM SATEN!!'
or
'DOWN FANG, DOWN!!'
and
'GO FER IT TYSON, GO!!'

Sure it was from the likes of them with names like that, that I made the important discovery that whatever I lacked in bulk, beefyness and brawn I could make up for by more refined qualities of brains, bluster and a good nose for sniffing out what was what in the order things.

NOW ROB was a good man for knowing what was what in the order of things. He lived next door to me and my man with his grown up son DARRYL, a young headbanger of a man who drove too fast and as a consequence suffered BANGS on the road from time to time. One time he got his head BANGED and couldn't speak. It was a week before his senses returned to him but even so no amount of damage, crawling from the wreakage or cautions from the Police would cure his passion for fast driving – not even when he was led away and BANGED up in a Police cell one night. His girlfriend was something of a BANGER too. That's probably why he liked her. When they wern't BANGING up the road together in his car they'd be BANGING away upstairs until ROB would come home from his shift at the bus garage where he worked and put some BANGERS under the grill so they could all have BANGERS and mash together for breakfast.

I was partial to ROB'S BANGERS and I got my man into a spot of trouble the day I found his front door open with ROB busy having a BANG on the pot and Darryl and his girlfriend having a BANG upstairs and their breakfast of BANGERS busy sizzling and crackling under the kitchen grill. This was one of those moments when temptation just got the better of me and ROB emerged round the corner still doing up his trouser button to see the tail end of me fleeing his kitchen wildly trailing his string of breakfast BANGERS as I began to get into my full stride for a successful get-away.

'Course, when my man heard about this incident from ROB, which he did straight away, I mean, ROB'S a big hungry man just finished his shift and bound to be a bit upset to lose all his BANGERS just when his mouth is watering at the smell of them a spitting and a poppin under the grill; well my man did the right thing and straight away went to the butchers for a fresh string o BANGERS and they all had a good larf about it because as ROB says about any crises in life:

'YOU GOTTA LARF AINT YA'

'Yes . . .' as I said later to my mate poor GINGER downstairs ' . . . Especially when you think that Darryl has had more BANGS than hot dinners – you gotta larf aint ya!'

Poor GINGER . . ., I say *poor* GINGER and it makes me take an involuntary breath and sigh. I say *poor* GINGER because the *poor* part of it for him was to be born into an unhappy and misfortunate household – no more no less than that; just rotten bad luck and not a lotta larfs! Some will say that to be born at a particular time and place is determined by the great scheme of things and others will go so far and say that we are active in an unseen way in chosing our time, place and circumstances so when we make our entrance into this world *we* have, in some way, willed to do so ourselves! WELL! I don't think poor GINGER knew anything about it because he may well have had second thoughts when the great aviator shouted from his cockpit in the sky:

'Here we are GINGE old bean! We're over FALORN HOUSE PLACKHAM PARK ESTATE, LONDON SW2 in the year 1994 – get ready for your drop. Chin

Chin, Tallyo ho and don't do anything I wouldn't do – GOOD LUCK!'

Had 'GINGE' known what was coming to him as he jumped into his particular allotment of time and place he might have said in reply:

'Hold up a mo' Guvn'r! I don't like the looks o' this one. Aint you got something a bit more cushy? I mean there's a bit of a bit of a ruck goin on down there in the yard, and I can see loads of loose roof tiles, know what I mean! Give us a squeeze and put me down for the next drop will ya Guvn'r, what d'ya say?'

Course old 'GINGE' may just as well have ended up being dropped over the rotting boat of refugees bailing out the shark infested China Sea; so its six o one and half a dozen o the other – the same difference no matter which way you look at it!

To describe GINGER'S lot you have to go back to his custodian called JAMIE. GINGER'S welfare and well being was umbilically bound to JAMIE'S and as things turned out that wasn't too good.

Years ago as a hopeful young man JAMIE left his highland home with its undulating vistas of heather and bracken and the air so clear you could drink it for breakfast in exchange for a van drivers job in the exhaust clogged atmosphere of LONDON'S congested streets and a ground floor flat at FALORN HOUSE, PLACKHAM PARK ESTATE, SW2. Before long Jamie had a wife and a family of two young children, and GINGER of course. For a while things went reasonably well and then came HARD TIMES. He came a cropper in the first cut of a recessionary swathe and he never quite recovered to regain a hold on his life. With no job and no income and no HOPE of finding regular employment at a time when employers themselves joined the dole queue JAMIE began to lose his health and self-confidence. He fought the pain with cheap cider. He stopped shaving and when he went out, which he did less and less, he wore dark glasses. When his wife felt that she could no longer cope in penury managing two children and a husband who'd retreated into his own despair, in an act of self-preservation she rounded up her weans and set out for her mother's house by the coast, never to return.

Jamie was left with Ginger and little to live for. In maudlin mood he'd write verses recalling the sunlight dancing over the heather growing over the free moors and mountains in the distant highlands he used to know so well; about the love which used to course so freshly in his young body when he courted and made love to his wife to be; and the prittle-prattle of the children when they used to play around him in his happier days before an iron cage of depression dropped around him like a portcullis isolating him from the rest of the world and those who he still loved.

While JAMIE still had some strength he'd climb the stairwell clutching his paper verses to show to my custodian who'd quietly read them in awkward silence feeling JAMIE'S bloodshot eyes closely watching for something that would stop him from drowning in his helpless misery. I could see that my man was often at a loss for words when he looked up from reading the verses into JAMIE'S swollen pools of despair but he made great efforts to say things which might reach out and touch JAMIE with hope and encouragement for the future and to free him from his present burden of shame and worthlessness. When JAMIE descended to his flat my custodian was left with an image after one of JAMIES love-sick verses which told of the last brief glow of light that seems to suddenly bighten in a last effort to rise above the descending sun on a receeding horizon, drowning in a sea of forgetfullness.

In his last days when he had no money to spend on cider, he drank from the bottles of aftershave in his bathroom. Poor GINGER! The last time JAMIE was able to do anything for him was when he stitched up his ear which had been torn in two by a rogue Tom who he came face to face with late one night when out in the court-yard. Stumbling and shaking in a supreme effort of self control JAMIE located his wifes sewing box and threaded a large needle with thick black thread. Gripping GINGERS body between his knees with beads of persperation gathering in the furrows of concentration on his brow he stitched and wove GINGERS torn ear together with the tenderness of a nursing mother. And as JAMIE cradled the convalescing GINGER on his doorstep that late summer afternoon a burst of warm golden sunlight quietly burst on their corner of the courtyard and sparkled brightly in the bottle of Eua de Cologne as JAMIE put it to his lips and swallowed the drops that remained after he had used it to soak a swab of cotton to clean GINGERS wound.

Gail from upstairs found JAMIE three days later lying cold and stiff and stone dead on his settee; choked on his bile. It was GINGER who'd raised the ALARM by his continuous cries and scratching from the inside of the front door; he had not been fed for three days. JAMIE'S body was bagged-up and bundled away in the back of an ambulance like meat being taken to cold storage through the streets that JAMIE used to work when driving and delivering.

The SCOWLER PROWLERS were the first to pillage JAMIE'S unguarded flat and what was left behind was picked by the local children of the yard and taken away, until the only things which remained were bulky pieces of furniture and some books and papers which no one cared for. His poems lay strewn around his doorstep until a seasonal change of breeze blew them away for good. A council lorry was sent weeks later and carted off the wardrobes and bedsteads while workmen fitted metal grills and covered the windows and barricaded the front door.

Poor GINGER in stitches but not a lot of larfs.

It was GAIL from upstairs who continued to look after GINGER. She had a soul devoted entirely to looking after everyones needs but her own. She took the world to her bosoom and it broke her heart. My custodian would cross to the other side of the street to avoid her lest she throw down her soulfull burden at his feet. If he rounded a corner and accidentley walked into her too late to avoid her he'd stand anchored to the pavement letting the swell of sickness and misfortune that submerged her family wash over him from the chalice of tears she carried within. A delinquint teenage son, a daughter and her baby returned home estranged from a violent son-in-law, a hypochondrical mother and an invalid cynical husband, this was GAILS lot; all of whom were squirming for life in a welfare net which was an ever tightening mesh around them, no more than holding them suspended above the teeth snapping jackles of hardship, constraint and poverty. They may just as well have taken their chances with the boat people in the middle of the shark infested CHINA SEA. Joining their menagerie of pets GINGER fitted in as best as he could; with the goldfish, a mongrel dog, and a plump yellow budgie.

One day my man was coming out of the Post Office when he saw GAIL walking towards him with the Family Credit book in hand. Her features were more engraved than usual and she carried the clouds of doom and gloom about her. Too late to be evasive, my man clenched his jaw and balanced his weight evenly on his feet in preparation for the latest onslaught from her which she looked determined to unleash on him as her rapid nervous stride swallowed up the space between them.

Tragedy came close to bursting it banks into hilarity as she spoke to him about the most recent mishaps to befall her, but he dared not show this because he'd never known her to see the funny side of things. She lived perpetually eclipsed in the shadow of anguish. Now if it were ROB, all he would say about it is:

'You gotta LARF; aint ya?'

and then he'd dismiss ole man trouble with a wave of his hand. But GAIL bore a heavy cross and it weighed like a ton on her that morning outside the Post Office. The more she sighed and complained as she related her woes the harder my man sucked in his right cheek and bit it to stop himself LARFING. Picture the events of calamity that unravelled from GAIL as my man saw them in his minds eye while he stood listening with cheek sucked in enough to swallow and his eyes popping out like ping-pong balls in an effort to control his expressions so as not to offend:

She said she'd taken in GINGER out of the goodness of her heart and treated him like one of her own since JAMIE had died. She was just thinking to herself how well he seemed to be settling in and how he'd already found a special place to sit next to the goldfish bowl near the budgie and what a domestic picture of peace they made with the dog dozing in front of the gas fire and her old man fast asleep in front of the telly still nestling his bottle of brown ale in the crook of his arm. Then there was a knock at the door. She thought it might be her son coming back from his community service. It was his last day of working all those hours the judge had given him to toil over an eight month stretch for stealing a frozen chicken from the Co-op, priced £2.86 'reduced' and he'd sworn never to get caught again. But when she opened the door she found a rather formidible man who was dressed like an undertaker. He was an INSURANCE SALESMAN and without drawing a breath he began to illustrate with the aid of graphs and coloured pens just how vulnerable she and her family would be should 'ANYTHING' happen to them. It was a completely new dimension of anxiety to GAIL when it was illustrated thus with the aid of graphs and coloured pens. Disaster in the abstract had a fascination that was alarming to her. Who would think that a sheet of paper with a few coloured lines and squiggles could tighten the chest, make the heart race with panic and cause the skin to prickle in a cold sweat? It was the moment GINGER was waiting for. With a well aimed clout from his right paw GINGER dislocated the budgie from its perch. In one pounce he was on it and secured the poor bird between his teeth. The tumbled bird stand glanced GAIL'S old man on the side of his head and he lept up in defensive shouts and confusion, catapulting the bottle of brown ale from the crook of his arm into the goldfish bowl. The suddeness of everything was too much for the mongrel dog whose nerves were tightly strung at the best of times and he started to yap madly and chase his tail. This was picked up as a signal for all the neighbouring canines to start a chorus of whines and barks bringing everybody to their front doors to see what the commotion might be about. In the meantime GINGER had bounded between the legs of GAIL and the INSURANCE SALESMAN on to the balcony and made off with his half consumed prey. As the import of what had happened began to be realised the old fellas language became colourful and GAIL went into a trance like state and started to make a long rising wailing noise like a air-raid siren warning of approaching enemy action. The INSURANCE SALESMAN who'd already sensed that he was not going to earn his commission easily, nervously gathered his illustrations and snapped them shut in his brief-case. He quickly retreated down the stairs following a yellow trail of fluffy feathers. After that poor GINGER was well and truly homeless and were it not for BOB and JUDY he would not have lasted from then on as long as he did.

Bob and Judy's charity towards GINGER was marginal rather than central. The vicissitudes of life proved to be a continuous roller-coaster ride which often proved too much for their tenuous hold on it and so they could not be relied on to always remember to put food out for GINGER when they could not always remember what day of the week it was unless it was the calender date for their prescription. Remembering the day of the week is difficult especially if you don't remember exactly what year it is. For BOB and JUDY time stood still around the late sixties and early seventies when summer was just one long music festival which flowed with wine love peace and pharmacetical nirvana. They entered a WONDERLAND where magic mushrooms grew freely in among the shrubbery but unlike HANSEL and GRETAL they never found their way back. Broken dreams lay all around them but they couldn't make a clean sweep of things as time moved remorselessly on at FALORN HOUSE where they kept losing their keys and were always locking themselves in or out of their flat in the middle of the day or night.

Poor GINGER never had a regular meal since the budgie incident. In the second winter after JAMIE'S death GINGER was seen less and less. He grew thinner and thinner and one day he just vanished. If he had stayed around I would have liked him to come away with me and my man on holiday to the country. Sure he would have thought he'd died and gone to heaven! MICE! Everywhere! Thouuuuss – sssaannnnddss of 'EM! You lay back in the grass and they are tripping over you! WIDE fields, Space, SKY, birds and NO CRAZY DOGS chasing your tail every time you step outside your door! When my time comes to enter the country from which no one returns I'd like it to be in the middle of the field where the harvest mice dance in the light of a full moon.

The only thing GINGER would not like about going to the country would have been the going . . . that was the worst of it. Once my man had to put me in the hold of a RAPIDO coach under orders from an officious inspector who said it was against health and safety regulations to have me travelling with the passengers. Well I could tell him from experience that four long lonely hours in the total dark, locked in with a shifting sea of luggage, going ninety miles an hour, seperated from the heat and noise of the engine by a thin alloy partition whose rivets rattled like hundreds of skelatol chattering teeth not only contravened health and safety and animal rights but was worse than a chute burial! There I was, like HOUDINI the ESCAPOLOGIST, freeing myself from the confines of my basket, crashing about with cases and rucksacs: it was murder in there! I only avoided being reduced to a mulch of KAT O MEAT by thinking up tunes and dancing to stay on top of the ever shifting pile of vibrating luggage. Who could blame me for losing control of my bodily functions, oral forically speaking? The inspector should have thought of that before he ordered me to travel with the luggage instead of the passengers.

Many summers have come and gone since then and the next time I make that journey with the luggage it will be in a wooden casket on a one way ticket headed for the middle of the field where I can hear the harvest mice dance over me in the light of the full moon. I'm getting on in years. My claws are brittle and I'm missing teeth. I don't eat much. Like the old lady downstairs my sight and hearing are fading. She lives alone and most of her adult life has been spent at FALORN HOUSE. She can remember the flying bomb that HITLER sent over here to clear the slums and create a better society. It landed short of the East End and wiped out an apple-orchard and allotment where tenants used to be able to grow there own greens. Now the place has been made into high rise flats where children can drop old televisions for a larf on to the abandoned wrecks of cars fifteen storeys below them. The old lady came up to ask my man just the other day if it was true that HIS HOLINESS THE POPE was on the stairs. She'd just seen him, or so she thought, but she was not sure because her eyes are bad and she gets confused about things from time to time. My man said that if she says she saw the POPE then he was quite ready to accept that she did see HIS HOLINESS in his red regalia and that it was a rare thing to have him visit FALORN HOUSE because most people have to go to ROME and even then they count themselves lucky to see a glimpse of him on his balcony. 'BUT . . .' he cautioned her, 'don't tell your family when they next visit you because they will want to put you in a home.'

And me; I'm off to the VET'S for the third time this week and it don't look too good for me. It never was a good experience, going to the VET'S. 'Third strike and yer out!' as they say in baseball. The worst memory of the VET was when he took away my manhood while I was in my prime and enjoying every minute of it, but thats another story. Suffice to say here and now to my ragamuffin progeny and all the future generations yet to come that if you can hurdle the chute burial at the outset then no matter what may follow life is there to unfold to the full and even if its a series of ups and downs like a roller-coaster ride or a dance in the dark with a load of other luggage, no matter what; as ROB says . . . 'YOU GOTTA LARF, AINT YA!'

THE END

The Scent of Strawberries

ALISON LOVE

It's hard to explain to you: in my time, you see, we were not taught the proper meanings of words. We lived among our silver towers, the air dry and perfumed, trying to breed. Fear? Betrayal? Don't ask me. The words meant nothing to me then.

After the War the sunsets were glorious. You could only see them through glass, but even so they stopped your heart, great swathes of red and orange churning up the sky. I can still remember it: crossing the bridge over what had once been Fleet Street, and watching the bloated sun drop so quickly you could see it fall. Count from one to five, and it had vanished beyond the chrome rim of the city.

I was sixteen, and I was coming home from Citizens class. As I walked, I recited the day's lesson in my head, matching its rhythm to the rhythm of my footsteps. Every day we learned a new statement, which we had to have word-perfect by the next class.

'Acknowledge but do not valorise . . .' muttered Blini, my classmate, who used to come with me as far as the escalators. She was a stringy pale girl, with hair the colour of lemonade; not as quick-witted as me, but much more docile. Everyone we saw smiled at us. We all smiled, all the time. Even the fifty year olds smiled, on their way to the hospital.

As Blini and I crossed the bridge, I pointed to the murky

ground beneath us. You couldn't see much, just a swamp of blackish mud and, occasionally, the charred remains of an old building.

'Flavian told me that there used to be a river down there, an underground river,' I said. 'And after that, there was a prison.'

Blini looked at me with her blue empty eyes. Then she said, in a flat voice:

'He doesn't know.'

'He might know,' I said, as we walked on. 'He might remember.'

'Nobody remembers,' said Blini, and she began once more to murmur our lesson under her breath. Acknowledge but do not valorise your blood relations. I often had a terrible urge to tell things to Blini, things I couldn't possibly have proved but which I knew would rattle her. Blini's father was a security man. As far as she was concerned, the world had always been like this, a sleek labyrinth of windows and silver walkways, slung so high that you need never touch the ground. I don't know why I did it: to shatter Blini's serenity, or to reassure myself? I can't tell. Either way, it was never satisfying.

Blini stopped chanting to herself, and turned towards me, her yellow head cocked sideways.

'You ought to try harder, Darrow,' she said. 'You'll be in real trouble if you fail Citizens.'

'I won't fail,' I said. 'Don't worry.'

'I'm not worried,' said Blini placidly, and she stepped on to the shining escalator which whisked her away, across the coloured sherbet of the sky.

I took the stairway to the top of the Ludgate Tower, where I lived with my mother. You won't remember the Ludgate Tower, but in my time it was a byword for luxury. Some of the junior statesmen lived there, although I never actually saw them. We had been allocated our apartment because my father was a hero; an official hero, I mean. He died in the Western Reaches, killed by terrorists. As a result, we had special privileges: extra rations in the winter months, seats in the main stadium for the remembrance ceremonies, when you might otherwise be trampled by the crowds.

In the Ludgate Tower the air smelt sweetly of strawberries. They changed the perfumes in the system there every week, so you could never get tired of them as you sometimes did in other buildings. There were four scents: cinnamon, peach, gardenia and my favourite, strawberries. The smell cheered me up after Blini's oblique warnings.

'Hullo, Darrow,' said Flavian, as I stepped into our living unit. He was watching the television. 'What did you learn at Citizens, then?'

'Acknowledge but do not valorise your blood relations,' I said, in the sing-song voice Blini had used. Flavian laughed.

'Very good, Darrow,' he said. 'Very good.'

There was something unexpected about Flavian. He smiled, of course, like everyone else, but his smile was not the same as other people's; it was as though he meant something quite different by it. He looked different from other people too, with a brown leathery face which was unusually soft to touch. I'm still not sure exactly what relation Flavian was to me. My mother was always vague about it, although on the residence documents she called him her cousin. He came to live with us when I was five, after my father was killed, and my mother was given permission to remain celibate. That was another of the privileges granted to her because of the circumstances of my father's death.

On the television screen a doctor appeared, with a needle in his hand. It was the birth programme; they showed it all the time. Every day they picked a different woman who was having a baby, and filmed it, to show to the rest of us the nature of the miracle. I put away my satchel, and sat next to Flavian on the vinyl sofa.

'Where's my mother?' I asked.

The doctor was giving the woman an injection. Her face was luminous with joy.

'Tcha,' said Flavian, and with one hand he zapped away the picture. In its place came the image of a fireplace, flames burning endlessly in the grate to the accompaniment of electronic music. My mother came out of her bedroom.

'How was Citizens?' she asked.

'All right. They said I've got to stay late next week, for more assessments.'

'Ah,' said my mother. She was wearing a shiny scarlet tunic made of polyester; like all her clothes, it reflected the light. My mother was a very beautiful woman. She had the most remarkable smile, which spread slowly, blissfully, from her lips across the whole of her face. At least a dozen men had protested to the authorities when she was given the right to remain celibate. They said they wanted her because she had proved her fertility, but really it was because of her wondrous smile.

'How are the assessments going?' she asked. I gave a shrug. All sixteen-year-old girls had assessments, to find the best partners for us. One of my Citizens classmates, a plump dark girl called Jazz, had already been paired off with a junior statesman. Young mothers were supposed to produce the healthiest children, and besides, it stopped us forming spontaneous attachments.

'Fine,' I said. 'High on physical strength, average on motivation. They say my intelligence quota's still too great, and they need someone high-drive to cancel it out.'

Flavian gave a short bark of laughter. My mother glanced across at him, abruptly. Then she said:

'So they probably won't fix you up for a while?'

'Probably not. I don't know.'

My mother let out a short, dreamy sigh, and came to sit beside me on the banquette. With one hand she began to unpick the slithery braid of my hair. I loved it when she did this, releasing my scalp from the sharp pull of my plait.

'Ah, Darrow,' she said, in her soft sleepy voice. 'I wish you could stay with us forever.'

'You're being unpatriotic,' said Flavian, cheerfully. 'Darrow will report you.'

My mother's fingers were busy unravelling my hair.

'You'd never report us, would you, Darrow?' she said. I did not answer. My throat felt sharp and dry. I tried to concentrate on the exquisite relief of having my plait loosened.

'I wouldn't be too sure,' said Flavian, in that same jolly voice. 'What was it you learned today, Darrow? Do not valorise your blood relations.'

'Acknowledge but do not valorise . . .' I started mumbling. My mother let her hands drop.

'Ah, Darrow,' she said, softly. 'Must we corrupt you?'

I twisted towards her. Lately I had noticed that her smile had lost some of its lustre. It seemed now to involve only her mouth; her eyes remained dark, as though they were perpetually on guard.

'I don't understand,' I said.

Both Flavian and my mother looked at me. Perhaps, after all, they were cousins: certainly, at that moment, their faces seemed very much alike, staring across at me with an expression which, even now, I can't describe. It might have been apprehensiveness; it might have been hope. There was a silence, as though we were all three holding our breath. Then Flavian said:

'Don't trouble yourself, Darrow. We're only teasing.'

'Yes,' said my mother. 'Of course we want you to be a good citizen.' She put out her hand and tweaked at the last knot in my hair. 'Just like your father.'

That night Flavian told me a story. Flavian often told me stories; not the approved ones which all new parents had to learn by heart, but ones he made up himself, stories about a different world, a different city. He talked about a time when people could breathe in the open air, when the river turned to ice and they lit bonfires upon it. He talked about how they set off special toys made of gunpowder in a place called Hyde Park, and how the toys burst brightly in the sky, like fake sunsets or enemy gunfire. He talked about mythological beasts, white police horses and different species of dog, roaming through the streets. That night, though, he told me another kind of story. It was about an old king, who had three daughters. I didn't really understand it; I certainly didn't understand all the words Flavian used. But there was something mesmeric about his voice, so that you never stopped to ask. In the story, the old king asked his daughters to look after him, but one was angry and ran away, and the other two were cruel to him. The angry daughter came home to rescue him, because she realised she was wrong to run away, but by the time she reached him it was too late. I can still hear the note in Flavian's voice as he said those words: too late.

The story gave me strange dreams. In my sleep I saw Blini smiling up at me from the Fleet Street quagmire, I saw Flavian's brown fingers preparing an injection, I saw my mother, spinning out of reach on the gleaming escalators. Dreams were the sign of a bad conscience: I had been told that in Citizens class. I got out of bed to find a pill to take.

My bedroom was the smallest in the apartment; it overlooked the river, curling through the darkness like a greasy ribbon. Sometimes I could just hear the creak of the great metal barges they used to ferry out the city's waste. Quietly I opened my door, my feet cold on the perspex tiles. The air still smelt encouragingly of strawberries.

I reached for the box of pills which my mother kept in the galley cupboard. As I did so I heard a sudden, gruff noise coming from Flavian's room. Flavian's room was a mystery to me. As the man of the household he was allowed to keep it locked, and I had never been inside. Once or twice I had glimpsed strange objects through the door – a green glass flagon, an old-fashioned videotape – and occasionally I noticed a musty, musky scent which seemed to come from the room. Now I crept up softly. The sound had grown sharper, sweeter, like the whinnying of the pretty horses Flavian had described to me. Then it changed again, became two noises entwined in one, a deep grunt with a high, sobbing descant. I pressed my cheek against the shut door. All at once the sounds died away, as though someone had swallowed them in two or three mouthfuls. I took my pill, and slipped back into bed.

At Citizens class the next day I kept remembering the noises in the night; it was hard to concentrate on learning my lesson. Today's statement was: A civilised society cannot condone sickness, of body or of mind.

'What are you thinking about?' asked Blini, as we were walking back towards the escalators. She was chewing pink flavoured gum.

'Nothing,' I said. 'Well – nothing much.'

I didn't want to tell Blini about the noises, so instead I told her Flavian's story, about the king and his three daughters. She didn't listen quietly, as I had done; she kept asking questions I couldn't answer, about how old the king was, where the daughters lived. When I told her about the good daughter coming home, and weeping to see her father, Blini stared at me.

'Weep?' she said. 'What's "weep"?'

'I don't know,' I said. Blini looked at me for a moment. Then she took the pink gum out of her mouth, rolled it into a little hard ball, and dropped it into the chrome wastebin beside the escalators.

'Do you think your mother and Flavian have formed an attachment?' she asked.

'Of course not,' I said. 'They're cousins. That's what it says on the residence papers.'

'Unorthodox matings are a crime against the state,' said Blini, in the droning voice she used to recite our Citizens lessons; and once again she whirled away on the escalator, out of my sight.

When I got home to the Ludgate Tower I found that the table had been laid for our evening meal. Flavian and my mother were already sitting there, waiting for me. My mother's face was more watchful than ever, her smile a bare flicker of the lips.

'Sit down,' said Flavian, and he reached to pour me a drink. I saw that on the table stood one of the glass flagons I had glimpsed in his room. He filled my cup with a red liquid, darker than chewing gum, brighter than cola.

'What is it?' I asked. The tight feeling in my throat returned, sharper than ever. I could feel my own heart beating.

'Drink, Darrow,' said Flavian. Obediently I bent my head, and I drank. The liquid was strange, almost bitter; I had tasted nothing like it before.

'What is it?' I asked again.

'It's wine,' said Flavian. 'It came from France.'

'What's France? It doesn't exist any more, does it?'

'It's not habitable, if that's what you mean,' said Flavian. He drank from his own cup, slowly, savouring the dark liquid. 'It was very beautiful, once. I travelled across it as a young man, before the War.'

I took another mouthful of the wine. It was so odd a flavour, somehow more complicated than the sweet drinks I was used to.

'Darling,' said my mother, putting her hand over mine, 'darling, we have something to tell you.'

I can't explain how it felt. It was like always knowing and never guessing, both at once. Partly it was the pressure of my mother's hand; partly it was that word, darling. I looked, not at my mother, but at Flavian.

'You're fifty,' I said.

Flavian smiled.

'That's right. I'm fifty.' He lifted his cup. I noticed that his front teeth were stained a dim purple colour.

'Aren't you going to the hospital?' I said.

'No,' said my mother, in a voice which bit. 'No, he's not going to the hospital.'

Flavian made a noise in the back of his throat, intended to calm my mother. Then he said:

'Darrow, you've never seen anyone old, have you? You've never seen anyone ill?'

'Of course not. We live in a civilised society. We don't allow people to endure that.'

'Yes, that's right,' said Flavian. 'No sickness, no pain.'

'What's "pain"?' I asked. Impatiently my mother stood up.

'We have to leave,' she said.

'What?'

'We have to go. All three of us.' She stood by the galley door, in her glittering red tunic, like one of the banned deities. 'Did you know, in the Western Reaches you can breathe the air? Did you know that? You don't have to stay behind the glass. You can get drunk if you want to. You can have sex for pleasure. You can smell muck and shit and wet leaves. You can be unhappy if you want. You can wallow in unhappiness.'

I was still staring at my mother when Flavian reached out and held my wrist. I wanted to pull my arm away, it was so peculiar to think that I was being touched by someone who was fifty, someone who shouldn't be alive, but it wasn't as frightening as you might think. His hand was warm and dry, just as it had always been.

'Darrow,' he said, in a deep quick voice, 'tomorrow night we'll go down to the river. The three of us. We can get through the gate where they load the waste barges. There'll be a boat. We'll get away from the city, and travel west overland.'

'But the terrorists,' I said.

My mother gave a snort; an echo of those fierce horse-sounds I had heard through Flavian's door.

'Don't tell me, Darrow, that they've turned you into a good citizen after all,' she said. 'There are no terrorists. There are people who think differently.'

'Hush,' said Flavian. His voice seemed to reverberate in my head. I felt suddenly as if my mind was clouding over, the way the sky grew smoky and dense after sunset. I heard my mother say:

'It must be the wine.'

Then I remember arms lifting me, and my head lolling, and Flavian's voice saying, too much, in the same way that he had said, too late. Then nothing.

When I woke up my face felt stiff and unusual. It was very early. Slowly I got out of bed, put on my clothes and went out, towards the escalators. I had only been to Blini's apartment twice, but I knew the way. Her building smelt of roses, the scent pumping noisily from the vents.

'Darrow,' said Blini's father, when he answered the door. He was a tall pink man, dressed in overalls. He didn't seem at all surprised to see me.

'Is Blini here?' I asked. I wanted to talk to Blini, to find out what she would say if I told her it was possible to leave the city, possible to breathe fresh air in the Western Reaches. But her father shook his head at me.

'She's still asleep, Darrow. Come in.'

Their living unit looked like ours, with the same sort of furniture, the same shiny perspex floor. On the television screen a senior statesman was talking about the population figures. Blini's father poured me a tumbler of cola, and he patted the beige seat of their banquette.

'Now, Darrow,' he said, in a friendly voice, 'I think you'd better tell me about it.'

I suppose you'll ask me why I told him. The answer is, I don't know. At the time – at the time, you understand, I needed to tell him. It was what I had been schooled to do. He sat there, watching me with Blini's opaque unrelenting eyes, and I told him everything.

When I had finished he gave my knee a pat.

'Good girl,' he said. 'I can tell you're a hero's daughter. I'll go and wake Blini, and she can walk with you to Citizens.'

'But they'll be all right, won't they?' I said. 'Flavian and my mother. They'll be all right?'

'Oh, yes,' said Blini's father, smiling. 'They'll be all right.'

We were halfway across the Fleet Street bridge when I saw the security men, coming down the escalator from the Ludgate Tower. They were carrying two clean white sacks.

'What is it?' said Blini. 'What are you looking at?'

The men had disappeared now, in the direction of the

river, where the waste barges were moored. I ran. I ran back along the Fleet Street bridge, up the stairway which led to the Ludgate Tower. The door to our apartment was open, the wood splintered around the lock. Inside my mother's shining clothes had been flung across the living unit, like scraps of coloured paper. The glass flagon had fallen from the table, and the rest of Flavian's wine had spilled in a crooked red lake across the floor. The air still smelt of strawberries. I reached down slowly to pick up the glass flagon. I was suddenly aware that there was water on my cheeks, and that the water tasted beguilingly of salt.

Mates 4 Life

JOHN RIETHMÜLLER

Hello there. Nice to meet you. What's your name then? And how are you keeping? My name? Ah, that would be telling, wouldn't it?

Anyway, let me introduce you to Dexter here. Me and Dexter have been together, so to speak, for about six months now. No, we're not 'together' in *that* way. But don't get me wrong. I've got nothing against gay people. Quite the reverse. Oh yes, I've bopped away many a Saturday night in Heaven in my time. But I'm not gay. On the other hand, I'm not heterosexual. I just am. Sounds a bit religious, doesn't it? Like something out of the Old Testament. You know, 'I am that I am' as God said to Moses from the burning bush. I do hope I'm not confusing you. It's simple really. I love love. Everybody loves a lover to quote the Doris Day song, and I'm no exception.

Not a word of this to Dexter, mind. He wouldn't understand all this philosophical stuff. He's a man of action not words. That's not to say he's the silent type – quite the reverse – but he's no great thinker. He's certainly got the gift of the gab, always ready with a mirthless joke. Frankly, I don't think we share the same sense of humour. He's dead straight as he'd be the first to tell you, but you wouldn't think so right at this minute. Just look at him queening it up in front of the triptych mirror of the bathroom cabinet.

He goes through this whole ritual every Saturday evening before going out to the pub. First of all he does five hundred sit-ups on his bedroom floor to get those abdominal muscles really defined. Beauty knows no pain and all that. Then he showers with wash gel by appointment to Her Majesty and dries himself with an ermine-white bath towel. He tooshes up his flat-top, scrutinising it from all possible angles. It's tinted blond at the front like a tiara. He smooths a dollop of royal jelly aftershave balm on to that face of his. And then he blows himself a kiss. Oh, he worships himself, does Dexter. He's got a tan and he exercises four times a week at the Bethnal Green leisure centre. He's always stripped off when it's sunny and he's working down at the building site. He's the one who gets wolf whistles from cockney office girls, and discreet *oeillades* from scurrying men in suits.

Meanwhile, in the kitchen, his mum is busy ironing his ripped jeans and his white T-shirt which has got CALVIN KLEIN written in large black letters on the front so nobody's going to mistake it for any Mr Byrite rubbish.

Me and Dexter have – how can I put it? – a symbiotic relationship. Know what I mean? Oh, you don't. Well, the dictionary defines symbiotic as 'two organisms living attached to one another or one within the other to their mutual advantage'. Now, to be perfectly honest, I need him a lot more than he needs me. All right, I'll come clean. He doesn't need me at all. He behaves as if I don't actually exist. And he certainly wouldn't be too pleased about having me as a pal. Not very good news for the old ego, eh? But I'm tough. He can ignore me for the time being. Oh, yes. For years if he likes. But I'll always be there with him. Changing his life in lots of little ways. He won't notice at first. But then, one fine day, to quote that hit by the Chiffons, he'll realise I'm with him. I wonder what his reaction will be? We can't always choose our companions through life, can we? Funny how me and Dexter have become mates. It was just one of those things. Oh, there I go again – quoting all these song titles. You must think I'm quite a cheery soul. Well, I always was the joker in the pack. As I was telling you, it was just one of those crazy things. Kismet. Fate. In the lap of the gods. Well, not strictly true. If Dexter wasn't so 'devil-may-care-couldn't-give-a-toss-about-anybody-except-numero-uno' things might have been very different. Very, very different. But that's just what I liked about Dexter. He was an easy bloke to team up with.

How did we meet, I hear you nosy parkers asking. Dexter doesn't realise this but it was some bird who introduced me to him one Saturday night about a year ago. She turned out to be a one night stand. You know how it is. We met at Puffin's, a flash East End pub, all mock-posh and neon. I hadn't been there before. It's a bit cliquey and you might think I wouldn't fit in. But you'd be surprised. Oh, yes. I fit in anywhere. I'm good like that. Cocktail parties in Belgravia. Warehouse raves in Barnet. Booze-ups in Balham. You name it, I've been there. I'm very protean. I think that's the right word, though it's not one Dexter would use. He'd think I'd swallowed the blooming dictionary.

Now Dexter's a regular face down at Puffin's. And I've met one or two young ladies thanks to him. Oh, he's quite a Jack the lad. I'll never forget the night he introduced me to Charlie . . .

. . . Dexter and me are at Puffin's as per usual for a Saturday night. Or to be more precise, we're outside Puffin's on the pavement with our mates, having a laugh and a bevy and checking out everybody and talking about the clothes we've bought this afternoon. The atmosphere is menacing with designer perfumes and aftershaves. It's a hot August night. Could be Ibiza. Only it's not – it's Bethnal Green. Love is in the air, as that quaint old seventies disco hit put it. The music is thuddingly loud. They're playing my favourite record: 'People Are Still Having Sex' by LaTour. You see, I'm not quite the old fogey you thought I was. In fact I'm not sure exactly how old I am. I could be a teenager. Or in my twenties. Or, shockerama, even older. Nobody knows.

Yes, the joint is jumping. Dexter's out for a good time. He's ignoring me. I don't care. I'm used to it. Then he spots Charlie. And her girlfriends. They're a chattering conclave of carefully tousled hair, sparkling eyes, full pink lips, flamingo legs and sunbed tans.

'Here, Charlie. Get a load of that bloke. He's not half bad. And he's giving you the eye,' her best friend Samantha twitters. Charlie's eyes flash in Dexter's direction. He smiles back his Marti Pellow smile and saunters over to her.

'How's tricks?' he says, removing his Ray Bans. She notices his long, curly lashes with the appraising eye of the trainee beautician that she is.

'All right,' She's deliberately deadpan. She knows that facial expressions accelerate the ageing process.

'Let me introduce myself,' he says. 'Dexter. That's me. And what's your name then?'

'Charlie,' she mews.

'Funny name for a girl,' he says.

'Yeah, I know. Mum called me Charlie after the fragrance. I used to hate my name when I was little but now I quite like it. Anyway, what about your name, then? Dexter. It's a fizzy drink, innit,' she says with a teensy-weensy pout of her pussy-cat mouth.

'Okay, okay. And talking of drinks, what's yours?' he asks.

'Mine's a pina colada,' she says, ignoring Samantha's titters and suppressing a desire to snigger herself. She lights up a Silk Cut and blows a feather of smoke through her nostrils.

'Right. Your wish is my command. Don't go away now,' Dexter shouts as he shoves through the crowd and into the pub, nodding to various pals and slapping them on the back. He knows a hell of a lot of people. A popular bloke, our Dexter. Always game for a laugh. And what could be a bigger laugh than karaoke? He can't wait to grab the mike and sing along to 'Bachelor Boy'. Up on the screen behind Dexter is a compilation video of clips from early Cliff Richard films such as *Summer Holiday*. And the crowd at Puffin's is loving every swivel and thrust of Dexter's performance which is modelled on George Michael in his artless Wham! days. Dexter has been practising in front of his bedroom mirror. His routine may be a bit of a send-up but he takes the singing part dead seriously. Everyone joins in the chorus and Dexter soars above all the others. He loves the sound of his own voice and who knows? Perhaps there'll be an impresario in the pub crowd who'll sign him up on the spot to a lucrative recording contract. Well, we all have our dreams, don't we? The song comes to an end and his mates cheer and whistle and Dexter takes a bow and blows Charlie a kiss. She turns on her white spiked heels to say something to Samantha and they cackle. He ignores the cries of 'more, more', and jumps down from the stage. He's a bloke who knows just when to stop. He pushes his way to the bar, grabs his drinks and goes back to Charlie.

'You're a cocky bugger,' she sneers.

'I'm going to be a megastar one of these days,' he says.

'Oh yeah?' she drawls. She's not impressed. 'Well, I'm hoping to become a model myself. The Adam and Eve Agency in Bow are signing me up next week.'

'Snap!' says Dexter. 'I might be going on their books

myself. Perhaps we might do a modelling assignment together . . . very soon. Just you and me.'

He takes a meaningful swig at his lager can. She sips her pina colada provocatively. And burps daintily.

'Manners,' she giggles. Her nose whiffles prettily. They both laugh, showing strong, white teeth, a tribute to fluoride and the NHS.

. . . Tempus fugit. It's half eleven. Dexter and Charlie have been talking on and off for about a couple of hours. I haven't said a word. Dexter has made a couple of snide jokes about me and the famous people I've known. Let him. I'll have the last laugh one day, don't you worry. Right now he's very much in control. He doesn't drink much. Interferes with the work-out routines. But Charlie. Oh dearie me. She's pretty far gone. All those pina coladas. But I don't mind. Makes my job easier if you catch my drift. Dexter takes her elbow and she teeters to his white Ford Escort with him.

'Smart car,' she mutters grudgingly.

'It's bog standard at the moment,' he says, opening the door for her. 'But I'm going to start customising it. I can get my hands on a lot of spare parts, if you know what I mean.'

She collapses into the passenger seat and he clunk-clicks the safety belt for her.

'By the way, don't take it personal, but I'd rather you didn't light up. I don't like the smell of smoke in the car.'

'Suit yourself,' she says sulkily, popping her cigarette packet back down the front of her lycra dress.

'Where to now, doll?' He nuzzles her ear as he slides a Salt'n'Pepa cassette into the sound system and flips the volume up full blast. 'Let's talk about sex, baby! Let's talk about you and me . . .'

'Your place?' she screeches.

So they drive to Dexter's mum's council flat in Hoxton but an aurora borealis is flickering up in the living room which means his mum is watching the late night movie on the telly and Dexter doesn't think it would be right to you-know-what with his mum still up and about. So they snog a bit in the car and then Dexter suggests: 'Your place?'

'No,' she says. 'My, er, auntie lives with me and I don't want her thinking I'm a slag or anything.'

It's one o'clock and Dexter's desperate and it's going to have to be a quickie in the car. Then he remembers the secluded patch of waste ground up the road from the pub. The night is balmy so what the hell. In next to no time we've whizzed back to Puffin's. The street is deserted apart from an old man, fag in his mouth, dawdling with a mongrel. There's the faint chick-a-boom of music coming from a distant party. The old man turns round to stare at us and coughs his heart out. Charlie gives him a vicious V-sign and then kicks off her stilettos. We squeeze through a gap in the corrugated iron fence. A crow caws and we hear the whirr of its wings as it flies up and away. Charlie gasps.

'It's all right. Nothing to worry about,' whispers Dexter, putting his arm around her waist. We pick our way through the burnt-out mattresses and sofas and find a spot under a rapacious buddleia. A full moon is shining. The night is made for love. I bide my time ready to strike . . .

'Oi. Mind how you take my dress off. It's a Miss Selfridge original and it cost me a fortune', Charlie hisses as Dexter tosses the dress away. He slips out of his own jeans carefully and folds them over a bush. Then he peels off his T-shirt and lays it under Charlie's head.

'Mmmmm. Your hair smells nice,' he murmurs, caressing her cheek hungrily.

'It's my Body Shop banana conditioner,' she sighs. 'And, by the way, what about a rubber?' she adds as an afterthought. I hold my breath. Is she going to insist on a condom? That would certainly put the kibosh on me. 'Don't be daft. Only queers use johnnies,' he growls. Like millions of others, I'm glad to say he never ever uses them.

'Well, that'll be extra then,' Charlie says pertly.

'What did you say?' Dexter is momentarily put off his stride.

'Only joking,' mumbles Charlie as she succumbs to Eros. 'Ouch! Don't be so rough. Go easy. You're hurting me,' she squawks. 'For Gawd's sake, stop it.'

But Dexter ignores her and plunges on and on, lost in his own pleasure . . . and that's how I grabbed my chance and got to know Charlie. Just like I've got to know thousands of other people. No one ever believes that I could possibly be there with them. How wrong can they be?

. . . Dexter thinks about that summer night under the stars and smirks. Bit too nippy for that kind of thing in October, though. He pats some Eau Sauvage on his chin and puts on the gold – the ear stud, the box chain and the Victorian sovereign ring. He tells his mum to get him a Special Brew from the fridge and slumps into an armchair to watch *Blind Date*. He slurps impatiently at his lager and glances at his fake Rolex. He'll be ready to hit Puffin's in about an hour. Charlie's gone away with her auntie to Southend for a few days so Dexter's footloose and fancy free. I wonder which lucky girl he's going to get off with this evening. It'll be a night she remembers forever if I get my way.

Some Londoners

LAURETTA NGCOBO

On this Wednesday morning, as on every other morning, Sandra sneaked into her classroom at 9.40, hoping the teacher would not see her coming in so late, just before assembly. She could see the teacher's back facing the other way, and for a moment she thought she had won her hide-and-seek game. She was just going to sidle into her seat, when she looked again, and realised that it was not the familiar back of Miss Davidson, but that of the weekly supply teacher, Mrs Sweetman. It was the third week of term at John Neville Junior School in the south of London and she hated the new idea that every Wednesday they would have this 'old dumpy excuse for a teacher'.

At that moment, she swung round and her little figure seemed to surge up high as she walked straight up to the teacher. With her coat sloppily hanging half-way down her shoulders, as always, her little arms akimbo, she shoved right into the half-turned figure of Mrs Sweetman, visibly jolting her. In the same movement she sprang right in front of her and hissed, 'Miss, what does non-contact time mean?'

'Why, it's you? When did you come in? The dinner register's gone in . . .'

'Miss, I said what is non-contact time? . . . What d'you want here? Why does Miss Davidson have to do non-contact time? . . . Away from us? . . . Just what is non-contact time? . . . Why don't you go and do it yourself?'

'Hurry up Sandra, take off your coat. It's time for assembly. Class, put down your pens . . . assembly time.'

'Miss . . .'

'I'll explain later Sandra. Go to the line. Line up everyone.'

'We don't want you here. We want our teacher.'

'Mandy, you'll lock the classroom door please. The key's on the table. Right, Shall we go?'

Mrs Sweetman turned round quickly to lead the class. She could feel the palms of her hands beginning to sweat. Sandra made her nervous. The child was unpleasant, and there seemed no way to predict her behaviour. What was worse was the power to influence the other children that she seemed to have. As soon as she came into the classroom, the whole atmosphere changed. A restless shudder seemed to go through the class and the whole air heaved. She had that effect. Suddenly the peaceful hum of a contented group of children would turn hostile and spiteful, as if ashamed to be caught 'betraying' Miss Davidson. She made the whole class feel that co-operating with Mrs Sweetman was the greatest act of disloyalty to their teacher. Her appearance seemed to marshal the group. This was reinforced frequently through the day, each time she chose to go to the toilet, which was often. Her toilet visits, of course, were longer than those of any other child. As soon as she would come back in, the volume of noise would suddenly rise several decibels. The children would lose interest in whatever they were doing, moaning that they did not know what to do, or did not understand the work, or that it was downright boring. Then they would start rolling bits of paper from nowhere, making pellets that they threw at each other and occasionally at Mrs Sweetman herself when they thought her back was turned. Suddenly the classroom floor would be littered with all sorts of rubbish that had not been there before. A few would find reason to stand up and wander around, looking for 'I can't find what'. If Mrs Sweetman should say one word of rebuke, some child might even answer testily with a tell-tale smirk on its face, seeking approval from the one girl in class whom they all, strangely enough, did not particularly like. It would take another while to settle them again back to a calm, working class. For some unknown reason, they owed allegiance and paid dutiful homage to her. But, what was remarkable was that they withheld their true friendship, that all-life-giving tribute that all children crave. In spite of her strange power over them all, she was decidedly lonely.

There was only one Asian girl in class, Neema, who in her own loneliness, sought her friendship for all it was worth. She was a new arrival in the school, straight from Bangladesh. With Sandra on her side she was not so taunted and isolated. Sandra helped her with her work as well. Mutual needs, mutual satisfaction. On occasions at play times Mrs Sweetman would observe the two standing together, leaning against the wall, invariably eating sweets, which was against the school rules. Sandra would be talking endlessly, and Neema would be listening intently. All the better for Neema's language acquisition. They were never more isolated than when out there standing and sharing each others company where no one else would.

In the few weeks that Mrs Sweetman had been there, she could feel she was losing control of the class. That morning the fear of losing control burnt her like a fever as she walked into the assembly hall. Mr Boyd, the headmaster, was taking assembly. There followed a twenty-minute period of non-contact time for all the other teachers. They all raced back to the staff room and with cups of tea in hands, they came out racing back to their classrooms or stock rooms to do whatever they needed to do, while their charges were out of the way. But Mrs Sweetman had no thoughts of coffee that morning. She dashed along the corridor to look for Miss Davidson in the office where she, as deputy head-teacher, was doing her other administrative tasks for the morning. That's why Mrs Sweetman was at the school, once a week, to relieve the deputy to do her other chores.

'Miss Davidson, please tell me about Sandra.'

'Sandra? What's up with her now?'

'Well, I need to know more. She's done nothing specific so far, but there's no doubt that something's going to explode any time. She's aggressive. She's provocative . . .' Mrs Sweetman was awash with a mixture of shame, failure and embarrassment. She wouldn't tell the other teacher, in the presence of the secretary and a few others, all the details of the humiliating behaviour. For the experienced teacher that she was, it was not easy admitting failure to deal with a puny eleven-year-old. Sandra, for all her bravado, was quite small for her age.

'When did she come in this morning?'

'Same as usual, if I go by what I see in the register. Why's she so disruptive? I need to know more in order to contain her. What's the matter with her?'

'Nothing . . . most of the time. Nothing, as long as I'm there. She fastens on to one person, and she will accept no one else after that. For now, that person happens to be me. I don't know if there's anything that anybody can do once she starts. But to be honest with you, she's not been too bad in the last few days.'

'She resents your not being in class. She said as much just now when she came in.'

'I'll have a word with her when they come out of assembly.'

That remark alone cut Mrs Sweetman to size. In the very act of Miss Davidson offering some help, Mrs Sweetman was aware that she was conceding her own power of control. It was humiliating. The act of asking for another teacher's assistance was also an admission of failure on her part. So she walked out, hoping for the magic wand that Miss Davidson would use to sweeten the disaffected child. Anything, anything to humour the child just for the day.

As soon as assembly was over, and the children were pouring out of the hall, Miss Davidson was there. She pulled Sandra gently out of the line and led her back to the office with her. As they walked together Sandra clung on to the teacher's crook of the arm, closely leaning against Miss Davidson as to a long-lost friend.

When Miss Davidson finally spoke to her she warned her firmly but kindly.

'Look Sandra, there's no point in you pretending all is well, because you know you're not being good in the classroom. In fact, you're being rude to Mrs Sweetman . . . Get this clearly. Teachers are not there for you to like or dislike. Teachers are there to teach you . . .'

'Did you say she's sweet Miss? Huh! She's horrible.'

'Now, that's enough of that Sandra. And you had better get this here and now, Mrs Sweetman is there in the classroom to teach you and there's jolly little you can do about it, but behave yourself . . . Now, let her do her job without having to swallow your insults.'

'Miss . . .'

'I don't expect you to be rude to anyone, least of all to teachers.'

'But Miss . . .'

'I'm very serious Sandra. Now go.'

'But . . .'

'But me no buts. The sooner you get used to the idea that

I'm not the only teacher in the world, the better for you and for all of us. Now, you go in there and behave yourself.'

When Sandra walked into the classroom she was fuming. She found a very quiet class, with their noses in their maths books. She walked in silently and Mrs Sweetman had her back to the door, so she didn't see Sandra coming in. Sandra sneaked up to one of her soft targets and jabbed him hard on the side with her elbow, pushing him right off his seat. Pandemonium broke loose. By the time Mrs Sweetman turned back, Mark was hot on Sandra's heels, weaving in and around the tables, the other children laughing and shrieking in excitement. The class was in chaos. Mr Boyd just 'happened' to be passing by in the corridor at that very moment.

'It's Sandra, it's Sandra, Mr Boyd. It was all quiet until she came in. I don't know what she did to Mark . . .'

'Sandra, take your books and come with me. You're going to work outside my office this morning. I'm tired of your ways.' He held the door and ushered her out, without even as much as a word to the offended teacher. Mrs Sweetman felt no more significant than a crawling snail. Another drain on her store of confidence. She could feel a flow of resentment coursing through her whole body. It was the children, the teachers, the whole school. This day set the pattern of her social position in the school for the rest of her days at the John Neville Junior School. An incompetent teacher. Perceived by both staff and children as such.

That lunch hour Mr Boyd met Mrs Sweetman in the corridor and without any preliminaries he said, 'Please don't take anything that Sandra does personally. It's nothing to do with you, but everything to do with Sandra herself. She has lots of problems.'

'What is it exactly?'

'She's an only child. Mother's on her own. A very nice

woman but she keeps herself to herself and she likes to think she can manage her own affairs. She puts infinite trust in Sandra. A nurse. You know what nurses' hours are like. She's got no one to look after Sandra when she goes to work. Neither does she want anyone to do it. She'd like to think she's coping. That's from what we can glean from some of Sandra's talk and the occasional remarks from some of the other mothers. I don't think she's very popular in the estate. Other mothers have nothing good to say about her. Very isolated. She lives for Sandra. For these reasons, and others that we don't know enough about, she's chosen to work night shifts. In this way Sandra can mind herself in her sleep at night and not need a child minder. So she thinks. This arrangement gives her more time off of course and she's paid more for night work. It also means she can see Sandra off to school in the mornings when she gets back from work, before she goes off to sleep during the day. She wakes up when Sandra returns from school. It seems a perfectly neat arrangement for herself, but I don't think it's working for Sandra.'

'I'd have thought this is a clear case for social services. Forgive me asking, what've they got to say about it?'

'Well, for one thing, it's only recently that the picture is becoming clearer. And, frankly speaking, our social worker is very laid back, I'm afraid to say. I haven't seen him for the last three weeks, would you believe.'

'Is there no father in the picture?'

'Clearly not. I understand when she first came into this country, she came to join her husband who was studying at the time. She worked hard as a nurse, helping him maintain the home while he studied. But no sooner had he completed his studies than he abandoned her. I believe they're from Ghana. Apparently she was left with Sandra, who was a baby at the time. She has, ever since, lived in this isolation, and will not have any officials of any kind sniffing around her. Frankly, I doubt if her legal status in this country is what it should be.'

'But, after all these years?'

'No one knows. It's all conjecture.'

'I understand Miss Jones is the teacher with responsibility for special needs. Has she been to see the mother?'

Mr Boyd visibly stiffened. 'I believe she's been, but got no joy.'

'Just what would make a sensible mother like that leave her child so exposed?'

'And how? Sandra is everywhere every evening, I understand. As soon as her mother's off to work, Sandra's off playing with whoever.' That's if we can call it that. She's the bane of one or two old ladies in the flats at the Studdley Estate. She taunts them in every way. She enjoys reducing adults to distraction.'

'Her vengeful way on the adult world, I suppose. Her mother, of course, wouldn't know any of that, would she?'

'Very vulnerable, Sandra is. I've been worrying about her a lot since I've been able to piece things together. At her best she's a very sensible child. At least she's been until recently. Very bright, when she chooses to do her work. The mother's taken in by Sandra's general grasp of things. They're very close.'

'Really? But they hardly have time together?'

'Well, there you are. Somehow they are. Clearly Sandra knows how to manipulate her mother. She makes her believe one thing and she does another.'

The following Wednesday, Sandra came in late again, decked in a very expensive necklace and earrings. Mrs Sweetman looked at her twice. They were real gold too. She hesitated talking to her about her jewellery. A case of letting sleeping dogs lie. On this day she seemed less concerned with Mrs Sweetman, as she tried to draw the attention of the other children to her jewellery. There were rings on her fingers as well. While Mrs Sweetman pretended not to notice what was going on she could see a small group of her classmates showing great interest in her. At playtime they stood up and flocked mischievously towards the coat-rack. There Sandra opened her bag to show the others loads more items of jewellery. In little whispers she shared them out. It was when they began arguing about which piece was whose that Mrs Sweetman intervened and stood them aside. She then wrote a note and sent a child to Mr Boyd, inviting him to come and sort it out. Several items were of pure gold as Mr Boyd confirmed. They were all her mother's pieces, Sandra admitted. In this one spiteful act, she was both bribing the other children for the price of friendship that she craved and getting her own back on her mother. Perhaps she was resentful of being left on her own, and the lonely lifestyle that affected Sandra's own relationships. Mr Boyd confiscated the whole haul from her and her friends. And, as was to be expected Mrs Sweetman paid the price throughout the rest of the day. Sandra was dreadful to everyone. She turned on the other children and taunted them, snatching things from them and even throwing pencils and rubbers at them. But that day Mrs Sweetman was determined she would ride the storm. Sandra's position had been weakened by the event and Mrs Sweetman was determined to assert her own authority.

As for Mr Boyd, his efforts to reach Sandra's mother by phone were fruitless as she had her phone off the hook while she slept. Sending a letter would be pointless as Sandra would never give it to her. So around 3.30 Mr Boyd drove to the estate, after having been stung by Mrs Sweetman's question earlier regarding the extent of Miss Jones' and perhaps his own pastoral care. The visit was a salutary experience for him. He was face to face with the conditions that many of his own pupils lived under. The place was walled in virtually on all sides with the towering blocks, so that the square in the middle had an air of restriction. Anyway, most of that confined square was taken up by large cars in their second or third phase of service, so that the same square served at least in part as an open garage. There wasn't a blade of grass, let alone a flower. There were 'sleeping policemen' every few yards to safeguard the young children who played freely around the yard among the large old cars. The once-enclosed play area had long lost its fencing, which lay flat and trampled. He went round and round searching for Spelman Court but could not find it. He saw all the familiar names that he knew from the many children's addresses on his register, but he could not find Spelman Court. He went from courtyard to courtyard equally enclosed by endless blocks. It was amazing how little the inhabitants of the estate knew about the blocks beyond the one immediately before them. It was amazing how many times he was misdirected. Finally, he found it. He entered it at the bottom like a maze. Endless stained corridors with graffiti everywhere lay in winding extensions in front of him. The place was soulless, if not downright hostile. They were on the third floor. He was hoping to find the mother awake, perhaps preparing the evening meal before leaving for her night shift. He carried her precious load in his pocket. Sandra had not reached home yet. No doubt still playing along the way or dillydallying in someone else's flat.

After a few knocks at the door, Mrs La Touche ambled sleepily to the door. She thought it was Sandra arriving.

'Aha, Mr Boyd?' she said, widening her eyes. 'Is something the matter? Where's Sandra?'

'Sandra? She should be home by now. It's four o'clock.

School was out at 3.30 as always. Anyway, I imagine she'll soon be here.'

Mrs La Touche craned past the teacher with a frown on her face.

'Just as well she's not here for now because I want a word with you alone.'

'Alone? What's happened to Sandra? Not injured or something?'

'No. Not injured. But I am concerned . . .' The headmaster poured out all his concerns fast, not giving her a moment to defend her Sandra. He emptied his pockets and put the jewellery on the table, so that they both stared at it. When it was all out he stopped as suddenly as he had begun and waited. A few moments ticked on and a slow smile began to play on the corners of Mrs La Touche's mouth.

'Well, Mr Boyd, I can appreciate your concern. But really, there's nothing to worry about. This is not my jewellery. It's Sandra's. You see, my sister loves Sandra so much and always feels sorry for her as an only child in this wild city of London. She maintains that she needs a lot of things to amuse herself. She wants to provide for Sandra, so that in future she will want for nothing. She buys her gold. Gold, Mr Boyd, which does not depreciate like our money. You see in my family we believe in things that endure. Real things . . .'

Mrs La Touche rambled on more about her family and their values than about Sandra and her ways. In the end Mr Boyd suddenly stood up, his hands spread out in despair, and left. Sandra still had not come home.

A couple of weeks later, Mrs Sweetman noticed that Neema would hang around her in the classroom and would not go out to play at break times. It was lunchtime one day as she 'helped' the teacher, arranging books and clearing up. Then Neema opened up.

'You know what, Miss?'

'Yes?'

'Sandra, he open your bag and take out your purse.'

'What? . . . when?' Mrs Sweetman hurried to open her bag. And indeed, her purse was missing. 'Where did she put it? Do you know where it is?'

'I know Miss. In library. The books Miss,' she said, gesturing to show that it was behind the books. So quietly and swiftly the two went to the library. And sure enough the purse lay nestled behind some big books. Mrs Sweetman was obviously shocked but relieved. Her mind was agitating as to when Sandra could have so stealthily opened her bag and, in full view of everyone in class, taken her purse out of the classroom. What to do next, she pondered. She doubted the effectiveness of reporting the matter to the headmaster. Then on their way down the corridor, her mind still in a flurry, she heard the little voice piping up again, no doubt encouraged to say more, sensing the urgency in Mrs Sweetman.

'You know what, Miss?'

'What?' asked Mrs Sweetman distractedly.

'Not tell Sandra I tell you.'

'Eh? Yes of course, I won't . . . But, but why not Neema? I have to ask her about this. I have to tell her where I found it. I have to tell her that she told you it was in the library.'

'Miss, Sandra he say he tell men to burn my house if tell you.'

'What? What men?'

'Men who burn Ashok house.'

'Oh, no. That's impossible . . . How terrible. How does she know who burned Ashok's house?'

'She know Miss.'

'I don't believe this,' Mrs Sweetman said under her breath. 'But she can't possibly know that. She's just frightening you. Don't worry. She won't tell those men to burn down your house.' There was a long silence between them as Mrs Sweetman gazed into the large innocent eyes, seeing the depth of pain and fear in them for the first time. Then Neema broke the silence again as she seized the chance to pour out all her dammed fears and confusion.

'Sandra he go to park.'

'Ugh? Who? What for?'

'A man take her. A big man take her.'

'Take her? Where to Neema?'

'Eh Miss?'

'Where did he go with Sandra?'

'To . . . to . . . to trees. To Clapham Road. To his house Miss.'

'In the park? Which park?'

'In park. To play,' she said indicating the direction of the local Lark Hall Park where many children played.

'Did you go with her?'

'Ya, ya. Many day I go with her. He give her sweet.'

'He gives you sweets too, does he?'

'No, no, Miss. Man he angry with me.' Again she gestured that he sent her off. Shooed her off.

'Are you sure about this, Neema?'

'Er Miss?'

'Did you see this yourself?'

'Yes I see this Miss. He say he take your purse for man. He want to buy her sweets.'

'Did he play in the park with Sandra? . . . Or did he take her to his house?'

'In the park Miss. But Sandra he say he take her to his house.' It was altogether too much for Mrs Sweetman. She did not know whether to believe everything that Neema had told her about Sandra. It was hard to believe everything she had heard of any child. Even for Sandra. Yet, she could not pretend she had not heard it. The fear that she had seen in Neema's innocent face told her some of it must be true, even if she made some allowances for the misunderstandings that must result from Neema's own language deficiencies.

Immediately after school Mrs Sweetman took Neema to the park and asked her to point out exactly where Sandra often met the man. She then took her home and asked her not to come to the park with Sandra that day nor on any other day. She told her it was not safe to come to the park to meet anyone whom she did not know. From there Mrs Sweetman went straight to report what she knew to the Child-Care Unit at the police station. She then went back to the park. She had made up her mind that she would take this matter on in her own right as a private citizen, without reference to the school. That was the advantage of being a supply teacher, with only a few hours a week dedicated to the school. Limited responsibility, limited liability. She felt she owed nobody any explanations.

It was about six o'clock that evening that she saw a tall man hanging around near the spot that Neema had pointed out to her. He was a man in his mid-twenties. She sat on a bench 'reading' a paper with faked detachment. A policewoman and a policeman in private clothes were sitting a distance away, on another bench, facing the other way, feigning disregard. Soon Sandra came hopping along. As she drew close to the man, she began to laugh, clutching something that looked like a small purse in her hand as she rushed forward with her outstretched hand which he took in a most natural way. That laughter. It struck deep into Mrs Sweetman's heart. It was so sweet and happy. It was innocent. She could not believe it was Sandra laughing. She looked up again, almost neglectful of her detective role.

Sandra virtually threw herself into the man's outstretched hands. They immediately walked together like old friends rehearsing an old routine. Mrs Sweetman even had a flickering doubt about the nature of the relationship of those two. Was it as suspicious as it seemed, or was the man a relative or friend of the family? While she dithered, she allowed the couple to pass her by for a couple of paces. But when she puzzled why it was that a relative or friend would meet the child away from home in a park, her mind was soon made up. They passed right in front of Mrs Sweetman, and Sandra was too absorbed to notice her.

'Hallo Sandra.'

She turned and the sound of that voice made her flinch even before she saw Mrs Sweetman's face. She jumped in spite of herself.

'Where're you going with that man?'

Sandra did not answer. But the man took one leap away from Sandra. She turned to look at him, surprised by his sudden abandonment of her. Mrs Sweetman stood up swiftly and stood by Sandra, taking her hand in hers.

'Don't you know you're not to talk to strangers?'

'I'm no stranger. I know the child . . .'

At that very moment the two 'innocuous' police figures sprang from nowhere and advanced quickly towards them. The man gave them one look and summing up the situation, he sprinted away. They soon caught up with him.

Mrs Sweetman was left with a crumbling little girl in her hands. Sandra was hysterical and Mrs Sweetman spent a long time comforting her. She was suddenly a frightened, bewildered child, sobbing uncontrollably in Mrs Sweetman's arms.

'Miss, don't tell my mum I went with a stranger.'

'But Sandra I must. Your mum must know that you were in danger.'

'I promised her, Miss. I promised her not to go with strangers.'

'Sandra, listen, your mum will be happy that the nasty man is now with the police. She'll be happy you're safe. I'll take you to some ladies who're going to look after you until your mum comes.' They sat down and Mrs Sweetman held her in her arms and rocked her comfortingly against her breast for a long time, like some trusted friend. Darkness had gathered and Mrs Sweetman was stirring to take Sandra to the Child-Care Unit when Sandra turned to face Mrs Sweetman and asked.

'Miss, do you have children of your own?'

'No Sandra. I've no children of my own.'

'But Miss, why not?'

'I just didn't get any.'

'Then how do you know how to love children?'

'I love children, Sandra. You're right, I love children. All children. That's why I'm a teacher.'

'But then, who will look after you when you grow old? . . . My mum says she needs me . . . That I'll look after her when she gets old.'

The Mongoose Factor

SIMON MILES

I find all sorts of things in the back of my minicab, my nice Nissan. I keep them in a plastic bag: the flotsam and jetsam of the city's nightlife tide, that washes people through one door and out of the other. While they linger in my mirror, floating around in the back of my cab for a while, I watch them, and they tell me things.

I had a guy in the back of the minicab one night who told me to take him to a 'lost' square. He said a mistake in the one-way system many years ago had left this square stranded, away from any through traffic, and concealed by a lucky combination of hoardings and old walls that meant no one knew of its existence; except for him, the motley bunch of misfits who lived there with him, and an old drunk who had once been a policeman and who still stumbled blindly in and out of the square once a day on his old beat.

Eden Square E1 he called it, and described it as a haven, in which a small piece of pastoral sanity was being preserved within the city's mad embrace. 'God's allotment,' he called it.

He made me drop him off nearby, by Bishopsgate, and paid me £5 to drive away, so I couldn't see where he went. I tried to find the place the next day. But I couldn't.

In my plastic bag I have an old *A–Z* that he must have

left behind. In its index he has scribbled 'Eden Square' after Edensor Rd W4. But a gust of wind whipped pages 62 and 63 from me as I opened the book, so there's nothing I can do.

Maybe the square exists.

Or maybe he was lying.

Another time I had a hooker in the back, her name was Mary. I picked her up near Spitalfields, on a road with gleaming empty offices on one side and neglected ruins on the other. She made me drive around while the police vans left her patch, and we talked.

She'd been on the game for six years she said, and was still a virgin, who fooled men in dark corners with hollowed-out bits of fruit from the old Spitalfields market lodged beneath her skirts.

She said her parents had died when she was young. Her father had been a window-cleaner whose ladders became too short for the new buildings being built around him. He began to take risks, and one day slipped and fell on to one of the many young artists who had begun to move into the area. The end of a long paintbrush that was sticking out of the artist's rucksack had gone through his eye. Her mother died soon after, of, said Mary, a form of sadness.

Mary was only allowed to take one possession to the orphanage: a picture of someone she called 'the man on the mantlepiece', who had long fair hair, blue eyes, and a chocolate heart which he held out in his hand. 'I've seen men like him since,' she told me, 'on keyrings and in churches. But none of them are quite the same.'

Mary said she had a secret garden of hope – for the moment just a dusty scrap of land between slums – into whose grit she'd pour the seed captured in the hollow fruit she kept after each encounter. One day, she believed, 'the man on the mantlepiece' would lead her to a client whose specimen would take, and flowers would grow; and she'd track down that sad man as her prince, and surrender her virginity at last.

Mary was a romantic. She may have been a virgin prostitute as well. I found pomegranate seeds in the back of the cab the next day. I keep them in my plastic bag.

Or she could have been lying.

I had another romantic, of sorts, in the back of the minicab once: a guy who spoke to me of his own strange love, for trees. We had been talking about how green London was, compared to some other capital cities.

The only girl he'd ever loved, because of her name, was called Theresa.

When they were in bed he made her . . . say things.

'Knock knock,' she'd have to say.

'Who's there?' he'd ask.

'Theresa,' she'd reply.

'Theresa who?' he'd enquire.

'Theresa tall and beautiful and rough in the wind . . .' and she'd have to go on and on about them, their power and majesty; and he'd get off on that!

Theresa first tolerated and then condemned his obsession with trees. He himself questioned it. Where had it come from? When he used to go away why had he yearned to see the oak tree in his garden again, rather than his lover?

One night, during a terrible storm – a Tennessee Williams night of lightning and revelations – his mother and father screamed the truth at last into each others weeping faces.

It had been a crap marriage: father away, and possibly unfaithful. Mother at home, young and full of sexual yearning. She'd go out in the night and wrap her legs around the trunk of the oak tree, and rub herself against its bark. The child she bore was not the tree's of course, but the passion she felt at the time strangely was: poulticed from her by its dependability and strength, cf absent weak-willed husband.

After her child, the guy in the cab, was born, she'd sit with him beneath the tree; and this guy's first strong sights were of the leaves in the wind that made the sun wink, knowingly, at him; and he smiled back, in total love with what he saw.

These truths came out. The father, in a rage – 'You loved a fucking tree! You mad cow' – tore into the garden to hack at his oak rival with an axe, and he felled it there and then, and she never forgave him, and he went away, and was found hanging from a tree a month later, on the Heath. And now the son and mother tend the stumps of lives wasted on a crazy kind of love. I dropped him at his Hampstead home. It was autumn. I later found some lovely golden leaves in the back of the cab, which I keep in the plastic bag.

The stump in the garden may have been his sort of stepfather.

Or he could have been lying.

I had a guy in the back of the minicab once with an altogether different type of passion. He was one of those characters your cab scrapes off London's seedy underbelly at times. I picked him up from a brothel.

In my mirror his eyes had the dead lead weight of dead-end self-indulgence: his face a soiled old flannel wrung dry of sweat and base desire by over-exertion. I turned a corner and a gash of neon caught one eye and made it flare briefly in my mirror, and he awoke into a new perverted quest.

'Excuse me,' he sneered.

'What?' I replied.

'For ten guineas would you come home with me, strip off and let me piss all over you?'

'But,' I said, 'I'm not young. I'm unfit. My body's not in trim. You've never seen me naked. When you do you may be disappointed.'

He leant forward: a gourmand greedy for a fourteenth course. 'Oh don't worry my man,' he growled. 'I'll piss over anyone.'

I turned towards him. 'Are you a happy man?' I asked.

He paused, casting his eyes slowly over the shifting lights of Soho through which we sped, and said: 'Yes'.

He accidentally dropped some very imaginatively illustrated hookers' cards from public phoneboxes in the back of the cab when he went, which I keep in my plastic bag.

Maybe he was a happy man.

But then again, maybe he was lying.

I've only ever had a policeman in uniform once in the back of the cab. His name was Dave, and he said he never took his uniform off. When I asked him why, he told me a very strange story.

His father had been a comedian, who had once played the Palladium: a man with an irrepressible sense of humour which sometimes made him neglect to consider other people's feelings. Dave's mother had died in childbirth, leaving Dave's dad to do the rearing.

I never knew this, but apparently the skull of a baby is a very soft and malleable thing. Dave's father got very excited when he discovered this fact, and amused himself while babysitting by slowly and carefully, so as not to cause brain damage, moulding the baby David's head into the shape of a point on which, David complained, his hair sat in a ridiculous tuft.

He confronted his father about it when he was thirteen,

but the way he shook his head in anger made his hair bob about so comically that his father just burst out laughing, pleading forgiveness with the cry: 'but it was just a joke!'

To avoid school playground jibes of 'pinhead' pursuing him into adult life, Dave decided to take a job where the hat would fit, concealing his peculiarity: that of a London Bobby. The welcome side-effect of Dave's disfigurement was a passionate sensitivity towards the underdog, and he claimed to work tirelessly in the fight against London's emergent racism. I found an Anti-Nazi League pamphlet in the back of the cab, and a pointy Father Christmas hat, which I've got in my plastic bag.

So he may have been telling the truth.

But it was December, and the pamphlet had been ripped in two.

So he could have been lying.

Prejudice is something I often see in the back of the cab. I've had some very dangerous people sitting behind me.

Once I picked up an unemployed man who had decided to become a mercenary in Bosnia, where he was a sniper who killed people of one type because he was paid to by people of another type, in a city which was as full of different types as London is.

He said that he had fallen in love with a young woman who he often used to see in his sights. Although he couldn't see her perfectly he thought she was probably very beautiful.

He said he used to shoot at her, not to kill her, but to make her move for him. By aiming just behind her for example, he could make her arch her back, flinging her arms up and thereby forcing the shape of her breasts out against the cotton of her dress for his enjoyment.

I watched his eyes in the mirror as he told me this, and felt cold. He said that lying so still on his hill day after day had brought him close to nature for the first time in his otherwise London life. He had become part of the land, over which tiny insects walked, unafraid. Sometimes they walked out along the barrel of his gun, and even up inside it. One day he fired a bullet that bore an ant, holding on for dear life, down into the valley and into the body of an old man. Apparently, and incredibly, the ant lived and crawled out of the wound and back up the hill.

'How do you know?' I accused.

'Because I saw it arrive,' he bellowed, 'covered in blood and with its little antennae waving in excited anticipation of telling its friends of its adventure.'

One day soon afterwards, he said, the infantry attacked the part of the city where the girl he loved was living; and he waited for the smoke to clear before going down to see what had happened.

He found her lying with other women in a burnt-out school, with her mouth full of chalk.

In the mirror I saw him break down, with his head in his hands and crying uncontrollably.

'It was then,' he sobbed, 'that I realised how wrong, how wrong I had been all the time . . .'

I waited, and hoped for his repentance, but all he said was: . . . 'she wasn't beautiful after all.'

I left him by a pub in the Isle of Dogs, surrounded by howling men with short hair and mad smiles. He dropped a small crumpled black and white photo of a young girl in what looked like a national costume in the back of the cab. I have it in my plastic bag.

It may have been of someone he loved.

Or maybe he was lying about ever having loved anyone.

I find it difficult to know who's lying and who's not. Once I had an old lady in the back of the minicab who told me she'd met a talking mongoose.

It lived in the rafters of an old house in Hendon. People came from far and wide to hear this mongoose talk.

A zoologist and a psychologist had even come to listen to this mongoose; and all contested as to how clearly it expressed itself.

I was impressed.

'What did it look like?' I asked.

'I don't know,' the old woman screeched. 'It lived in the rafters. I told you it lived in the rafters. The rafters. And spoke through holes to the people below. I told you that. It lived in the rafters, and spoke through holes. I told you. Didn't you hear me?'

'Then how,' I asked, 'did they know it was a mongoose?'

The old woman paused, and sighed, impatiently, as if she thought me stupid, and bent forward, her old breath in my ear, and hissed: 'Because we asked him, and he told us.'

'He told us!' People are always telling me things – from the back of my nice Nissan. But are they true? My minicab seems to attract 'the mongoose factor': people late at night, hailing dreams from films and shows, and from the eyes of strangers in whose dark and inconclusive pupils they mix their hopes and dreams, or fears, into a heady cocktail of delusions, fuelled by adrenalin, or drugs, or booze that pours down throats and comes back out again as fantasy or lies, in clubs and pubs and minicabs like mine.

The city's in a fever: sweating and possessed by demons, and crying out through the mouths of its deranged menagerie of people pretending things.

And I can hear the mongoose too, speaking in my head. I can hear voices. And they tell me they are mongooses. But are they fucking mongooses? How am I supposed to know?

And my ruddy Nissan's on the blink again. Exhaust fumes billow over the pavement like the morning mist around fairies and goblins taking on the guise of humans on the city's streets, at night.

Look at them: a busker down from Hull who says his mother slept with Jimi Hendrix; next to a rhinestone cowgirl for whom Texas just means home care; by a tall man crooning in his cups trying to be Sinatra; by a piper down from Airdrie who once fucked Charlotte Rampling, or so he told me; near a big man in a tweed suit who has proof the world is flat; beside an old woman singing Gaelic to buy food to feed her fifteen cats, that she believes love her as much as she loves them. It's a scattered, fey, night-fever that grows into a full-blown basket case of crazy self-delusion. A Saturday bright fever . . . in which I must keep calm. Keep calm. Pack away my plastic bag and take another fare.

'Good evening sir. Morden? Oh, no more than three quid, honest.'

The Bracelets

MARION MOLTENO

These bracelets I'm wearing – Najma gave them to me. She has just come back from Pakistan, her first visit home since she arrived in England thirteen years ago. 'My mother is getting old,' she said. 'I knew if I didn't go now, and something happened to her . . . God may forgive me, but I won't.'

Her father is already dead. He died a month before she left for England, just after her marriage. She was his favourite, she says, the youngest of many sisters. A long line to find husbands for. The others all married cousins and stayed in Pakistan. Perhaps by the time it was Najma's turn he had run out, or perhaps he thought he was doing specially well for her when he wrote to his own cousin in England to look out for someone suitable. And when it was all done, and she was about to set off across the world, he died.

She rustles about in half-unpacked suitcases looking for something she has brought back for me, all the while telling me about her father, her mother, the sisters whom she has seen again after so many years. I sit on the edge of the double bed that almost fills the small bedroom, watching as she pulls out embroidered shawls of green and gold, a blue silk *shalwar* – loose Pakistani trousers gathered in at the ankles, and long *kameez* top of matching fabric. Mirror-work cushion covers, pile upon pile of hand-printed cloth, their intricate patterns crowding out the overblown flowers of her English wallpaper . . .

She emerges triumphant, having found the bracelets. And now she is putting them on me. First this gaudily painted red and blue and white one. Then the delicate gold ones, each so slender, but together making a metal band on my arm, fully an inch wide. Then the other gaudy one, to close the set. She squeezes and presses my flesh and knuckles with one hand, while with the other she manipulates each bracelet over the humps. She has bought an identical set for herself, 'So that we will be like sisters,' she says. Her hands are like mine, big and competent, but the bracelets slip on to her arm in a few wriggly seconds. She laughs when she sees me staring. 'It's an art, putting on bracelets,' she says. 'You have to start when you're a little girl.' Her knuckles can flex into a soft O-shape, as easily as my daughter Jane can flip her body upside down and stand, crab-shaped, stomach arched, or as the African women of my childhood walked gracefully erect with a heavy jar of water on the head and a baby on the back. I can do none of these things. Najma is right, you have to start when you're a girl.

When the bracelets are on, Najma holds my hand, extending my arm so that she can admire the effect. 'They look beautiful on you,' she says – with regret, for she is sure I will not wear them once I have left her house.

'I'll have to wear a skirt,' I say. 'They don't look right with jeans.'

She looks up hopefully – 'Have you *got* a skirt?' – and we laugh at her undisguised pleasure at the discovery. There is hope for me yet.

'It's a woman's first right,' she says.

'What is?' I ask, cautiously. She doesn't usually talk of women's rights, only their duties.

'To make yourself beautiful,' she says. And then, sensing

that I am about to interrupt, she rushes on. 'You're so nice, everyone likes you. You could be beautiful too, but you don't pay any attention. All you need is a little makeup, and just to brush your hair this way – .' She is on her feet, seizing a hair-brush, before I can object, before the moment is lost. She puts me in front of the mirror. I submit passively and let her become absorbed in her work. Her hands move swiftly, competently. 'My sisters and I dress each other,' she says. And because she has just come back from her visit to her family, to Pakistan, she uses the present tense. For a moment she has forgotten that she is in Balham, that she has lost them once again. For a moment I am her sister.

When she is finished, she gazes at me intently. 'You see?' she says. 'You *can* be beautiful. Now why don't you do that for yourself?'

I washed off the makeup before I went downstairs. Najma didn't mind; the game was over. But the bracelets were still jingling on my unaccustomed wrist as I looked into the living room, where Jane and Yasmin had been watching *Neighbours*. Jane's eyes darted to them before I'd even had time to say 'We have to go'; and the moment we were in the car she demanded, 'Where did you get those?'

'Yasmin's mum gave them to me,' I said. But of course she knew that; what she really wanted to know was, why had I consented to wear them?

'They're a present from Pakistan,' I offered. 'In Pakistan all the women wear these. Yasmin's mum wanted to give me something to make me beautiful!'

I could feel her become very still in the seat behind me, a sign for me to go on. So I told her about Najma sitting me in front of her mirror.

'Well?' she asked.

'Well, what?'

'Well, did you explain to her? About why you don't wear makeup and things?'

'It was a little difficult,' I said. 'You see, it mattered a lot to her. She really wanted to feel that we were sisters. And I did too.'

'If you're like sisters it's no use pretending.'

'That's true. I did try and tell her, a little.'

'So,' said Jane, triumphantly, having known it all along. 'What did you say?'

'I asked her if she thinks her mother is beautiful. *I* do – she was showing me photographs of her, and all her family in Pakistan. Her mother's face is lovely – kind and smiling, but full of wrinkles, and no makeup and no jewellery because she's a widow. And her older brother – there's one she's especially proud of. Najma doesn't think her mother or her brother need makeup to make them beautiful.'

Jane was close behind me, her breath soft on my neck, no longer urgent. The world was safe again because I had explained it. Perhaps she even felt sorry for Najma, defeated by such eloquence, for she said, 'Did Yasmin's mum know how to answer?'

'Oh yes,' I laughed. 'She thinks she's right just as I think I am. She said, "Of course it is the *person* who is beautiful, not the makeup, but what's wrong with a little decoration just to make life more interesting?'

Jane said nothing. She leant over to touch the circles of gold on my arm, tinkling softly as I changed gear. For a moment or two she lost herself in their glinting movement, the shiny reds and blues. When she spoke her voice seemed that of a much younger child: 'They're pretty,' she said.

Though she has been at secondary school almost a year, Jane still has the slim-shouldered body of a child, moving with unconscious cat-like grace. Not so her friends, most of whom seem to be growing several inches a month and, when they appear on Saturdays to ask if Jane would like to go shopping with them, stand awkwardly in the doorway as if not knowing where to put their suddenly rounding bodies. Their eyes are ringed with black pencil, their lips unnaturally red. Arrayed in an extraordinary ragbag of styles – skirts long and ungainly one month, short and suggestively tight the next – they look to me like overgrown children, playing at dressing up.

Left to herself Jane is still not bothered about what she looks like, wearing whatever clothes she finds on the floor each morning. Yet her friends' strange new chameleon activities fascinate her. She notices everything – Tracey's brash dangling earrings, the widths of Rebecca's belts. She pretends complete detachment, giving wicked imitations of Charmaine trying to run in her new skirt without her bottom sticking out. Yet I know that she is watching from the sidelines, trying to deduce the rules so that she, too, will be able to play. And I watch her, by turn amused, touched, and angry that she cannot simply continue to be herself. Of course she will not discover the rules for there are none, only conformity to what the others will approve – and she cannot possibly ask what that is for fear of admitting that she does not already know. How the others know is a mystery to me. Perhaps this is another of those skills you have to learn very young, from a mother who herself spends hours wandering around the shops, who notices small changes in fashion, whose dressing table is equipped with eyeliners, lipsticks, and nail-varnish.

Jane bears me no grudge that I am not as other mothers are, but she observes me as sharply as she does her friends. The last time we went to buy her some new trainers she took me over to the rack of Ladies' Sandals – pointed toes, stiletto heels, elegant gold chains. Titillated by the impossibility, she dared me to try them on. Perhaps beneath her glee at having teased me in public she is also testing my reaction, in case she should want to wear shoes like these. It is still my approval she needs, as she tells me that Tracey is taking *fourteen* different outfits on a one-week school journey to France. But already she is making overtures towards that other world, the world I will not take her into but which she senses she will have to enter herself if she is to avoid ostracism. Avidly she watches television commercials, her personal initiation rite. At night in front of the bathroom mirror her toothbrush dangles from her fingers like a cigarette, and she becomes the suave, inexpressibly bored-looking woman accepting a Martini, or the Bird's Eye Mum with neat skirt and fresh apron, serving her eager children their favourite meal. If I come in on her during one of these scenes she finishes acting it with élan, playing to her audience. But for that first moment before she notices me I know that she is not merely fooling. She has to learn these things from somewhere, if I will not teach her.

Najma's daughter, Yasmin, is a little younger than Jane, a little further away from that world into which her mother, too, cannot initiate her. Still at junior school, Yasmin is as yet unaffected by the need to examine the length of her skirts or the width of her belts, and perhaps that is one of the reasons that Jane is still more relaxed going to Yasmin's house after school than to any of her other friends. She's also more used to being there, ever since the year Najma and I were both working part-time and took it in turns to have the children home after school. In Yasmin's house Jane slips back effortlessly into a state of childhood in which the pressures of secondary school life have no part.

But Yasmin has her own double life. To school she wears what she calls 'normal dresses', in which she runs shouting in the asphalt playground, jostling in the queue for school dinners, replying with spirit to any boy who ventures a tentative insult in the direction of the girls. Such repartee is the first stage of courtship, and she knows it. At home Najma sews for Yasmin Panjabi clothes in brilliant green or red satin – *churidar* trousers that wrinkle tightly around her calves and ankles, and matching *kameez* with shiny gold trimmings at the neck and wrists. Yasmin changes into them when she gets home from school, and instantly looks older and more graceful.

Najma worries about her, I know. She doesn't say much, but I have seen it on her face on the days we used to wait together in the playground at three-fifteen, and she would see the children come hurtling out of the grimy Victorian building, boys and girls together in innocent defiance of the nineteenth-century signs carved in large letters in the stonework, BOYS above one door, GIRLS above the other. It is a relief that next year Yasmin will be going to an all girls' secondary school; but she wishes it could have been sooner.

'She is a good girl,' Najma tells me, perhaps to convince herself that there is nothing to worry about. 'Look how she helps me.' And it is true – Yasmin has learnt young and willingly many of the things her mother can teach her. These days when I go to collect Jane I often find her reading on her own, or doing puzzles with Yasmin's younger brother Aftab; while in the kitchen Yasmin is helping Najma to prepare *pakoras*, her head tilted in concentration, her rope of never-cut hair swinging in a plait down her back between the ends of her long chiffon *dupatta* scarf. 'She's a good girl,' Najma says, as I admire Yasmin's deft hands neatly dropping the spoonfuls of mixture into the hot oil. Beneath the softly rustling green and gold Yasmin is still child enough to enjoy the praise without feeling self-conscious. 'I used to make *pakoras* often when we were at my auntie's in Pakistan,' she tells me proudly. 'Here – taste one. They're good with tomato ketchup.' And as she chatters her hands are busy, the bracelets on her wrist tinkling gently as she arranges *pakoras* on a little stainless steel tray which she will carry demurely to her father and the other men sitting in the front room.

The morning after Najma gave me the bracelets Jane came into the kitchen in her usual half-asleep state, got down the box of Shreddies from the cupboard, and was half-way through filling her bowl when she suddenly stopped.

'You're still wearing them,' she said, staring at my wrist.

'Yes,' I said. 'I was wondering when you'd notice. I couldn't get them off last night.'

'Use soap,' she said, matter-of-fact. 'That's what Yasmin does. You rub dry soap all over your hand and they slip off easily.'

'Okay,' I said, 'I'll try it. But I won't bother now. I have to be at work a bit early this morning.'

She stared again. 'You're not going to wear those to *work*?' she asked.

'I thought I might,' I said. 'Just for once. I've got used to the feel of them now. And I thought it would be interesting to see what people said.'

Jane said nothing, but kept staring at me as she munched her way through her Shreddies. She seemed to be considering something. 'Okay' she announced finally, 'I'll go to Yasmin's after school today. Then you'll have to come and fetch me, and Yasmin's mum will see you wearing them.'

Strange Attractors

HARI KUNZRU

By December Carla's city is fraying around the edges. The lights of the tower-blocks seem to flicker and dim at random. Sometimes as she is driving over the Westway giant cracks appear in the road. The cracks will grow to cover the entire surface, fracturing the white lines, widening steadily before her horrified eyes. It takes all her willpower to keep control of the car. Usually when this happens she is coming back from one of Pablo's parties, high as a cockatoo and concentrating hard on avoiding the phantom shapes flitting about in her peripheral vision. So the cracks are just one more thing, and it doesn't seem to matter whether it is her, the pills, or the city itself which is causing it.

Mornings, after she has been working in the casino, she always sits on the balcony smoking spliff and watching the light change on the office blocks near the river. As the sun rises it bleeds across the huge glass panes, ripples of light warping the unforgiving squares into new and beautiful shapes.

By December the sunrise has begun to look like a wound, and she has a sense of thousands of years of history lying in wait just over the horizon.

She would like to have the answers. Different answers, clever ones. To claim all this was forced on her by the tense faces on the tube or the date on the calendar. Someone (party conversation) once tried to convince her that between about AD 100 and the invention of Hovis the whole of Northern Europe had been tripping on Ergot fungus, which (he claimed) explained religion, art and the duration of the Middle Ages. 'It was on the wheat,' he said 'Hallucinogenic. Whole communities of isolated peasants fantasising witches and spirits and divine visitations.' At the time she had humoured him, then found a way to move on. All the same, the idea had stayed with her. If this was a hallucination, some chemical in the food or the air, then she could disbelieve it and it would leave her alone. Better, if this was something shared, rising up from the grimy unconscious of the city, then she could disbelieve and be absolved of all blame.

Almost true. But never true enough. Sometimes, dealing out cards to another hard-faced row of punters, she can convince herself, and for a few minutes or hours she is free, just the bird paid to run the second game of Vingt-et-Un and see to it the House doesn't get screwed. This blankness never lasts, and eventually she has to call a break, make a run for the toilet. After she has locked herself in the cubicle and cried for a while, she just has time to chop out a couple of hasty lines on the loo seat before going back to the table.

This has been going on for almost three weeks, since the morning she got the letter. Deep down she knows the letter is the cause of it all, the cracks, the darkness, the bloody skies. It is still lying there on the dresser, tucked behind the Christmas cards. It is the same as the letters JD and Hughie and the others received, plain white envelope, little window for the address. Carla cannot bear to open it. It is as if she is frozen. Inside the tension is welling up, eating at her, spilling out into the air. Unbearable. Yet any amount of stress is preferable to reading the letter and finding she is seropositive. As long as it stays sealed, she still inhabits the land of the living.

People can almost see her tension. It hangs round her like a cloud, oppressive and heavy. Linton, Janine and the other croupiers avoid her at breaktimes. Fewer punters seem to be coming to her table. At home she stands for hours looking at herself in the mirror.

Carla: Twenty-five years old. Angular face topped by a crop of bleach-blonde hair. Big mouth ('full', supposedly), straight nose, clear skin that's not so clear these days. Looks tired. Big dark circles around her eyes. Three piercings in each ear, one on her cheek which she takes out for work. Black teeshirt with a Tibetan design on it. Likes: summertime, caffé latte, Bhangra Techno, sushi. Dislikes: politics, driving, Coca-Cola, winter. Ambitions: Not to die.

Tonight she tries to make up stories. They all feature her, a younger version of her. Usually she is with someone else. The stories always falter at the same point, which is the point of sex. Sex has become unimaginable, a thing she cannot connect with herself. After a while she can't focus on her body any more. It rejects her attention, which wanders to the other things on the dresser. Make up. A row of pill bottles, mostly prescription, two or three boxes of slow-release drug patches. The line of cards. '*Hey Girl, Merry Xmas and a Hap-E Millennium Love Laura xxx*'. '*Step into tomorrow, With all our love, Matteo and Cee-Cee*'. One of them has a little sound chip embedded in the cardboard, playing the theme to *2001*. The corner of a white envelope peeps out from behind it.

Carla lights a cigarette and walks back across the room, little snowflakes of ash falling on the dark blue carpet.

In the corner the console is burbling away to itself. For some reason the music service has gone offline, and a plastic-white face is singing a hymn. Its lyrics scroll across the bottom of the screen in big faux-Gothic script.

yet will I fear none ill
for thou a-art with me and thy –

Church Channel. She scrabbles for the remote and blows the little choirboy away, swearing under her breath. Suddenly every fucker seems to have found God. Almost every day she gets e-mail from another new online religion. The police occasionally conduct raids on some armed bunch of suburbanites, holed up in a semi-detached waiting for Divine Judgment. The pictures come on the Reality Programmes, police armed response squads storming bright-red Barratt homes. Wobbly camera. Firecracker sound of gunfire. The bodies afterwards.

She switches to a local pirate. The screen fills with harsh abstract squiggles, flashes and spirals of light. Over the speakers come speeded-up machine-gun beats, a deep grinding voice.

Win' your body na Sista, win' up ya wais'
Sound of the Murderer gwan mash up de place
Hear me now!
Me gwan mek you sweat yeh me gwan mek you scream
Dem a call me Natty Murderer de dancehall king.

Absent-mindedly Carla shuffles about to the storm of drum and bass. The music fits. Music to crack up to. The beats fall on her like fists, the hollow boom of the eight-o-eight juddering the thin walls of her flat. Gradually the music forces her to the floor, where she lies very small and still, warding off this sound which is the sound of her body shaking apart.

Batty boy gwan tek som licks
Police officer gwan tek som licks
Step right up see Natty go like dis
prom prom!

Curled into a ball, she listens as the toasting fades behind a new pulse. These sounds are always there in the spaces between the legal stations, a sort of hysteria threading its way through the margins of London. *Big up all you Chingford posse. Big up all you Walthamstow posse. Big up to the man like Ragi. Big up Lisa, Gina and all Limehouse massive.* It is the same hysteria that is coded into the newspapers, that hangs over street-corners, bubbling in the faces of the commuters who come into the casino after work. A constant subsonic panic.

A couple of months back there was a frenzy, you couldn't go anywhere without hearing about the year Two-Thousand and what it meant and how it was a turning point and what everyone was going to do to celebrate. Now the millennium seems to have run out of steam. Christmas is over and the suicide rate is up. Some headcase burnt down several nightclubs, then on Boxing Day gutted the Albert Hall. He's threatening one more a night until the 31st. Wants everyone to stay at home and pray, apparently. All that is left is the drum and bass. Carla was wondering about staying in for New Year, also whether she might kill herself. An idle, abstract thought. She couldn't decide how to do it.

8:50pm. Soon time to go to work. Carla gets out of bed, lights a fag and crosses the room. The console says 29–12–99, which means the letter has been here for sixteen days. When she goes online it downloads an invitation from Pablo into her mailbox.

The Last Party

Arrive Promptly

'If you can remember it, you weren't there'

(trad.)

Carla considers this, even prints it out and sits with it on the balcony. After a while she carefully folds the invite into a paper aeroplane and sends it out into the night. It is sucked towards the roofs below, a little white smudge fading into the darkness. The millennium party with Pablo Linden. JD would have been so bloody excited. The thought sends her into floods of tears, and she stays outside until she is freezing cold, looking at the lights swirl towards the river.

(In Memoriam to JD: Jaydee even when I first met you you were very far gone, getting thin. You loved me for loving you even though you had lost your looks and got angry when you were scared. I loved you for the times we just stayed in and ordered a takeaway then fucked on the floor among the empty wrappers. I loved you for still wanting to live.)

JD was three years ago, when they still called it HIV and thought it was one thing. Now they call it HIV Complex and talk about families of viruses. Now it is changing faster than they can study it, and they are worried, because their sons and daughters, their straight, fun-loving sons and daughters, are growing listless and sick. Oh Jaydee, quiet, pensive Jaydee, how cool you would have thought it was to get an invitation from Pablo Linden, King of the West.

Pablo Linden. Jaydee read his book and quoted reviews to his mates when they were seshing out on the balcony. From *Edge City* magazine: 'As a legitimate businessman the author of *Molecular Enlightenment* is conspicuously successful, and his flamboyant philanthropy has endeared him to alternative causes throughout the European Economic Zone. Linden's business empire runs so smoothly that he can spend all his waking hours (which can be up to seventy-two at a stretch) engaged in conversation with the constant stream of socialites, bums, bohemians and freeloaders who turn up on his doorstep.'

– Fucking cool, man.

Pablo owns half of London. He has his picture taken for fashion magazines, and his opinions regurgitated by the singers of indie guitar bands. From his wedding-cake pile in the leafiest square of Notting Hill, he stretches out his mysterious threads of influence over the capital, a benevolent and slightly overweight Godfather dispensing clean, precisely-measured doses of excitement to a grateful public. These days it seems pretty much everyone is high most of the time, which is largely thanks to Pablo. Before they were banned a couple of years ago, he was the biggest importer of the various new synthies coming out of Japan and America. Obviously, the moment HM Government said no, he stopped. Obviously.

– So can you do me ten of the starships? Nice. Sorted.

Carla starts, hearing JD's drawl in her ear. So clear. He ought to walk through the door. There is a clatter, a tiny rattle in the background, which puzzles her. Eventually she realises it is her teeth. God knows how long she has been out there. She gets up and yanks open the stiff glass door. Right on cue it begins to snow, and she stands inside watching the flakes dissolve on the warm pane in front of her face.

How Carla came to know *The* Pablo Linden (or 'To Cut a Long Story Short'):

Through GameBoy. That's what he said his name was. He made Hardcore tunes, and did she want to go to a party? Since they were already *at* a party (which she pointed out to her new friend), Carla decided she was fine where she was and persuaded him to fuck off. Then the amp blew, half the guests left, the other half started freebasing in the kitchen and she changed her mind. It was surprisingly easy to get back into GameBoy's good books, and soon Carla found herself being dragged through Kensington as he explained his 'personal philosophy of Bass'. Above them, CCTV cameras jerked round on their mountings, and every few paces they triggered another security system. Weaving their way through pool after pool of white light, they felt as if the enormous virginal houses behind the gates were trying to blind them to their nakedness.

Eventually GameBoy decided he'd found the place, and they lurched up to the intercom. Carla was too far gone to care, but had she given it any thought she would probably have run away. No one who lived in one of these places would want to see her at 3am on a Wednesday morning, or any other time for that matter. GameBoy mumbled something incoherent and slumped against the buzzer. Carla resigned herself to the long walk back. But as if by magic the high gates swung open, and clinging on to the sleeve of GameBoy's Hoodie she tottered into a dimly lit hallway.

Inside, the party was a complex swirl, silver-and-gold-sheathed bodies tumbling about in high-ceilinged rooms. Every surface seemed to be encrusted with jewels and ornaments. Diamante studs were set into tables, chairs, the lintels of the doors. Renaissance nymphs frolicked in heavy gilt frames and strings of fake pearls were wrapped round brass statues of Hindu gods. Throughout the house, enormous cut-glass bowls of brightly coloured sweets had been scattered like ritual offerings. Every room was a treasure-trove, crammed with impossible junk. A giant stuffed bear guarded the entrance to the toilet. Caryatids held up a painted stone lintel under which women dressed as eighteenth-century dandies served pastel-coloured cocktails.

Through this dressing-up box of a house moved precise, elegantly-wasted partygoers, bright-eyed and wittily incoherent. Carla lost GameBoy in the second or third room, and never actually saw him again. She danced to ProgHouse in a big dark room. She had meaningless conversations with people who claimed to be poets, film directors, ex-convicts, a politician. The poets looked like politicians and the politician was the spit of the DJ at a club she used to go to. None of their identities were verifiable, and Carla didn't actually care enough to poke about for the truth. Finding the bathroom, she offed the rest of a wrap she'd procured to keep her going for the night, only realising when she'd got the tenner wedged into her nose that a number of smiling naked people were sitting in the sunken bath at the other end of the mock-Grecian room. Joining them she found out one was her host. And that was how Carla met Pablo Linden . . .

She arrived back home three days after she left it, so fucked-up she was barely capable of ringing in sick to the PleasureDome.

That was a year ago. There have been other parties, each as full-on as the first. But at the moment Carla fails to see the point of a party, however good. She goes to work with the letter in her pocket, determined to open it. She comes back in the morning with it still unread. And again. A night of torment, handing out cards, keeping the rictus smile fixed on her face. The envelope burns its imprint through her body, a square of absolute zero where her heart used to be.

She tells herself she will stay indoors, that there is no way she can see anyone, do anything, think of anything until she has faced this. In the shower she examines her wet skin, half-believing her eyes will bore their way through it to the diseased flesh beneath. She imagines the virus replicating, threading its chain of code through her body. For the last two weeks she has spoken to nobody, and her machine is stacked with her friends' talking heads, telling her what they're up to, asking her to call, wishing her happy Xmas. Dripping from the shower she plays a few back, until she thinks she sees JD's face, and has to switch off. Asleep, eidetic bacteria dance and multiply on blue and yellow screens behind her eyes. They mingle with Jaydee's smile, her own face, thin, stained by sarcomas. She gets up, smokes furiously, drinks vodka, trying to hammer herself into unconsciousness. Eventually she drifts off, a pile of roaches in the ashtray beside her.

Yet somehow on New Year's Eve, the eve of the New Millennium, she finds herself in front of the mirror, putting on her best clothes, applying makeup with a care she never remembers taking before. She slips the letter into her bra, feeling its hard, crinkly shape against her breast. Strange how this sort of communication is still done via snail mail. There is something about the act of tearing open a sealed message. Fax, vid, e-mail, a phonecall, none of them would be as real. Wrapping herself in a thick coat she sets out to walk to Pablo's party. No cabs now, no buses. No one wants to work tonight.

Outside it is lightly snowing. Pablo's house is visible half a mile away. It has been strung with coloured lights, which shimmer and pulse, sending waves of red or blue or yellow skittering across its high white walls. It looks like a gigantic jewel case, fantastic, only semi-real. Carla rings the bell and is immediately absorbed into the body of the house. This time it seems to have a new order, an order which affects all the people inside, the things they do and say. The party is a mêlée of exposed flesh and laughing voices and light and smoke and movement, yet every aspect, from the smell of sex on the dance-floor to the way the candles gutter in Pablo's kitsch chandeliers, seems to follow the same pattern. The further she travels through the party, the more this order asserts itself. Certain things are repeated, particular words, smiles, ornaments. Somehow Carla knows she has come to the heart of whatever is happening on this night, a system infinitely complex and tantalisingly close to revealing itself. She could go on forever, falling towards its impossibly distant heart.

Always accompanying her is the roughness of the envelope inside her clothing, reminding her of what has got to happen at midnight. Beneath the narcotic mantle wrapping her brain she is aware that every nerve is singing with tension. Somewhere upstairs she sees Pablo, swathed in red velvet, holding forth to a throng of laughing people. He is the Red Death, 'out of Poe, darlings, out of Poe.' As he says this he executes a theatrical flourish of his cape. Carla finds herself giggling, then laughing hysterically, red wine slopping out of her glass. People nearby begin to turn round, amused, then concerned as her body starts to jerk about like a spastic puppet. For a moment the room is very far away, then, as quickly as it started, the spasms are gone and she is back again, gulping air in sharp, ragged breaths. Pablo is telling a Gothic tale about Japanese gangsters and a bungled scoring mission. Slightly nonplussed, Carla looks at her empty glass, then goes off to search for a refill.

Again and again she returns to the pale front room to stare at Pablo's enormous Louis Quatorze clock. Everything around its ornate face seems vague and distorted, as if the entire room is being sucked towards this one spot, sedately revolving about the narrowing gap between the minute and hour hands. Eleven o'clock. Half past. Ten to midnight. Around this room is the house, around the house the street, around that the city, all its thousands and millions of lives tumbling into this ever-decreasing fissure. A thousand years of history culminating in this moment, the apex of a vast pyramid of time . . . The chemicals pumping round Carla's system spiral her into a huge rush as the moment comes closer and closer and she finds the letter in her hands, dog-eared and damp from her sweat. The noise is deafening, as the guests scream and bray and weep for the approach of midnight. In front of her a young woman snivels and wrings her hands, her makeup sloughing down her face. A couple slide to the floor, struggling out of their clothes. Suddenly Pablo appears beside her. He has pulled the hood of his costume forward to cover his face. He seems taller, truly immense, a mythic figure at the centre of the storm of light and colour he has set in motion, yet Carla barely sees him as her fingers worm open the envelope and close on a piece of printed paper. This is the touch, the singularity towards which everything has been converging.

Changes

FRANCIS KING

For thirty-seven years Mar had been married to a builder with a headache and a squint. Then he had decamped to the one-room flat off Shepherd's Bush Green of a Spanish girl, at least half his age, called Carmen, who worked in a nearby tapas bar. Miraculously, Carmen had cured him of the headache; but about the squint she had been able to do nothing.

As in the case of so many losses in her life – her tattered old moggie, kidnapped or run over, a ring which had mysteriously vanished from her finger during a visit to the Antiques Road Show in Kensington Town Hall, the front teeth which had all been yanked out on the same morning (it was a case of 'ginger-vitis' she explained to everyone) – Mar was stoical. Just as she had managed without all these things in the past, so now she could manage without her husband.

Today she was equally stoical as Dr Bhose removed the dressing from her leg. She grimaced but made no sound. 'Good girl,' he said in his high, precise voice, as he gave a series of tentative pulls. The cheek of it – good girl! She was old enough to be his grandmother. 'It's getting along nicely.' He had been saying the same thing about the ulcer for the past five weeks. 'Very nicely.'

'It doesn't *look* at all nice,' Mar said. Then, deciding that he might think that ungracious and ungrateful, she added: 'But it's certainly looking less angry than last week.' She had learned the 'angry' from Dr Bhose himself. She would never have before thought of using that adjective of a varicose ulcer.

'You should rest your leg more,' Dr Bhose said, as he began to prepare another dressing. 'Do you have to go on working?' Mar was eighty-one.

Mar replied tetchily, as she always did when people put that question to her: 'I couldn't possibly let my gentlemen down. They rely on me.'

'I'm sure they do. But at your age . . .'

'Not so much of "at your age", *if* you please, doctor!' Mar burst into laughter. 'I don't like to be reminded of the years. There've been far too many of them.'

'So what do you think of our new premises?' Dr Bhose asked, sleek head once more bent over Mar's leg.

Mar sniffed. 'Very nice. Very posh. But I miss the old place. It was so convenient for me, you see, just the next-door street. With this place I have to hop on the 31.' At that moment an underground train rattled past on its way from High Street Kensington to Notting Hill Gate. Even with the double-glazing one could hear it, just below the window. 'Don't them trains bother you at all?'

'Not really. Not now. One gets used to them.'

'People say one can get used to anything in the end. But I'm not one for getting used to new things,' Mar said. 'I've lived in the same council flat for more than forty years. Can you believe that? Moved in soon after the War – when my husband, my *then* husband, had come home from Germany. I'd never want to move from that flat, never, whatever they offered me. I hope to be carried out of it feet first when my time comes.'

'Well, that won't be for a long while yet.'

'You're the doctor, you've said it. Remember that – when you come to sign my death certificate.'

Dr Bhose laughed. He stood back from her leg and, head on one side, stared down appraisingly at it. 'Well, that should be all right for another week. These ulcers take time.' Then he added: 'You know, if you don't want that journey on the 31 bus, I could send the nurse to see you.'

'Oh, no, doctor, I wouldn't want to put anyone to any trouble. That's something I never like to do.' The truth was that Mar rather enjoyed these weekly visits. With Dr Bhose, as with one or two of her 'gentlemen', her manner became girlish, even skittish.

As she laced up a well-worn brogue, she asked Dr Bhose: 'Have you seen what they've got written up in the window of that Paki shop two, no three, doors down from here?'

Not looking up as he scribbled something in her notes, Dr Bhose shook his head.

'It says BACK TO BASIC PRICES and then below that MAJOR REDUCTIONS.'

Mar laughed, but Dr Bhose did not do so. He might never have heard, as he went on scribbling.

'I like that,' Mar said. 'Shows they have a sense of humour. Perhaps I'll look in to see what those MAJOR REDUCTIONS are. Probably on things years past their sell-by date.' She pulled on her ancient fur coat. Only last week, on the 31 bus, some little pig with a ring in her nose had asked if she wasn't ashamed to be wearing such a thing. 'Whatever animals they were, they were dead long before you was born, my girl – and no doubt long before your mum was born,' Mar had retorted. 'So what can we do about it now? Anyway, I see you're wearing leather boots.' The cheek of it!

'Now do try to keep that leg rested,' Dr Bhose said, holding open the door for her.

Mar gave her head a vigorous shake. 'No rest for the wicked,' she said.

That morning Mar went for the first time to a new gentleman, the friend of another of her gentlemen. 'Oh, I don't know that I can take on anyone else,' Mar had said, 'I'm that busy.' But when she was told that the new gentleman had first lost his wife and had then spent several weeks in hospital recovering from a near-fatal heart attack, she had relented. 'Poor old chap!' she had said. 'Well, in that case . . .' All her gentlemen were either widowers or, as she put it, not the marrying kind.

It was really spooky when she learned the address; and it was even spookier now as she turned off first Church Street and then Holland Street and eventually found herself, for the first time for – well, how many, many years? – in Salmon Place and approaching that house.

As she entered through the door which the white-haired, red-faced man with the purple, swollen hands was holding open for her, she announced: 'I know this house.'

'Oh! Have you worked here before then? I suppose that was for the Coopers.'

'My grandad lived here,' Mar said, asthmatically struggling out of her fur coat. 'Before the War. Not only the last War, also the one before that. He worked on the underground. The Metropolitan Railway it was called when he first moved in. These houses belonged to the Metropolitan Railway. They were built for the workers, the railway workers.'

'Well, fancy that! I never knew that, I doubt if any railway worker could afford to live here now. Well, well! One lives and learns.'

'After his retirement, the Railway let him stay on. He lived here for, oh, at least fifty years with my grandma and one of my aunties. That was my Auntie Beryl.' Mar looked around her, from time to time uptilting her head on its tortoise neck. 'This hall was always narrow. You've got something lovely things,' she added. 'Is that Chinese?' She pointed at a celadon vase on the hall table.

'Japanese actually. A well-known potter. It's rather valuable now, I'm told, even though the potter's still alive. You'll have to be careful not to break it!' Mr Leonard then laughed, to indicate that he was joking.

'I'm not a breaker.'

'I'm sure you're not. That was only a – a *quip*.' As he spoke, Mr Leonard was trying to remember whether he had saved what he had been writing on his Macintosh. There was always the possibility of a power failure, he was constantly reminding himself, ever since a woman novelist neighbour had bleated to him of how, because of a power failure, she had lost a whole morning of improvidently unsaved work. 'Shall I remind you of the geography of the house – and, er, show you where things are kept?' He began to limp off down the hall. 'I'm afraid you'll find everything in rather a mess. I had this, er, French girl, a student, who came in. She was very bright, but I'm afraid she had little idea of how to use a Hoover or to clean out a bath.'

'Young girls are not all that domesticated these days,' Mar said. She looked around her. 'What's been done here?' she demanded. Mr Leonard had conducted her into the sitting room.

'What do you do mean?'

'There were two rooms in the old days, two separate rooms. One was the parlour and the other was a bedroom. My auntie slept in here.' She crossed over to the window, peered out, then turned. 'There was gas here, all through the house. Even in the Thirties there was only gas. Imagine!'

'Well, well!' Mr Leonard's desire to get back to his Macintosh had now become an agony. 'Things change.'

'I hate change,' Mar said. 'Why do people have to change things which were already working perfectly all right? The other day one of my gentlemen said to me "Most change is a change for the worse", and I agree with him.'

'Things can't always be at a standstill. Nature abhors a – a total lack of motion.'

Eventually, after he had heard how there had been no bathroom and no running water in any of the bedrooms so that, if anyone wanted a wash, a proper wash, water had to be heated by a geyser in the kitchen, how linoleum had covered all the floors and even the stairs, how his study under the mansard roof had once been an attic store-room, how there had been a coke-burning Ideal stove in that corner over there in the sitting room and a gas-fire in that other corner over there in the dining room, Mr Leonard managed to get it across, as he had so far repeatedly failed to do, that he really must push on with his work.

'What is it you do then?' Mar was amazed that, at his age, he should still have a job, even though he was at least ten years younger than she was.

'I'm a journalist,' he told her. 'I write about economics.'

'Oh, I've another of those,' she said. 'A journalist, I mean.' Then she remembered that the gentleman to whom she was referring was the gentleman who had put her on to this gentleman. 'But of course you know him,' she said.

Crouched over his computer, his purple, swollen fingers often hitting the wrong keys, Mr Leonard could hear distant thuds and clatters as ferociously Mar went about her work. It was disturbing but, well, he supposed it was a good sign. With that French girl there had been too many intervals of total silence, during which he had resisted the temptation to rush down to see if she was taking a break. Those silences of hers were even more disturbing than this racket.

'Mr Leonard!' Mar called at one point.

With a groan and sigh he limped out to the top of the stairs. 'Yes?'

'I can't do with these cloths.'

'What's wrong with them?'

'I'm not used to cloths like these.'

'Then do buy some others. Tell me the cost and I'll give you the money.'

'All right. As I told you, I'm a creature of habit.'

Later Mr Leonard creaked downstairs. 'I'm off now. To the London Library. I'll give you these keys. You'd better keep them. Then you can let yourself in and out.' Without bothering me, he all but added, since he was a man who never cared to be bothered. 'Do please be certain to double lock.'

'Oh, I always double lock. One can't be too careful these days, can one?' She turned round from dusting the banisters. 'You haven't got a burglar alarm, have you?'

'No. No burglar alarm.'

'Oh, you should have one. With all these lovely things.'

'Somehow I've never got round to having one installed.'

'Better late than never.'

'Well, that's true.'

As he turned away from her, pulling a face which she could not see, Mar said: 'You won't mind my reminding you, will you? All my gentlemen pay as we go. It's easier that way. No argument.'

'Oh, yes, yes, of course. That's fine.' Once again Mr Leonard pulled a face as he turned away from her.

Having handed over the three five pound notes for the three hours, Mr Leonard let himself out of the house. In the weeks ahead, he was often to escape to the London Library on one of Mar's days.

Mar worked even more ferociously, banging the Hoover against the legs of chairs and tables as she thrust it back and forth and abrading the two bath-tubs, the two lavatory bowls and the three wash-basins with a rough cloth thickly caked with Vim. That French girl must have been thoroughly lazy, no elbow-grease, a slut.

Having finished, Mar decided to make herself a cup of tea. Mr Leonard had said nothing about one, but all her gentlemen allowed her to have one and she saw no reason to make an exception for him. She would leave a note, that's what she would do. MADE MYSELF A CUP. HOPE THAT WAS OK? She added her initials: MP.

As she waited for the kettle to boil – it was in need of a descaling, she would have to buy something for that and then, as with the cloths, get the money out of the old bugger – Mar looked out of the kitchen window on to the garden. With its York paving and its little fountain and its prissily ordered beds – later she was to meet the deep-voiced, middle-aged woman in breeches, green wellies and a tweed cap who 'did' it every two or three weeks – it was totally different from the grassy rectangle, surrounded by overgrown laurels, of her grandfather's day. But how it brought back to her that life of more than seventy years back! From a branch of the chestnut tree, now vanished, which grew over the wall at the far end, Uncle Cyril had hung a swing, and in his shirt-sleeves, on a long, hot summer's day, he had swung her there for, oh, ages, it seemed. Tireless, he was. On and on. Even now she could see his muscular, hairy arms and the shirt sticking to his square torso with sweat. With him too, on another occasion, she had played ball out there. But it wasn't just with him, Aunt Beryl had also been present. Pig-in-the-Middle. The little girl was the Pig. But all the time, as she had rushed and lunged, with shrill laughter, in pursuit of the ball, she had wished that just the two of them, she and handsome Uncle Cyril, had been alone and that Aunt Beryl had been at her cooking or sewing or knitting.

Mar got up and, unmindful of the electric kettle, which had now switched itself off, she opened the French windows and stepped out into the garden. The spring air was cool, almost cold on her sweating forehead and bare arms. Slowly, pausing to look around her and to breathe in deeply, she walked down over the paving to the far end of the garden. She stopped. She was standing on a square of concrete, in the corner made by two walls, one shutting off the street and the other the next-door garden. It had been here, exactly here. This concrete slab was all that was left of it. She remembered it so well. The outside toilet! She had often run down here in the rain. She had often shivered in it as the winter wind slashed through the cracks and crannies in the wood! It was here – suddenly she remembered and her heart jerked and then began to beat faster and faster as it had done on that occasion so long ago now – that, when she had failed to lock the door, Uncle Cyril had come on her, her legs wide, her black woollen knickers about her ankles and the urine gushing out of her. 'Sorry, old girl!' He had slammed the door shut.

It was not long after that that he had gone off to a job as a builder in Edinburgh – a mate of his, from his days in the trenches, had offered it to him and with all this unemployment one could not be choosy, could one, one had to take what one could get. He had never returned. Later, long after she had ceased to receive any letters, let alone money, from him, Aunt Beryl had learned that he had moved on to Canada. Then he had vanished. Could he be alive now? Well, he'd have to be at least ninety-five.

Slowly, head lowered, Mar moved back to the house. She had forgotten her cup of tea.

Mar had soon told Mr Leonard: 'Oh, please, Mr Leonard, do just call me Mar! All my gentlemen do.'

'Oh, very well,' Mr Leonard replied, not really liking to call her anything of the kind. Like many people before him, he had not realised that Mar was called Mar from Marjorie, not Ma because of her age. Thenceforward his notes to her would always begin 'Dear Ma . . .' From time to time Mar was tempted to correct him. But eventually she came to enjoy seeing herself addressed as 'Ma'. She had only once been pregnant and then the child, a boy, had been stillborn. 'It's something to do with my avaries,' she had told everyone. Ma, Mum, Mother – yes, it was rather nice.

When Mr Leonard was out of the house, as he usually contrived to be in order not to have to talk to her, Mar would often wander out into the garden, sometimes with a cloth or a brush or even a cup of tea in one hand. How it all came back! Things she had long since thought to have forgotten. One Christmas she had played out here, oblivious to the icy air and the grass crisp with rime under her feet, with the Diabolo given to her by her grandfather. Where there was now a statue of a naked girl, one hand coyly placed over her private parts, there used to stand the two cages for the guinea-pigs which Aunt Beryl fostered with so much cooing and clucking love. From this garden she had stared up at the blue, blue sky while majestically a Zeppelin had blundered across it – until her mother, lost in conversation with Aunt Beryl at the sink, had suddenly looked up and screamed out: 'Mar! *Mar*! Come in! Come in at once! At *once*!'

One day Mar was in the house when a tall, thin, stooping middle-aged man in a charcoal pinstripe suit and bow-tie had called. He was Mr Leonard's nephew. Mr Leonard had mentioned him once or twice. The visitor coughed his way up the stairs to his uncle's study – 'No need for you to announce me, I know the way' – and a little while later Mr Leonard called down from the landing: 'Oh, Ma, Ma, could you be an angel and make two cups of coffee? The Mocha, I think.'

Mar ground the beans, as Mr Leonard had shown her how to do, made the coffee in the ancient Cona percolator with the spirit stove beneath it – although it caused so much trouble, she liked that percolator, it reminded her of one that one of her other gentlemen, now dead, had owned, oh, donkey's years ago – and then carried the two cups upstairs with a plate of biscuits beside them.

'Oh, you've brought some biscuits,' Mr Leonard said. 'I don't know that we really need those. But it was a kind thought.' Mar had long since decided that Mr Leonard was mean. People could get like that in old age, couldn't they?

'This is my nephew,' Mr Leonard said. 'Mark – this is . . .' Uncertain whether to introduce her as Mrs or Ma, Mr Leonard concluded: 'The lady who so kindly and efficiently looks after me and the house.' As Mar was leaving the room, having set down the tray, he went on: 'My nephew is an architect, quite a famous architect. He's trying to persuade me to build on an extension, a glass extension. He wants to give it to me as a seventieth birthday present. It's terribly generous of him but . . .' Mr Leonard shrugged and gave a weak smile. 'All that trouble. I hate having builders in, with their noise and dust and delays and inefficiency.'

'Why should you need an extension?' Mar asked, a note of belligerence in her voice.

'Why indeed?'

'It would be a kind of conservatory and study combined.

My uncle could work there instead of up here. All these stairs can't be good for his heart. And in any case these windows are so tiny – no view at all. A view of the garden would be far more cheerful for him.'

Mar felt tremulous and even more asthmatic than usual as, one hand clutching the banisters, she swayed down the stairs. Sweat began to break out on her forehead. A kind of conservatory and study combined – the idea of it! Why couldn't people leave things as they were? The house was already far too big for the poor old bugger on his onesome.

Later, having seen out his nephew, Mr Leonard limped into the kitchen, where Mar was kneeling before the cooker, Brillo pad in hand. 'So what do you think of my nephew's idea?'

Mar squinted up at him: 'I'm sure I don't know.'

'From that I assume that you don't think much of it. Neither do I.' He veered away, then turned and edged back. 'He's my only living relative – my only living *close* relative. One day he'll inherit this house and everything in it. I suspect he's planning the extension for himself and that common little wife of his, not for me.' He gave a barking, mirthless laugh. 'He's a pretty cold fish. Quite ruthless really.'

Some days later, Mar found a note, not from Mr Leonard but from the nephew, on the kitchen table. Mr Leonard was once more in the Lister Hospital, he had had another heart attack. There was no money left with the note.

Should she go to the Lister to visit the poor old bugger? Mar all but decided to do so. Then she told herself that of all her gentlemen he was the one she liked least, and in any case, if she did go, what would they have to say to each other? Unlike some of her other gentlemen, he never took any joy in a natter.

The next week, when she had let herself into the house,

it was to find the nephew there. Mr Leonard had died. The nephew told her that he and his wife were planning to move in before long – just as soon as some essential work, some long overdue work, to the house had been completed. Would Mar like to continue with the, er, arrangement which she had had with Mr Leonard?

Mar shook her head decisively. 'I'm sorry,' she said. 'Oh, no. I work only for gentlemen. Call me odd, if you like, but that's always been my rule. Somehow working where there's a lady in the household . . . I'm sorry.'

The nephew paid her off – giving her what was owed and adding thirty pounds. Mean like his uncle! Meanness tended to go in families, didn't it?

Months later, Mar happened to be walking down Holland Street, on her way from one of her gentlemen to the doctor's surgery. Normally she took the bus but today, since the sun was out and she felt like a breath of summer air, she had decided to walk. Far off, in a corner of her vision, sunlight glinted on glass. She stared, wrinkled hand raised to half-closed eyes, then hurried down the narrow alley which led to Salmon Place. There it was, the conservatory or study or whatever one called it. It covered more than half the garden. It covered the place where Aunt Beryl had kept her guinea-pigs and where she herself had played both Pig-in-the-Middle and with that Diabolo given to her by her grandfather. It even covered that concrete slab which had been all that had remained of the outside toilet.

Mar felt affronted and appalled. How could they, how *could* they? She had to resist an impulse to rush up the steps, bang on the door and demand an explanation. She all but picked up a stone and hurled it at all that glittering glass. Regressing to her childhood of seventy and more years back, she all but screamed, stamped a foot in fury, burst into tears.

'Well, that's coming along nicely, 'Dr Bhose said. 'This won't hurt.' A finger touched the skin around the puckered, healing flesh. Mar pulled a face, drawing in her lower lip and biting on it. 'Good girl.'

'Have you noticed at the Paki shop?' Mar asked.

'Noticed? Noticed what?'

'It's gone. What they had there written on their window.'

'What was that?'

'Don't you remember? You must remember. BACK TO BASIC PRICES, MAJOR REDUCTIONS.'

'Oh, that!' Dr Bhose laughed. 'Well, I suppose they thought all that business of back to basics out of date.'

Ma again drew in her lower lip and bit on it. 'Why can't people just leave things *alone*?'

Hearts and Flowers

DEIRDRE SHANAHAN

I didn't always look like this, I had a good body once with a face to match but two years here have taken charge of them. I must have something going for me because the gentlemen tell me so, but of course if I was that marvellous I would be doing something better, have one of them as me own gent instead of cavorting under the lights where red sizzles and shades of pink come and go. Orange crushes down with a flourish and a blade of lemon crosses my legs as I step forward. I could let go of it all, could run off from this tiny stage, shabby and crackling with paint like an old spinster, but I can't. I manage to keep ahead, flexing my legs at the tinkling piano music. Five minutes is two shillings. What else could pay so much? Not even a go with one of them, though I could do without these faces, round baldy heads or those thinning on top, eyes large and round, with pallid cheeks and sad voices.

I would like to give in, run off and say, stuff it Mr Somers, Shove your shillings up your arse, but I love the pay off of easy money. There is an easy flow. A drift of gents between nine and eleven while music leaks from outside and in the street men call out their wares, the organ grinder sounds on and the dark brown monkey dances.

When Blow and I started after coming over, we got a room

in a house in St Giles' but it was so cramped it looked like families were hanging out of the window. There was no room for even a line. I didn't want that. Blow didn't either. It was almost as bad as being in Kilduff.

'Come up, come up.' Clarice, the blonde woman, says, leaning over the banister, her eyes wide with blue and lavender and her petticoat showing from under the hoop of her skirt. Do we look too young? I wonder. But who would have told her? We spoke to no one. Blow and I were going to do our best, show ourselves, make some quick luck.

In the upstairs room above the costermongers, they make us turn around. Mr Somers tells us to walk the length of the room and our plumpy pale bodies reflect in all the long mirrors. Was that it? It was and I had better get used to it because when Mr Somers nods, a blonde woman and another man in a hat look at each other. The blonde woman fiddles with her ringlets and the man in the hat looks at her like he was trying to hurry off somewhere and that was the end of it, they must have thought we could do something for them.

I know we are an odd pair. We show all our amazement at having arrived at all. The truth is, in a hostelry in Dublin someone told us you could earn a lot in London if you showed off your underclothes.

The first I have gets his shirt off and then just lays beside me. His shoes left neatly at the end of the bed are brogues, which make me think of home. We just lie and I am waiting. He is confessing but I don't care that he has no feeling for his wife in Dulwich, or his elder son who is studying. I close my eyes and try to pray but he is still with me in the room, a fat man slapped on top of me, the bed sinking with the mattress almost reaching the floor and the beery whiff on him as beads of sweat run on his brow.

Others come and they are better, or at least active, I mean, which I do not particularly like except you earn more. The next one is tough but better. Andy is from Glasgow, though I wouldn't hold that against him. He is mad as a hatter and I like him even if he is getting on and looking at fifty. I met him in a hostelry. God, why do I pretend. I meet most of them there. It's easy. Fatal. I can't help it. He is tall and you couldn't miss him. His mother was a trapeze artist and his father helped her and the men with the animals, but they're both dead now. He says I look like her.

'Come on, don't give me that.' But he insists and we get friendly.

He takes me down to his place where he has this parlour done out with dyes, tints and pictures. He has learnt to do tattoos from some Chinese sailors in Limehouse and the walls are covered with designs. What did I want? Lilies or hearts and roses? Shields or garlands, or something with posies? What about a face or an animal, even a bird. I say neither but he insists and eventually I go under and lie down and stretch my arm out. He moves across my arm, working on a fatty bit near the top because he says it would not hurt. I tense, expecting the pain but it does not come. I think I will shriek, that my voice will wake angels but I am calm and in the end it takes only minutes, as if he was writing upon me, and when I get up from the tattered chaise-longue about half an hour later, it is done and my arm proves it. Cooked and made. Finished. Flowers like eyes look at me.

'What do you think?'

'I like it. Yes. I do,' I tell him and catch him looking at me in a strange far off kind of way.

'Nothing, just something about her. I mean you.'

I turned and followed his gaze to a picture of a woman looking at me.

'I told you.'

I couldn't think for a moment and then I did.

'It's just the dark here, the shadows.'

He comes close and kisses me and I think I will tremble away.

'See, I said she was lovely.'

We part, our bodies falling away like clothes.

'Somers treats you all badly.'

'Does he?'

'Doesn't he?'

I shrug. I have no complaints even if Blow has and wants to get out.

'You could if you want.'

'I know but there's nothing else.'

'Move in with me.'

'I'll think about it.'

'Promise?'

Times with Andy grew and spread. He had a cart and we used to go about in that, which pleased me for a while despite the clobber in the back, wicks, ropes, and boxes rumbling around as he drove, but I only see him from a distance now because I am busy and I suppose I wanted to move on, you know to someone better, someone who at least had a pony and carriage. I tried to get rid of the flowers he made on my arm but I couldn't, and in the end it was as if it was something I wanted and I still walk around in clothes which show off my arms and their delicate design, and I think of what he said when I got it done. 'I'll tell you something for nothing, girl. Have a bird or a heart. Hearts last longer than flowers.'

In between jobs, days pass slowly as afternoons. I meet the Chinese boys and we drink outside. They're nice and considerate, not like your big towering fellas that make you feel you would be down on the ground.

The boys are good to me, even though they are far from home, having left their little villages behind and trekking for days in North China. Yen Lee has his grandmother with him and she sits in the shop among tea and sauces, pale cups and plates with the pictures of fish on them swimming, adrift. She has small eyes and tanned skin, folds her arms into herself and says nothing but her eyes smile. She has no English but we talk anyway with our hands and her face changes like the shadows on a lamp, her lips flicker their own words. Sometimes she points to a picture of a man in one of the newspapers I do not understand and looks sad. It is about the war and how her parents died there, how her husband was left behind and I think how men are always in pain or crying. Last week someone was stabbed outside Ratzini's, he stumbled along the street till he fell down, and another time I was leaving after the show, I saw a Peeler and the next day I saw him again and it was almost familiar.

Yen Lee took me out but we spent an hour not going anywhere. We saw the buildings along the Euston Road and then we turned up other streets. There are lots of people around but they don't bother us. There's stealing and bit of crime but nobody's robbed us. No one I know's been murdered. We walk along Romilly, Manette and Lexington Streets which have grown into us like old stains, travel like stars. The sky is a roof, it's ours.

Blow and I were good at the job and the numbers of men coming in rose. La Belle Vie was doing as good as any of the other theatres. Clarice showed us her routines. She says she trained as a dancer with the Russians in Paris once. I said, 'Blow, once is probably just as much as ever.' We stay in the upstairs room and do moves she shows us. She shows and Blow follows. I do the best I can but it's not easy. I feel heavy in those strutting heels.

'Mary.' Clarice shouts. 'Two steps to the side and one behind.'

Then I take my gaze to the outside of the window, where I hear the men calling their servants and the lumpen clip clop of the horses. It can't go on like this, I think, but it does until the day Blow tells me she's packing up.

'Are you going home?'

My anxiety rises and my throat tightens. I can't survive if she's not going to be around.

'Course not. I've got a maid's job in Camden.'

'I'm glad and relieved that I'll still be able to see her.

'Will it pay much?'

'Good enough for me. Not what I pick up here but then I'm tired and I just don't have the figure. I eat too much.'

'So what? We both do.'

She exaggerates because she pecks at her food like a bird. I'm the one who hurls it in. But I can't persuade her about moving. She's fixed and decided. Besides in the end she's going to be happier and have more money.

Somers comes in when we are changing, but we don't say anything. Sometimes he has an idea for costumes or shoes and we have to try them on. I don't mind. I don't care what we wear as long as it comes off and we don't have to wear it home. This is the line up, slippers, boots, high heels, sandals and feet. Who thought of this? Clarice or Somers. It's so simple it could be either but he doesn't tell. Never lets on. If we're lucky, Blow and I escape. She tells me she has met this fella but she can't fancy him because he is blind.

'He's no eyes, he can't see. Look you meet him. Take him over.'

'What for? I don't like Italians. They don't know what to do with their hands.'

'Roberto's not like that, I'll say that for him.'

She was right, he wasn't. No wonder she got bored. Her last bloke was a boxer though he didn't mess with her. She got into the fights free and was always heading off to some place in Stepney or Dalston.

Roberto said I needed to feed so I let him take me for meals because he insisted. All I had to do was cut up his food, but other than that with him using a spoon it didn't matter. He told me about his village near Milan, and his father and how he came across as a political refugee and how his sight failed afterwards. He can never go back and misses the places of his youth, they have gone forever. Clasping my hand, he says, 'Let's walk.' When we cross the bridge I look at him but of course he has no eyes and could not see and would not know my expression of surprise, except he did.

Of course word got around and Somers called him a 'blind cretin'. I tried to explain but he wouldn't let me. Because Roberto wasn't rolling in the money or bringing it in, he wasn't worth it. But I didn't care. Roberto and I walk around, take carriages when he says he can afford it to his place at the Elephant and Castle, where lights from buildings guide us. It is very quiet and dark and everywhere looks shut up for the night and sleeping as we go south.

He puts on one of those gramophone records on a big new player and we dance with his hands around my face, and mine going lower. The music is a strange, moving Italian piece which bleeds out of the building to the reaches of others in the opposite block. We sway and he holds me. He weeps as he lays his face on my breasts.

That night as inevitably as the stars we lie together and in the tight confines of his bed in the single room I have to guide his hands to all the right places and then almost as if he knows, we take off. He is with me and my head feels as if it is a flood, startled alive to his hands, deep and dark delving into me.

Next morning, Sunday, is deathly quiet, with not the faintest murmur. We dress and go out, walking for what seems miles. We arrive somewhere further north.

'Is this a beautiful place?'

'Depends what you're used to.'

At my feet lie grubby papers, the ends of cigarettes, crumpled boxes. His face is bright and open.

'It's different. But you could say so. Yes,' I add.

I look at the run of grey blocks against the sky. I like them because their windows are as if they were inside out, dark and smudgy, reflecting back the clouds and other buildings, watery, and airy, dreamy as if you're leaving the heavy bits of yourself behind.

'Roberto.'

I edge him away from the steps because I am terrified he will fall down the steps and break a bone and then everyone, Somers included and especially Blow, will say the accident is my fault.

It is easier now, going back. He seems more contented and to be walking faster but he still clings with the press of his lean hand on my arm. It's a shame he can't see. Such a waste on one so young, Blow used to say. They should be out making families for themselves. Leave the boring kind of stuff to the older ones.

'The air is softer here. There is no sound.' Roberto says. 'I love being out of the centre, somewhere else. I'm glad you've brought me.'

He grabs me so I have to lead the way and we go down some steps and I think, he knows this place, I can tell. It is not the first time he has been here. We go through a kind of entrance with a high arch. There are trees, benches and it's very green.

'You lighten my darkness.' A voice comes elegant and light. Who said that? Him? We walk along, stumbling really.

'I'm only holding your hand.'

'This is where I heard a cello one day like a stream.'

I don't know what he means. I am surprised. I thought London was all buildings. That's what they tell you back home. No one ever took me to a garden and I did not know there were any. The stillness is so quiet, it might break. It is strange, a place with nobody in it. My eyes dazzle and I have to stop and think, did I take anything? Were we on something before we came out? Did Yen Lee give me anything? I can't breathe for a second, and then it passes and Roberto edges around the flower beds inhaling, straining and leaning forward as petals tumble over themselves, fat, billowing and sweeping the ground. I see them too and smell their sweetness and light fragrances, as if for the first time, and deep in the essence is the scent of honeysuckle trailing the stone walls that are written like messages across the land I know so well, and thought I had left behind.

The Traffic is at a Standstill at the Hangar Lane Gyratory System

ELSPETH EDWARDS

Isobel felt acutely embarrassed. She had a plate of salad to eat and had to eat it in front of Victor. How was she going to achieve a relatively empty plate when tendrils of endive kept whiplashing vinaigrette around her face?

'I've been thinking about what you said,' she heard herself say, 'and mother agrees, that we could possibly diversify into main courses.'

'Entrées too.' Victor pronounced the word with a perfect if inappropriate French accent.

'Er . . . yes . . . we could. We'd need another pair of hands and I'm not sure how mother would feel about that.'

Victor and Isobel were sitting side by side in The Holly Bush, a low-ceilinged, well scrubbed pub that once had been stables, close to the close-knit heart of Hampstead.

Two weeks previously Victor had rung Just Desserts to order a cake for his son's bar mitzvah, and had intrigued Isobel by saying that this occasion would be 'less a celebration, more a farcical imbroglio. My soon-to-be-ex-wife will arrive with my cousin's husband, but we're all going to pretend that we're a happy family to please my parents. Hard going with a woman like Shirley Kaye.' He enjoyed calling his wife by her full name. When she eventually married his cousin's husband, he relished the alliteration, Shirley Shaw.

Telephonically, he had coaxed Isobel into revealing something about her small catering business. 'Wonderful name! Ties you down a bit though. Ever thought of expanding? Oh dear! That sounds rude. Bet you're no bigger than a size 10?'

Flattered, Isobel agreed to this present rendezvous. Victor, as it happened, was a freelance business adviser.

Isobel gave up the salad struggle and Victor ordered her a de-caff. He narrowed his eyes and smiled at her.

'Mothers can be killed with too much kindness, you know,' he said. Dangerous ground, he suspected, and changed the subject. 'So what have you been up to, since I picked up your gorgeous cake?'

'I went to the Everyman on Saturday and I saw *In a Lonely Place* and *Kiss Me Deadly.* I love Film Noir! And they've got a nice café downstairs.'

Suddenly, the thin, colourless woman bloomed. Victor, a cultured man with a variety of pleasures and pastimes, saw obsession, and trembled. 'I saw *A Room with a View* on Saturday. Wonderful Tuscan landscapes. Beautifully acted.'

'Hmm. I think the book's better really.'

Victor wondered what attracted him to this pale, pedantic creature. Could it be the blonde hair and the cheekbones, just the gentileness of her?

Isobel was silenced by an overwhelming attraction. Sometimes she had Mother crying with laughter when she described the airs and graces some of her customers put on. Now she wanted to see him smile just a little, and she would like to have asked who he had gone with. He wouldn't have been out alone on a Saturday night.

Watching her crestfallen face, Victor remembered that Hilary couldn't make the tenth. 'I've got a couple of tickets for a film at the NFT. *Manhattan.* Would you like to come with me on Wednesday?'

Isobel didn't find Woody Allen funny, but she pulled out her diary. Wednesday's entry read: Deliver wedding cake – Mrs Lipow.

'Yes that would be lovely! Where shall we meet?'

'I'll pick you up, seven o'clock. Have to dash now. Meeting a potential client at two thirty. I'll drop you home first.'

After delivering Mrs Lipow's cake and before going to the hairdresser, Isobel decided to go shopping on her own. She told the woman who worked part-time in Next how she had trained to be a teacher, how the kids got her down, how mother had thought up the catering idea. She bought a bright pink coat and a rose pink mohair jumper. The mohair tickled and made her sneeze. When she looked at herself in the shop mirror she thought it made her look fatter, but for once she didn't mind.

At seven, Isobel was as ready as it was possible for her to be. She had even filed her nails and painted them rose pink.

'You know you've got beautiful hair,' Victor said as he unlocked the passenger door of his antique Daimler. His flattery made her dizzy and wordless again, as they drove across Waterloo Bridge to the South Bank.

They sat on the hard curved wooden benches in the bar, as Victor recounted the bar mitzvah fiasco. The spotlights in the ceiling shone down on their heads. One silver, one gold. Isobel laughed, relaxed, and remembered forever his alien face against photographs of those so familiar to her, Buster Keaton, Jack Lemmon, Greta Garbo.

They both enjoyed the film, even Isobel, but they kept glancing at each other to see if the feeling was mutual. Afterwards they ate at the restaurant. At the time, the NFT had a help-yourself salad bar. Isobel piled her plate up with more endive, shredded carrot, tomatoes, no dressing. Victor had boeuf en daube. They shared a bottle of Rioja. He told her of his troubled marriage, his amiable son, his difficult daughter and his honeymoon on a kibbutz. Isobel repeated the story she had told the assistant in Next. Their heads closed in over the table. Did she need glasses, or could it be love?

He drove her to her door and kissed her. How strange, how extraordinary, having someone's tongue licking the inside of her mouth. And how strange to enjoy it so much. Victor pulled away and struggled out of his seat, round the car to open the door for her. 'I'll ring you soon,' he panted.

Isobel's mother was still up, sitting in the kitchen with a cup of tea.

'And what time do you call this?'

Christmas and New Year came and went. Days peeling off the calendar, flying away. Isobel did not sit by the phone. Instead she spent a lot of time in the bathroom bringing up whatever her mother had put down in front of her. It occurred to her that maybe he wasn't separated from Shirley after all.

He rang on 20 February. 'Isobel, sorry I haven't been in touch. Miserable time playing Trivial Pursuits with relations. Finding homes for ties and socks. Then busy, busy, busy, you know.' He didn't mention Hilary.

Isobel didn't know, but she murmured sympathetically.

'Thought you'd like to know that my divorce has just gone through. Wondered what you're up to this weekend? Thought we might celebrate!'

Isobel, who was never up to anything at weekends, accepted his offer of an outing to a fringe play on the life and times of Tony Hancock. The theatre was a small room attached to Raymond's Revue Bar in Soho. Probably not there any more.

'He was very funny, but what a sad life he had.' Isobel toyed with a fearsome plateful of alio, olio, e peperoncino! Victor carefully wiped the juices of the osso buco from his chin, as he filled her in on Hancock's radio and television sit-coms.

On Sunday, Victor took her to the Tate. She was ashamed to admit that she had never been before. She was impressed by the circularity and the height of the foyer and intrigued by the tourists. Earnest Japanese, nonchalant French. The Tate was not really Victor's cup of tea but Isobel seemed a 20th-century creature. He liked to see her pale blue eyes widen, and to answer her questions. They passed through the Rothko rooms. Victor sucked in his cheeks and rolled his eyes, conveying both the desire not to laugh and the distinct impression that he knew nothing about art but he knew what he liked. They looked at the squares of colour within squares and finally arrived at a perfectly black canvas.

'Look!'

Inside a glass case lay a feather on a plinth, above it was suspended a shiny metal brick. It was titled *The Ineluctability of Fate.*

Victor had had enough, 'How about some tea?'

'It's just like sitting on the launching pad of a rocket!'

'And they must have had a clairvoyant on board. The medium seems to have left her crystal ball behind on the ziggurat.' Victor pointed at the edifice slap bang in the middle of the gallery's café. 'Perhaps we could go back to my place. If you've had enough for one day, that is.'

Isobel felt the mirrored walls closing in on her. Feeling squashed and breathless, she declined, relieved though that he wasn't married after all.

In the fading afternoon light, the Daimler climbed back up Rosslyn Hill.

'Things are a bit flat at this time of year.'

Isobel recalled his 'busy, busy, busy'.

'Would you like a ramble around Kenwood tomorrow?'

She remembered the christening cake for the Buxtons, urgent for Tuesday, and said, 'Yes, that would be lovely.'

'The library is one of the finest Adam interiors in the country,' said the guide proudly.

Isobel wasn't really listening. Victor had put his arm round her waist and suddenly the muted and tasteful olive and mustard decor achieved lime and canary yellow brightness. She slipped her hand as far as it would go round his back. They were supposed to be admiring the Iveagh Bequest and indeed Isobel did recognise some famous names. Gainsborough and Reynolds, and the famous face in a self-portrait turned out to be Rembrandt himself. She also noticed the anachronisms. The recessed spots (just like the NFT) and the big, chunky, warm radiators. Victor felt her ribs through her coat, felt her responding and, true to his name, felt victorious.

Lightheaded now with lust, Victor's jokes came thick and fast. They were walking back up the path to the car park. Isobel noticed that the couples coming towards them were smiling too. The whole world was amused.

Inside the Daimler's masculine interior, Victor pulled her towards him, and kissed her. 'Please come back to my place!'

'I'd love to Victor, but I have to ice the Buxton's cake for tomorrow.' She cupped his round forlorn face in her hands and kissed it lightly all over. 'I'd love to, but not today.'

Mrs McNally was ambivalent about leaving her daughter alone. Isobel had appeared almost translucent recently, as well as taut and snappy; like a loose guitar string. But Jessie, her sister, persisted that she need a weekend away from London and all that cooking. So she stocked the freezer with home-made soup and individual portions of cooked mince, and left for the seaside.

Late on Friday, the phone rang. 'So what's cooking this weekend?' Isobel remembered the soup and the mince. 'Mother's gone to Bournemouth. Would you like to come round for supper? I could try out one of my new recipes on you.'

Isobel was awake until one in the morning with Delia Smith. She was first in the queue at Waitrose, fretting that her shopping list might not all be kosher. She laboured all day over tomato and mint bulgur salad, trout cooked in greaseproof paper parcels and home-made profiteroles with French chocolate sauce. She wasn't fond of wine but had bought two bottles of Rioja. She wore the fluffy pink jumper for the second time and what she hoped was a sexy short skirt, but her legs were thin and didn't curve in and out in the right places.

Victor's frame filled the door, horizontally anyway. Heavy rain had subdued his camel hair coat but only glistened in his irrepressibly curly hair. 'Filthy night.' He shook himself like a dog, and laughed.

She lit two pink candles and they sat down to eat, Victor impishly teasing and praising her cooking. Isobel was only capable of teasing her food. Her mouth felt so dry she drank the wine like water.

'Sit somewhere more comfortable and I'll make some coffee.'

When she tipsied back with the tray, Victor was taking up most of the room on the sofa. She placed the tray on the table and squeezed in next to him. A big arm engulfed her shoulders and pulled her close. Familiarity, happiness, intoxication, led them from the sofa to the bedroom.

Outside the bedroom window the rain continued to pour down. This was the evening of the Zeebrugge disaster. As they were clambering over each other for the first time there were others, just off the Belgian coast, who were clambering over each other for the last.

Isobel kept the postcard Victor sent her from Jerusalem for six years. It depicted a holy man, bearded and dressed in black. He appeared to be arranging a bunch of gladioli. On the back he had written, 'One of you lot at prayer.' Six years later she posted it in the paper bank along with her back copies of *The Hotel and Caterers' Journal*.

As spring turned to summer Mrs McNally felt she had been ill-advised. Just Desserts had seemed such a good way of engaging Isobel. Giving her an occupation and purpose. Now it was Mrs McNally who was doing all the hard work. All Isobel seemed capable of doing was putting on her coat and visiting the Everyman and the Screen on the Hill. Sometimes she even ventured into the West End, returning with forlorn pieces of popcorn stuck to the pink coat.

On her birthday, Isobel carefully sorted out her cards from the bills. As well as Auntie Jessie's familiar writing, Isobel found another card. The handwriting reminded her of gladioli. Under 'Best wishes, Victor' was written, 'Please ring me, I need to see you.'

'He needs to see me!' She couldn't pluck up the courage to speak after his wisecracking answering machine message. She rang several times before she found him in.

'Thanks for remembering. It was a lovely card.'

'It took my fancy. I thought of you. Good old Robert Mitchum dancing on the sand. Sorry we haven't been able to meet for a while but there's an exhibition that I thought you'd like on at the Whitechapel. Epstein's sculptures. Could you make it on Sunday afternoon?'

'I hope I'm not being rude but I always thought the East End was a Jewish area, but all the shops seem to be owned by Asians.'

Victor swept her into the gallery. 'No, it's not rude. When the Jewish population became wealthier they moved north. Stamford Hill, Golders Green, and of course Hampstead. The Asians have moved in now, but they'll probably move on eventually.' Victor was telling this to a huge monolith called *Lazarus*. It was as if some magnet inside him had turned round and was pushing her away. She couldn't get close to him, and it was her turn to want to.

When they left the exhibition, he took her on a tour of Epstein's sculpture's in situ. First they visited the Strand. High up, nude figures, lots of them, posed in recesses. Then somewhere north of John Lewis, he showed her a Madonna and child. But he wouldn't meet Isobel's gaze. Didn't touch her. All the adrenalin drained from her heart, down her arms and out through her fingertips.

Finally they drove to Westminster to see *Night* and *Day* carved in Portland stone above St James's Park underground station. *Day*, a sphinx-like woman with someone stretched over her knees, faced north. *Night*, a flat-faced man with a small boy twisted into an impossible position between his legs, faced west.

'It's ironic,' said Victor, 'that *Night* created such an outcry at the time that Sir Jacob had to come back and cut a bit of the boy's willy off' It was. There were not many people about and none of them were looking up at the sculptures. The idea of artistic circumcision subdued them both even further as they rounded the corner into Caxton Street.

'I want to treat you to tea at the St Ermins. He gave her pink coat a quick tweak.

They went up the stairs and into the foyer . . . Isobel's jaw dropped. 'This . . . this hotel was in *Mona Lisa*! You know, the film with Bob Hoskins and Cathy Tyson.'

Cathy Tyson had been a prostitute who had used the hotel's rooms on an hourly basis, but obviously Victor didn't have this in mind because he ordered a cream tea.

'This is the oldest hotel in London. Don't you just love the splendid baroque . . .'

'Why did you need to see me?' she cut in, for the first time irritated by his didacticism.

'Well, it's a bit difficult.' He reached out and grabbed her hand. Someone who could have been a pop star wandered by. 'I'm getting married in September.'

Isobel smelt cigar smoke. An elderly American couple sat down at a nearby table. The chandeliers glistened and winked indifferently. She looked at the scones, the cream, the red jam. She wanted to smear cream and jam all over his chubby face. Instead she got up. Pulled the pink coat tight about her, and walked out, down the stairs of the hotel, and for once in her life, took a taxi home.

She caught sight of him a few times after that. On the first Saturday that *The Last Emperor* was shown in Leicester Square. He was with a small, pretty, redhead, vivacious and talkative. And again when *The Manchurian Candidate* was re-released. This time he was with Mrs Victor and a small party, they were drinking coffee and eating carrot cake. Victor was anecdoting them all enthusiastically but stopped mid-sentence when he saw her. She walked past him and sat in the front row, but couldn't concentrate. A long time later she dreamt that he took her to the theatre. He looked greyer, looser. Sadder but not wiser. It was a long thin theatre and he sat at the front while she sat at the back. He didn't want anyone to see them together. Isobel remembered nothing about the play, except the sensation that the auditorium was very dark in contrast with the stage, which was brilliant orange.

They said goodbye at Hangar Lane. He got into the Daimler, just as the traffic ground to a halt. She had the feeling that she was moving backwards and upwards like a crane shot. She could see Victor's bulk filling the stationary car. He and the car looked very small and very insignificant.

Isobel woke herself up saying, 'I really fancy a bacon sandwich.'

The Choice is Yours

MARK WALDER

Ralph was dressed only in shorts and T-shirt, but when he spoke you felt that he should be wearing something a little more theatrical, a wide brimmed hat and swirling cloak perhaps. By contrast, Rob, who was confined in a grey suit, starched white shirt and blue tie, seemed attired entirely appropriately. Ralph, at forty-two, was energetic, enthusiastic and expansive; while Rob, twenty years younger, was far more conservative and a little bit shy.

They first met in Russell Square on a sultry summer's day. Both were observing daily rituals. Rob came to munch his molten egg and cress sandwiches and Ralph came to recruit potential sexual partners. You could say that Rob came to eat his lunch, while Ralph came to meet his. You might also surmise that Rob had no idea that he was on the menu. But then again, you could be wrong.

'My dear, what a fabulous day!' was Ralph's opening line. 'Humidity prickling the skin and pollution tickling the palette. It quite puts me in mind of Bangkok. Have you been to Bangkok? My dear boy, you must go immediately. What is it about that place? It has the capacity to appeal and appal in equal measure. Do you know what I mean? It's a kind of evocative cocktail of the exotic and the chaotic, where foul-smelling exhaust fumes hang in the heat, as beauty melts your heart. One moment you're expiring on a packed bus in a traffic jam, or being jostled by crowds along the manic streets, the next you're standing barefoot on the cool marble floor of an exquisite Thai temple, breathing in sweet incense and gazing up at a serenely smiling statue of the Buddha. Very like London, in fact. Well, we have the pollution and the traffic at least. Buddhas are in rather shorter supply, but there are one or two small, but perfectly formed, specimens in the British Museum, over the road. Have you seen them? You really should. It's all free. As for beauty? Well, not in such density as Bangkok, of course. The ratio is, in fact, quite the reverse. Nine out of ten people are beautiful there. Exactly the opposite proportion over here, alas. But, if you think this is bad, my dear, step out into the provinces. Take an Away Day, no that's too much, an away half-an-hour, and take a look at Olde England. Everyone out there is virtually *in-bred*. It's really very frightening. It comes of not being invaded for a thousand years. Such a tragedy. Thank God for ethnic restaurants and overseas students, that's what I say. Without a little beauty life would be unbearable, don't you think . . .? By the way, what is your name?'

'Rob.'

'Robert. A pleasure to meet you. So rare one meets a kindred spirit. Let me give you my card. No, it's pronounced Raif. Like waif. Poor little me. Or like the actor, Sir Ralph Richardson, You know? Of course you do. Lovely plummy voice, always a chuckle in the throat, a twinkle in the eye, bit of a leather queen, except he actually did ride a motorbike. Where are you from? Hongkong?

'Grantham.'

'Grantham!?! They have Chinese in Grantham?'

'One or two.'

'Praise be! Been in London long?'

'About six months.'

'Like it?'

'S'alright.'

'Is that all? Where do you live?'

'Wood Green.'

'Oh. Well that explains a lot. First rule of liking living in London is never live outside of zone one. All that tedious tube travel. Grinds down the spirit so terribly. Buses aren't so bad, although bus stops can be murder. Cycling could be fun, if only there weren't so many cars. No, the only alternative is to live close enough in to have everywhere within walking distance.'

'You live around here?'

'Within a stone's throw. Is that the right expression? I don't think I've ever actually thrown a stone.'

'You like it?'

'I love it! It's fabulous! Where else could you go out to see a different play/film/opera every night of the week? Or choose from so many different kinds of cuisine? Where else will you find so much art, so many museums, nightclubs, fashion stores, or beautiful, exciting, interesting people? Nowhere in this country, I can assure you, my dear Roberto, nowhere! The only problem is finding the time to fit it all in.'

'You don't work?'

'Work!? Vile word. Never, unless I choose to. And then it's not work is it? It's recreation, or play, or it's just life.'

'How do you afford to live like that then?'

'Doesn't cost a penny, my dear boy, nay, not a farthing.'

'How come?'

'Meet me here tomorrow after work, say six? And I'll show you how to eat drink and be merry in London, for absolutely nothing. Rien de rien. Okay?'

Rob had to stand on the tube with his face pressed into some man's armpit the whole way from Holborn to Manor

House. It was the same every night. He picked up a takeaway near home. His landlady had offered to cook, but she insisted on strict meal times which he found too restricting. She was okay. She was a friend of his mother. Spent most of her time watching TV, or shouting at Lee Ton, her teenage daughter. Poor Lee Ton, she only wanted to do what all the other girls did. Rob went upstairs to his room, as he did most nights, and began to plough through another chapter of *The Mill on the Floss*. Going to university had made him realise how difficult it was to converse with certain people if you didn't have all these English cultural references at your fingertips. They always seemed to assume that you knew, and it got a bit boring having to keep saying, 'I'm sorry, I've not read that.' Rob's parents only read Chinese newspapers and they had encouraged him to go into science. But now that he had his degree and was working for a firm that dealt with patents, he knew his heart was not really in it. He had hoped that coming to London would offer opportunities for him to meet someone nice, but so far the gay scene had proved disappointing. Going into bars on his own was a bit daunting, and even when he did he found it frustrating, because the only guys who seemed to find him attractive were older men. Guys his own age treated him as though he was invisible. He started to think about Ralph. He was quite attractive, for his age, well muscular, but so camp! And well . . . a bit strange. Eccentric.

Rob had decided not to meet Ralph. He thought he might not be trustworthy and, well, he obviously only wanted to get him into bed, so what was the point? But when he arrived at Holborn station and found it was closed, due to a security alert, he thought he might just as well spend half an hour having a coffee in the park as stand around in Kingsway. So he got there at five past six, but Ralph was not there. Rob waited for forty-five minutes and still Ralph did not show up. Typical! So typical of people in London. They never kept their word. They were so cavalier and unreliable. He hated the lot of them. He was going home!

He was going home when Ralph's voice shot across the entire width of the park.

'My dear, I'm so sorry! I got waylaid by a lovely boy from Kuching. So charming. If you had seen him, you would understand. Do forgive me!'

'I'm sorry, I've got to go,' growled Rob.

'Now, my dear, don't be so grumpy. Especially, as I've just run at least a hundred bruising yards to be with you. I'm sure I've done some dreadful injury to myself in the process. Do you mind if I lean on you, just for a second? Help me to stagger over the road. I live in this crumbling old mansion block. That's right. In we go. I think we'll have to take the lift. Normally, I use the stairs, so good for the heart, but on this occasion.'

They entered Ralph's flat. Rob was impressed by the Chinese dragon masks on the wall in the hall.

'Such a cluttered little hovel, but don't be put off. I know it has all the allure of a Shanghai knocking shop, but we call it home.'

'We?'

'Masakuni! Chop! Chop!'

Ralph clapped his hands and a bleary-eyed Japanese boy holding a can of Carlsberg and wearing only a pair of white Y-fronts emerged from the bedroom.

'Masakuni, this is Rob. The boy I told you about yesterday. Rob, this is Masakuni. He's my rent-boy.'

Masakuni grinned.

'Not lent-boy,' he said. 'I rodger.'

'You certainly do,' rejoined Ralph.

Masakuni grinned again.

'He very bad man,' he warned Rob.

'But you love me.'

'No, no, I love only my girlfriend,' insisted Masakuni.

'It's true, alas. It's his only fault. And she's such a drab creature, too.'

'No, no, very beautiful.'

'Fortunately, she's in Matsuyama. Look at that smile. Have you ever seen such beauty?'

'Not beautiful, only women beautiful.'

'That smile could light up an entire theatre. Think of what they could save on electricity having Masakuni grinning up from the pit in place of the footlights. How can Paul Theroux claim that the Japanese always look in pain when they smile. That's a smile to make the birds sing. To make the blind see and the lame walk!'

'Lob, be careful. He very strange man.'

'Now Masa, don't you dare give away all my dark little secrets. Are you coming to eat with us? Yes? Well, much as I hate to ask you to desecrate the wondrous contours of your body by putting clothes on, we're dining with your ambassador this evening and I think something crisp and white is called for. Rob, come into my room. Search through that pile of papers while I have a quick shower and slip into something more uncomfortable. You're looking for an invite to the Japanese Embassy. It's just a little card. It's in there somewhere.'

Rob looked around Ralph's room. He had never seen anywhere so cluttered. Theatrical costumes, antique furniture, oriental screens and fans, a computer, a fax machine, a CD player, millions of books and a desk piled high with papers, photographs and magazines. He began to sift through the papers. The first piece he came to caught his eye. '*What is it about Bangkok? The place has the capacity to appeal and appal in equal measure* . . . Then there were piles of programmes, and invitations to press nights, exhibitions and openings. Finally, he came upon the little card.

'Have you found it? That's the one. Heavens! We're meant to be there at seven-thirty, I thought it was eight. Right, we'll have to swoop! Masa! Chop! Chop!'

They swooped out of the flats, across the park, past the museum, toward the YMCA, where Ralph chatted briefly to a boy from Malaysia, through Soho Square, where Ralph hugged and kissed two boys from Thailand, down Greek Street, where surprisingly Ralph didn't seem to know anyone, and then into Old Compton Street where any semblance of swooping ground to a halt. Ralph seemed unable to pass a single outdoor café without pausing to wave to someone, kiss, hug or chat, take down a telephone number, make an arrangement to meet, later, tomorrow, the next day. It was 8.15 before they got to the other end of the street and escaped into the crowds clawing their way up Shaftesbury Avenue.

'You seem to know a lot of Orientals,' remarked Rob, as they waited for the lights at Piccadilly Circus.

'He lice queen!' grinned Masakuni.

'I am not a lice queen. A lice queen only sleeps with tramps.'

'That's what I say, you lice queen!'

'Ooh! He's growing sharp in his old age. Masa we'll make a queer of you yet!'

'I don't think so!'

It took hours for the night bus a) to arrive, and b) to crawl home to Wood Green. Rob had declined Ralph's invitation to stay over and very much regretted it. He had arrived home at four-thirty and would have to get up again in another couple of hours to go back into work. 'Vile word'. The dawn sky was turning from dark grey to light. It had been a great night. Dinner at the Japanese Embassy had turned out to be a finger buffet followed by the screening of a Kyogen version of *The Merry Wives of Windsor.* They had sneaked out of the film after ten minutes and 'swept' along to Covent Garden to watch the second act of *Madama Butterfly.* Ralph seemed to know all the staff and to Rob's amazement they were shown into the royal box. It was fantastic! Ralph said that VIPs enjoying corporate entertainment often left at the interval. Rob thought the opera was brilliant. He really should have gone home at this point, but Ralph produced some free passes to a club called Grind and persuaded Rob to go in for a quick drink. The quick drink turned into several and before he knew what was happening, Rob found himself writhing around on a packed dance floor, stripped to the waist, sweat pouring out of his body like Niagara Falls and enjoying every moment of it. He had never had a night like it. He had never lost his inhibitions to this degree. He had never expressed himself so physically. He had never experienced such joy, or felt so free. And now back in Wood Green he had never felt more like death warmed up. And he had to get up for work in two hours.

Having overslept, he phoned in sick and then lay in bed until four in the afternoon. He had never missed a day's work in his life. Serving in his parent's restaurant since the age of ten had instilled a strong work ethic in him. He felt a distinct sense of guilt mixed with a strange feeling of elation. He had always been a bit of a goody-goody at school and for the first time he experienced what it felt like to be a naughty boy. His parents, his landlady and his employer would certainly not have approved, but with a mischievous grin, Rob thought, 'Fuck them!'

The thing he liked about Ralph was the way he seemed to be able to talk to absolutely anyone. One moment he was discussing the similarities between Kyogen and *commedia dell' arte* with the Japanese cultural attaché, the next he was dishing the dirt with a glamorous drag queen in six-inch stilettos. Rob was just happy to be standing by Ralph's side listening. He was involved in the conversation without feeling he had to say anything. Also, he was amused at the way Ralph addressed everyone as 'my dear', from the coat check girl to the Ambassador's wife, and got away with it. He was as camp as a row of tents and he made no apology for it. 'Fuck 'em if they can't take a joke', he drawled, imitating Bette Midler. But everyone could. Everyone seemed to see the funny side of it. It was another world. A world Rob had no idea was there. And it was so seductive, so sexy, surely it would lead to his destruction. Rob felt his skin prickle into sweat. How could anyone live this life and hold down a steady job at the same time, let alone develop a career, which had always been his intention. Or at least, his parent's intention for him.

Ralph said the whole point about being 'queer', Rob hated that word, is that we are different. Our lifestyle is different and we have no desire to assimilate into theirs, which is why they sometimes hate us and find us so threatening. Rob's parents had always wanted him to assimilate. That was the whole point of doing four hours homework every night and going to college and university. But could a Chinese-looking person ever really be accepted as English. Whenever he met someone, the first question was always 'Where do you come from?'

As they trailed back down Old Compton Street at 4am, the street was still packed with people drinking coffee and hanging around having a good time.

'Doesn't anyone have to go to work in the mornings?' he had asked.

'Mornings? Vile word!' Ralph had replied.

'Don't you ever have to pay for anything?'

'If the Queen doesn't why should I? Isn't that woman a fabulous role model?'

'Don't you ever feel that you're being a bit of a parasite?'

'My dear, everyone is a parasite. Everyone feeds off everyone else. Dogs and beggars lick crumbs off the floor under the master's table. We all do it, but some of us choose to do it with a little more style.'

'But how does it work?'

'Simple. You make a list of everything you want to do and then you get yourself put on a list of the people who are doing all the things you want to do.'

'You make it sound so easy.'

'Not easy, but simple and possible. Everything is possible. Welcome to the city of possibilities. Now, do you want to sleep with me?'

'I think I should go home. I've got work tomorrow.'

'As you wish. Here, you had best get a cab.'

'It's all right. I'll get a night bus.'

'My dear, that will take forever. Get a cab. I'll pay. And you won't often hear me say that.'

'It's all right. I've got a travelcard.'

'My dear boy, you have so much to learn. It's been a great pleasure meeting you. Goodnight.'

This sounded like a brush off, but Rob was not going to let anyone brush him off that easily. He went around to Ralph's flat that evening and was invited to attend the first night of a new play featuring Maggie Smith. Rob had never sat in the best seats before, nor seen such a great actress perform. Ralph was ostensibly there to review the production, but unlike the other critics, who scribbled notes furiously throughout the performance, penning their copy as they went along, Ralph made no attempt to write anything.

'I'll mull it over tomorrow morning. It'll be a fabulous review in any case. Just a case of choosing the right superlatives. Always write for the weeklies. No ghastly deadlines to meet that way.'

Over complimentary drinks at the interval, Ralph pointed out the various critics.

'Do you want to go and speak to them? I don't mind standing here on my own.'

'Not really. The thing about critics is that they'll talk about anything, except the play they're watching. I'm sure they're all paranoid that you'll steal their best lines. Which means there's nothing to do but exchange gossip. Boring. Ooh there's Michael Arditti, I must just have a word and see if he's heard what I've heard about a certain knight of the realm!'

That night Ralph made love to Rob very tenderly. They slept for a couple of hours and then woke up and did it all again, this time with increased ardour. After they'd showered in the morning and had breakfast, they went back to bed for more fun and sexual gymnastics. Masakuni popped in briefly with a cup of tea and Rob phoned work and said he was suffering from food poisoning. The following evening they went to eat in a very out of the way restaurant in Docklands, Ralph was apparently writing up something on the place for an American magazine that Rob had never heard of, then they went on to a leather club called Meat which featured an SM cabaret that Rob found stomach-churningly disgusting. Ralph said he wasn't too keen on it either. They went home and had more fun in bed and by the morning Rob had the distinct feeling that he was in love. He called in sick again, this time with an authentic sore throat, and then Ralph suggested he go home to Wood Green to sleep, because he needed to finish the article he was writing on Bangkok. They arranged to meet later that evening at a private viewing at the Royal Academy.

When Rob got home, he was greeted by his landlady. She was stony-faced and wanted to know where he had been. Rob told her it was none of her business. At which point she gave him notice to leave. She also told him that his boss had rung and that she had told him that Rob had not been home for two nights on the trot. Rob decided he had better go into work. His boss called him in, gave him a kindly talking to about telling lies to his supervisor and then gave him the sack. Rob left in tears and rushed straight over to Ralph's house. Masakuni answered the door and informed Rob that Ralph was 'otherwise engaged'.

'A Filipino boy,' mouthed Masakuni, pulling a face to indicate his distaste.

Rob walked over to the park and sat there in a numb state for several hours. He was still sitting there when Ralph walked into the park with the Filipino boy and kissed him goodbye. As Ralph turned to leave, he saw Rob sitting dejectly on the bench and went over to him.

'Hello. What's up?'

'Who was that?' scowled Rob.

'That's Joel.'

'Another one of your pick-ups!' snarled Rob, contemptuously.

'No, he's a friend.'

'How long have you known him?'

'About three hours. He's charming, and very funny. His aunt used to work for Imelda Marcos. She was one of three maids employed just to look after the bitch's shoes!'

'Don't you care about me?'

'Of course I do.'

'I just lost my job because of you and got kicked out of my house!'

'Because of me? What did I do?'

Rob scowled. He was too angry to find the right words to reply.

'At the risk of sounding very old and patronising, may I give you a small piece of advice, my dear? The first step towards becoming a grown-up is to not blame others for the bad things that happen to you.'

'What would you know about being a grown-up? You spend the whole day playing! Life is just one big party for you!'

'Well, it's not such a bad life. You seemed to be enjoying it.'

'I thought you liked me.'

'I've told you I do.'

'I thought I loved you. God, that was stupid.'

'Yes it was. You hardly know me.'

'I thought we could be boyfriends.'

'That's what you fell in love with. The idea of having a boyfriend.'

'Well, don't you want that?'

'No, my dear. I'm afraid I've done that one. I gave ten years to three different boyfriends. Every one turned out the same way. They came to me knowing nothing. I take responsibility for that. I am always fatally attracted to innocence. I nurtured them into adulthood. I imbued them with confidence and recognition of their self-worth and when I had given them everything and taught them everything, they upped and left. Same thing happened every time. I don't feel bitter, that is simply the nature of youth. But at the same time, my dear, I am not a charity. I am not a no-fees-required finishing school. I am simply not prepared to make the same mistake a fourth time. That's called maturity. My life now is made up of moments. I live neither in the past, nor the future, I am 100 per cent in the present. I am open to opportunities and every day they present themselves, all I have to do is respond.'

'And what about me?'

'What about you?'

'Don't you feel any responsibility for what you've done to me?'

'On the contrary, I think my befriending you has helped you a great deal.'

'What!?!'

'If you had never met me, you may have stayed in that dreary job and that revolting house for years. Slogging away through that mind-numbing routine of nine to five, work–home, work–home. I've shown you that there are alternatives. You just have to have the courage to choose them. Now cheer up. In a short while you'll look back on this as one of the best days of your life. A real turning point.'

Ralph stood up as though to leave.

'But what am I going to do? Where am I going to go?' wailed Rob.

'Either you'll find another job and another bed-sit and go back to the dreary world you just got kicked out of, or you'll go out and seek something a bit more exciting. Something that will allow you to really be you. It's all here, my dear. This city has it all. It's just a case of going out there and finding it. Now are you coming, or are you staying?'

'You mean with you? I can stay with you?'

'For a few days. Until we can fix you up with something else. No longer, mind. My place is too small and it's not how I choose to live. Do you understand? Now what are you going to do? The choice is yours.'

Millennium

ATIMA SRIVASTAVA

His face is off centre, smiling in the video screen, half in his world and half in hers. He doesn't realise he is being surveyed by the camera above his head, and he moves naturally, puts down his bag, scratches the side of his face, puzzled now. She didn't anticipate this warm feeling that is embracing her senses. He is her friend now. Nothing will tear them apart, because the past is over. He is exploding with colour, pink kerchief tied to his head like a gypsy. The video grain makes his day old stubble purple and blue, his Jackson Pollock jeans splattered with yellows and his red striped lumber jacket fight with the electrons dictating linear image inside her entryphone.

'Hey, you,' she says.

He turns this way and that, only slightly perturbed, steps back to assess the direction of her disembodied voice. Of course. He looks up and squints at the flat, shining grey metal ceiling of the lobby, grinning as if there were stars, not precise chinks of laser driven white light that confer the status of intruder on every visitor. Oh but this is Barley, no thief, no foe, no crazy person.

'Just place your hand on the white line on the door, and take the elevator in front of you to B5,' she says, watching the screen anxiously like a mother bird.

After a few seconds, the screen goes blank, and again the

bad design frustrates her. She wanted to watch the whole action of him entering the inner lobby and fumbling with the elevator lines. 'So much technology, so little thought,' she thinks. Remembers in a flash and smiles, because in these micromoments before he glides down to her, she has time to quickly flick through the picture book of the girl she used to be. Suddenly he is outside her door, she can hear him, shuffling about looking for the door knob.

'Hi there,' she is shyly smiling from ear to ear as the door slides back.

He puts out his broad arms and hugs her, wiping away her formality, some things never change about people. Bless you, Barley, for never giving thought to protocol, convention. She is glad they don't have to go through horrible, jarring moments of side-stepping each other while they put down the new demarcations of their relationship, friendship. The six years which have waited, before making their friendship known, now dissolve in the warmth and bigness of his hug.

'You look great,' he says, still holding her by the shoulders and tilting his head back to look more keenly. 'You lost weight, Rags?'

She smiles wryly, because Barley always knew what to say to women. Instead she says with a straight face: 'No one calls me that any more. No one's called me that for years.'

He drops his multicoloured baggage in the hall, it looks so strange against the criss-cross honeymilk wood of the parquet floor, and walks easily into the pale central room. He is standing in the middle of the white space, looking around her galaxy with the eyes of a child.

'Like it?' she asks, a little carefully.

'You design it?' he asks, in that voice that tells her that even if they were standing in that crumbling hovel in

Kilburn, with its gnarled walls and seeping dust, where they had kissed and gouged bits out of each other and said things they regretted, he would still have liked her eye, her flair for the day after tomorrow.

'Some,' she admits. She is hesitating, pushing back her hair.

'I promised I'd come,' he answers her unasked question. 'We made a promise, didn't we?'

'It was so long ago. I never intended to hold you to it. It was just the kind of thing lovers say,' she says casually.

'Why just?' he asks. 'At least we didn't plan it to be on St Valentine's day. That would have been tacky. At least we said any time before the New Year.' He looks at his watch and grimaces affectionately. 'Just about made it.'

'We thought it was so far away, the end of the time, the distant future. And it's here. Nearly. Tomorrow. How funny,' she smiles.

Without invitation, Barley walks around the room, touching things like a blind man, feeling them against his skin. The cool of the white screens built into the walls, the white computer on the white desk in the corner. The two sofas are made of fantastically soft buttery white leather. There is a window, which looks on to a glass kitchen, giving the illusion of space within space. It is like the old trick they used in fairgrounds, with mirrors, where the same image was repeated over and over, giving a feeling of depth and a neverending story.

The epicentre of this flat is the table with the computer. Its invisible umbilical cord pulls at your attention. From here, he can see all of the flat, its horizon, its belly, its slant and its curves. He listens to the sound of birds and realises there is no skylight or window to the sky. It is a CD. And there's something else too. There is a scent of a pleasant summers' day, of mown grass and faint honeysuckle and eucalyptus in the air, just the right proportion to skim your senses, not attack them like cheap aftershave.

'You actually don't need to move away from here do you?' he asks in wonder, seating himself at the computer. 'Bar the obvious, you don't need to cross any lines, go through any corridor, walkways, to get anywhere. You're the centre of your world here.'

He looks at Rags, a bewildered look on his face. 'You could make the coffee from here, couldn't you?'

She laughs. 'I can switch the timer on the espresso machine, yeah. So what? You make it sound as though it's spooky, instead of just functional. Tell you what, I'll make you a coffee manually,' she emphasises the word, loading it with sarcasm, 'and you can tell me about your travels,' she grins. 'Do you like the mood? I can change it if you like,' she adds.

'We're . . . let me see, how many feet under ground? It's frightening. To think it feels like a perfect summer in my shirt-sleeves. And we're under the ground?' he asks, following her into the kitchen. The area is a series of flat shining surfaces of white and grey, but there is the familiar paraphernalia of a half-eaten breakfast. A tray of untouched croissants, milk, half-eaten Cornflakes. The kitchen smells warm and cakey, as if they were in a farmhouse and about to eat a tea full of scones and lashings of lemonade.

She shrugs. 'Twenty maybe? . . . Oh and Barley,' she says, 'We don't use that terminology any more. We say Below Ground. Underground has all kinds of associations which people find offensive.'

She rolls her eyes to show him she hasn't changed as much as he thinks. Years ago, she had kicked up a fuss when the magazine which was publishing an article she had written on architecture, wanted to know how to refer to her in their introduction. Was she to be referred to, (they enquired), as Black, or black (lower case), Black British, Asian, British Asian, Woman of colour etc, etc? She had screamed into the phone that she wasn't interested in being a mount on a colour chart, and was more interested in putting forward her views on architecture than in pseudo-cultural politics. Barley had accused her of throwing the baby out with the bathwater. They had rowed. She had won by making him laugh, saying all he thought about was babies.

He is standing by the door watching her and suddenly he feels nauseated. The steam of the kettle seems to be fighting with the air-conditioning.

She wrinkles her nose. 'I need to turn that thermostat down. Too much,' she says, touching a strip of metal.

He wants to sit on the beautifully manicured wooden floor, which is uncomfortable but luxurious, and they lean against the velvety leather sofa as they sip their coffee.

'I've only been here for a few months. Getting used to it myself,' she explains. 'It's part of the contract. Accommodation and services,' she smiles.

'Is everything really space age or have I just been away too long?' he asks her, peering into her face with crumpled, stubble lit jade green eyes.

She laughs out loud. 'Don't be silly. What's space age about it? The underfloor heating doesn't work properly, the videophone's colour is out of alignment, the kitchen smells too . . . cakey'. . .

They burst out laughing together.

When they had been a couple, years and years ago, ten years ago, when they were just out of art school and living in Kilburn and having arguments about form and content, Rags had baked Barley a cake for his birthday. In a deserted carpet warehouse deep within the empty dead infrastructure of declined industry in East London, he used to paint vibrant purple landscapes and expressive faces that drilled their stare into your eyes.

There was a kind of open exhibition of artists work entitled Artists in the Nineties. The huge desolate warehouse was full of rooms rented to artists, and to mark the first anniversary of this initiative to '*encourage artists to experiment and fail*', the warehouse had been made open to the public. Every artist threw open their door, invited friends, provided some crisps and cheese and music, and friends met other's friends. That day was Barley's birthday. He was twenty-three, one day older than Rags. She had helped him set out his work, despite his reluctance – it wasn't good enough, what was the point – and then rushed via a knotted network of trains and buses to North London, Kilburn. Baked a cake with Cointreau and stuck candles in it, blown up balloons on the tube and managed to get back for when the guests began to arrive. Barley had said it was cakey cake, fat and luscious with jam oozing out and polka-dotted candles sticking out like antennae. Straight out of a storybook.

'Hey,' he says suddenly, 'I bought some champagne on the flight.' He pulls out the bottle and makes to open it, then begins to look around for a tea towel. She brings two tall impossibly elegant flutes to him, has a big smile on her face. Then: takes the bottle from him, opens it with no regard to the floor or furniture, jumps back childishly at the 'pop'. Foamy champagne splashes their shins and the sofa and the floor. He watches as the creamy leather absorbs the liquid in seconds, and Rags is smirking with raised eyebrows.

'Magic!' he exclaims.

They toast the millennium a day early, in this white underground cave, cocking a snook at the promise of hysteria and wild claims about to be made in their world.

'You came straight here? You didn't go home first?' she asks, not meaning to pry, but still . . .

They had parted tearfully, like best friends moving house, knowing they would lose touch but not wanting to. They had not traded in blame or recrimination. All that came later with next lovers. He had sunk into a gloom when she told him it was time to let each other go. She had cried for a week when she heard that he had got married.

Barley hadn't written or phoned for years, and then, in the last year, came a sudden stream of postcards, a few scribbled letters, phone calls. From villages and cities in India that she had only read about. Astonished at herself, she had responded by scribbling thin blue aerogrammes to P.O. Box numbers, never knowing if they reached their far-flung destinations. They were both hurtling towards the millennium, about to turn thirty. It was as though suddenly, vitally, they needed to know what books they had read and thoughts they had been having, which views they had been viewing, before the new world wrenched them inside its hungry jaws.

He is hunched over his champagne, concentrating on the floor. 'Do you mind me coming here first? I need to sort things out. I've been away for so long. Travelling makes you distant.' He looks at her, waiting for her to explode, disapprove as she always did. There is no flicker on her face.

'I don't mind. I just don't understand. Up to a year ago I thought you were happy, settled. That's what you wanted wasn't it? Babies, wife. All that. And then this travelling about. Why alone?'

He is nodding. Even now, even when he is distracted and disoriented over some things, he is certain about others. He always knew what he wanted in his life. That's what ended them.

'You say it like that, and I can't quite believe it. Still that disdain in your voice . . .' he says. Barley never bothered with the conventions of politeness needed between people to take the place of gentleness, understanding. Barley always said they should say what was in their heart even if it hurt. It was to do, he knew, with years of having to hide how you felt at school, keep back real emotion and not talk at the dinner table unless his father asked him a question.

'Barley, how is this conversation turning into an argument? I know you wanted to have kids and a family. Why should I care now about it? You've been gone for years. We've been living in different worlds. I'm different from who I was. I don't get angry about everything now.'

'You're not different,' he says kindly, suddenly. 'It's just your environment that's different.'

'It's a great apartment, isn't it? I think this contract could last for a year and the money's good. I can live here peacefully. I'm connected to whatever I want, whoever I want. The computer they've installed is top of the range. You wouldn't believe what it can . . .' She breaks off, smiling because she remembers that conversation when they knew their time was up.

Barley was painting strange headless bodies in their Kilburn flat. He had stopped paying for a tiny studio in a huge warehouse where he felt stifled by the deadness of the air. 'I can't work here, I can't think,' he had complained. 'I need to be where there are people, hurrying and alive, not among dead buildings and deadly ambitions,' and it had led to their now familiar, cruel conversations, battles, about the nature of art. Although Rags was trained in Fine Art, a First Class degree, she was interested in design, in function. She had always wanted to be an architect and, despite everybody's better judgement, had taken a badly paid job as a junior in a small architectural practice which went on to meteoric heights of achievement. She had learned to displace ideas and spatial differences on to the computer. It was a much better canvas, it gave her more scope. She couldn't stand it when Barley refused to learn. She thought it was a stance he liked to use against her. He the artist; she the hack. He made no money, she was in demand. He was happy, smug even, about being oblivious to computers; she was filled with a sense of excitement.

'You just don't want to work here because you've run out of ideas, and you're too scared not to paint. You think you'll become a graphic artist and never paint again. So you don't have anything to do with the outside world, the technology which is changing our lives, you don't even care about it,' she had shouted at him.

'So much technology, so little thought,' he had screamed. 'Yes I'm scared. I'm scared I'll never paint if I enter your world and start earning money,' he had cried foolishly, knowing how foolish it sounded to her. Its naivety, its arrogance.

'You haven't got it in you, Barley,' she had spat back. 'It's typical of you. There are so many like you. Middle-class English public schoolboys living out fantasies of purity in dirt. Working through their sterile childhoods, holding on to some rarefied world that I will never be part of.'

Barley had hit her across the face, and she had stood there smarting, satisfied with his blow.

'Why are we doing this?' he had said, full of sadness.

'I'm not from your world. I grew up poor and I'm never going back. I'm not afraid. You're afraid of everything. Even a little machine,' she had said.

He had never known till that day how afraid she really was. He knew from that speech that he couldn't help her in her sea of fear any more. The days when they had held hands and eaten fish suppers in the rain and gone to exhibitions as students were over. He knew her ambition was part of the barricade to the fear of losing herself in insignificance. They were so young, everybody thought it was such a shame, such a perfect couple. They both knew they were tired of arguing with each other, cutting the other down sometimes just for the sport of it. It was like a revelation to see that, after all, fear was stronger than love.

'Did you ever go to India, study the Low Income Housing initiatives?' he asks. 'I met Charles Correa, I sent you a postcard, did you get it?'

'I didn't go. I keep meaning to go. I've been working all the time. So many new things going on. I keep meaning to go.' She looks at him and smiles lopsidedly. 'Find my roots?'

'I went for you,' he smiles back. 'Your roots are fine, they're still there,' he adds laughing, his broad tan, his long legs.

'Will you stay long?' she asks, knowing he won't.

'Just till the evening. I want to go . . . home,' he says, eyelids flicker.

Home. Home to the country, the cottage. His wife would be waiting, with his children. They would have missed him, but they accepted it. He needed to feel free, to be by himself sometimes. That's how he had explained his long trip in a scrawled postcard to Rags.

'Of course,' she says. 'How are your kids? I'm sorry. I forgot to ask.'

'The kids are fine,' he says, aware of how strange it sounds. Suddenly: 'You never wanted anything of me, did you? We had so much together, we had so much to look forward to. I wanted to learn Hindi, and travel around India with you, so our children wouldn't miss out on things that were important to us. Your family, your birthplace.'

'Barley!' She is shocked, appalled by his emotional outburst. Then, evenly, she changes the subject: 'This is my country. This is where I live. This is where my terms of reference are.'

He looks away from her. 'You can keep it,' he says bitterly. 'This green and pleasant land. It throttles me. This England. You can keep it.'

'Thanks,' she says and they laugh. 'Anyway,' she adds, 'I live in England, but I don't do any work here. All my work is in Europe and Hong Kong. Don't you see? It doesn't matter where you live any more, you can be where you like. Citizens of the world.'

'Only you never *go* anywhere. You always said you would go to India and find out about the places you came from, where your mum and dad were born. You used to talk about it all the time. You said you wanted to find out about the significance of cities, how they functioned through their architecture. Were made.' He wrinkles his brow to remember her feverish article. He likes to be the one who remembers it better than she does. He had been impressed by her ideas. 'Were made immortal, given continuity through their intersection with people's lives.'

She cringes, covers her face.

He continues, 'About those connections you wrote about. You were going to do a project on open-to-the-sky architecture remember? How buildings can be used to bring communities nearer each other,' he says.

'Oh yeah, well. What for?' she says dismissively. 'What do you need to do all that stuff for? I don't experience life the way I did. I used to be angry all the time about discrimination, about injustice, racism, blah blah. I used to think the answer lay in looking back, in examining the past, examining the environment. I was just young, and looking for something to do. Don't you see? The answers lie in looking ahead, towards the sun. Things are different now. So much dead wood has been eliminated. In my work, in the way I work, I don't experience any of those things. My work stands on its merits, I don't have to deal with office politics, or harassment in the streets or traffic or labels. I don't have to deal with that stuff.'

'You're protected,' he says, 'beavering away in the house that Rags built.' He's grinning proudly, so that she doesn't take this the wrong way. Suddenly he's serious. 'Who's in your life?'

'What's the weather like up there?' she asks after a while.

'It's cold. England,' he smiles.

'I've hardly been out of this place,' she explains sheepishly. 'No need.'

'But at least the corner shop? The Patel shop. There must be one, even in this posh neck of the woods?'

'No need. Milk and cigarettes and newspapers available in the inner lobby.'

'Inner Lobby. Sounds weird.'

Her eyes light up despite herself. 'It's not weird, it's wonderful. Think about it, Barley, I'm living in the future. I'm living in the kind of flat which is going to be commonplace in this coming century. I can see the person I'm talking to in Hong Kong, I can transfer a piece of work to New York in micromoments. And just with that, that little computer. It feels so exciting to be here, to be celebrating the turn of the century in this turn-of-the-century flat.'

'Who's in your life that doesn't mind you keeping an old sentimental appointment with an ex-boyfriend on the eve of the millennium?'

'Oh,' she says unsmilingly, 'no one very important. He's interesting and good, but he's not perfect.' She looks at his face kindly. 'You mustn't mind so much, Barley. I chose to live an impossible life, looking for the ideal. It just means that you're alone a lot. In your heart. You get used to it. You mustn't worry for me.'

He says, 'I think that's why I went off travelling. I'd forgotton how to be alone, so busy being . . . part of something that I thought would make me feel safe. Continuity. Immortality. Same old stuff . . . But it's still there. I need to know it's still there, wherever I stray.'

She laughs easily. They are sitting, sipping champagne, cross-legged on the floor, finally through the dark tunnel, into the light of friendship. 'It would never have worked out between us Baal,' she says mischievously, 'I wouldn't have allowed any such freedoms.'

'You're wrong, Rags,' he says, grinning. 'It has worked. We know each other without explaining things. We don't fight each other. We let each other be.'

They make love, the last hurdle, to see what is on the other side. When they open their eyes in the white room, everything is just the same, and they breathe in the honeysuckle with equal amounts of relief and gladness. Sad too, like the disappearance of dreams when you wake determined to remember. They look at each other and laugh nervously, wondering how they managed to reach this place of near perfection where love at last is not used against each other as a weapon.

As she clears up the drinks, he turns on the TV, a large rectangle in the wall. Every channel is building up to celebrations. He stares at the videophone, its little revealing screen. The computer screen winks chequeredly in his direction and he smiles. Rags had been playing chess on it with someone in Berlin. She sees him looking and wants to explain how Virtual Reality works, but Barley has had enough of being in this beautiful cave. He is longing for winding roads and amazing pathways and green parks.

'Shall we go. Up . . . Out for a walk?' he suggests suddenly. 'See what's happening in the street?'

'Mmmm . . . could do,' she looks doubtful. 'We could go

for a drive. I know what's happening out there, anyway. They're going to have a street party, soup kitchens, food aid that kind of thing.'

'*They're* having . . .? Are *they* entering a different century? Soup kitchens?' he wrinkles his brow,

'Barley,' she is impatient with him now. 'Obviously, *we* won't be going to their street party tomorrow. It'll be more of a feeding of the five thousand. Maybe I'll walk through it. Most people will be with friends at home, or in restaurants. Only the poor will be in the streets. Didn't you see them on your way here? All the people who live on the streets? The itinerants, the homeless, the drunks, the loonys. It's not safe out there. Your compassion is only lip service, it's a wasteland out there.'

'Lets go for a walk,' he says slowly.

Rags's face is filled with a mild horror, and then she checks herself, armed with sarcasm.

'Oh I see. Social conscience, right? Does it make you feel good?'

'Let's get off the spaceship and see what's happening,' he grins, not allowing her to spoil things.

The first time they went to Paris together, they were just out of art school, and neither of them had been anywhere much. They held hands all the time as they crossed the streets and sat in cafés. They dropped a tab of acid and went to gawp at the Pompidou Centre. It looked so ununderstandable, and they giggled at each other in the square, a little scared of exploring this strange sinuous steely beast. Barley had taken her hand and whispered, 'Let's get off the spaceship and see what's happening,' and they felt like Martians landed on earth, dazed, strolling around the people and the buildings.

'You sure you want to do this?' she says a little nervously. She wasn't joking, she really hasn't been out for a while.

Days seem to go by so quickly. There's a pool in the back and an entertainment room, an exercise room and a sun room where sunlight filters in through solar panels . . . but Barley doesn't want to see any of it.

Rags dresses strangely. A huge white padded jacket, like a Michelin man. Her white jeans tucked into pale boots. A hat that pulls over all her hair. Sunglasses too. They glide up to the light together, Barley resplendent in his splattered colours, close to her, but not holding hands. In the inner lobby, they check themselves in the floor to ceiling mirrors, and see two people from different lands. Barley's shirt is open at the neck; her mouth is covered by the puffed up collar of her coat. There is a lovely cello playing around them, and a mist of dew and the scent of fresh, clean, crisp mornings. They look at each other, and press the white metal strip.

The light outside is grey, drab and unreal against the inside reality of heightened perceptions. They take steps outside the block of flats, and immediately Rags sneezes. The air is full of flecks of dust and smoke and a metallic cold that sears her throat. Her whole head feels full of vacuum. After a while she gets accustomed to it as they walk apprehensively into the street.

Like fingernails on a blackboard, the first thing that jars is the noise. People shouting, laughing, horns blaring, dogs barking, bicycle bells, cars accelerating, a baby screams, loud hard music collides with other music, melodic or rhythmic or guitars and flutes. It is as though they have plunged back into the decayed fabric of a charcoal past. Along the streets, faded pale bunting has been strung across the few broken lamp-posts still remaining, portions of their Victorian wrought-iron detail not yet crumbled. In some places there are fairy lights, chinese lanterns, even candles and burning torches. Nothing has shape or form. It is a rambling, cascading stream of rabid consciousness. People scurry past. The helpers and the helped. Men and women with scrubbed and tired faces are milling among the needy, carrying boxes and decorations, industrious as ants. Little half-made settlements have built up along the pavements, with corrugated iron and plastic waste. A few fires inside large metal bins smoke the air. Soup stations have been set up, in large doorways, behind which there used to be houses, roads, parks, picnics . . .

Rags hasn't remembered writing that article for years. What was it called, something pretentious like 'Significant Connections'? It had started with how the retelling of folklore and mythologies made connections between subsequent generations. From there sprung the notion of a house being like a little city, its corridors, arches, patios, colonnades, shadows, connecting the rooms and their inhabitants with the language of movement. In the same way, what was interesting and meaningful about a city was the way its architecture made connections through its amazing paths and winding roads and rolling hills and turquoise waterways and purple riverscapes which people had to pass through in order to experience themselves in their societies.

'I can't remember the last time I went for a picnic,' she says suddenly. Ribbons of laughter, uncles and boys and cricket, mothers unwrapping chappatis and sandwiches. Arguments and songs. Poetry recited. Blistering afternoons, rainy evenings.

Barley is taking a newspaper out of a vending machine, speed-reading the headlines. A young man waits greedily by the sidewalk, glancing to see when the paper's finished with. Barley picks out the bulky ENTERTAINMENT section and goes to discard it, while keeping back the rest of the paper, rolled up under his arm. 'Thank you,' says the waiting man, seizes the section and walks off from Barley's bewildered stare.

'That happened on the trains all the time,' he says. 'In India. People would just take what you didn't want of the paper.'

They smile at each others thoughts masquerading as conversation.

'I'm glad we made a sentimental promise,' she says.

A man approaches them, his face wan with fatigue.

'Want to help?' he enquires of them sternly, about to hand over a box full of bread rolls. 'We need ten people on this street, five on the next.' He is waiting impatiently for their assistance.

Rags looks at Barley. They are shocked, stunned to be addressed like this by a complete stranger.

'No . . . er thanks. We're just walking,' says Barley.

'Why not?' demands the man calmly. He is used to this. Asking favours of strangers and being rebuffed happens all the time. There seems to be no protocol on the streets. No ratification of social services. No official badges. Help is given and asked for on an individual, arbitary basis. Results are random, disparate.

'Why don't you want to help?' the man asks with weary aggression.

They just walk by. They don't know what to say. The man carries on, unperturbed, unabashed, carrying his box, saying hello to people.

Strange faces stare at them without any shame. Distorted faces, eyes bulging; men who can't stop shaking their heads, women who sit crying by the roadside. Among them are figures rushing on briskly, in overcoats, in a hurry. The pavements are full of the shadows of people wrapped in sleeping bags, and holding conversations or lying in corners. There are a few shops open, only half full. Miserable, wretched in their half-hearted attempt to entice customers. Peeling posters and notices on the walls proclaim faded dance-halls.

'Did you see them?' she whispers into his ear. 'Those people we just passed. There was something wrong with them. Their faces. Not quite right.'

They walk along the length of the crowded street, almost pushing past the tide of unmoving, stagnant, noisy tamped-down people and sleeping bags and half eaten food and dogs and balloons and crackers. The odd misshapen sub-personalities of the grotesque street surround them, leering. The press of the street like the still sulphurous press of war lumbers on with its silent tragedies.

Rags walks quickly, buried now in her white tyres of foam, peeping out of her sunglasses. Barley turns to look away from the staring eyes around him, as he suddenly puts his tanned muscled arm around Rags. His colourful garb streams past people with dirty knotted hair and children with running noses, like the strobing light rays of discotheques. Rags and Barley huddle by like two refugees clinging to each other.

A car pulls up, and children scatter. It is a white, gleaming car with tinted windows, and soft upholstery. It is similar to Rags's car. They hear the click of locks, as all doors are automatically sealed. Presently, one of the doors is unlocked manually, and a woman steps out with a golden child. They look gracious and lovely against the fading grey and yellow light of the grimy street. The child is pulling at her mother's arm, towards a shop. She is pointing to a rusting chrome sweet machine outside the door of a closed shop. It dispenses an old brand of confectionery with sugar and spice, behind the mottled glass. She has begged her mother for this treat, to put her old twenty-pence piece into the slot. Barley and Rags stand near them on the pavement, staring and listening to their conversation. It is mellifluous, dripping with honey and gilded with diamonds. They stand staring, because they can make no sense of the mother's words, even though they use the same language.

The woman is dressed in a svelte grey material, swathed in its soft folds, looking anxiously around the street, her hand on her daughter's head, as she pushes her twenty pence through the slot. Suddenly the arc of her anxious gaze stops at the crossroads of their stare. She squeals and quickly covers her face, begins pulling her oblivious, happy daughter away from the machine, towards the car.

'Come on honey, come on. We've got to go. Did you see those people? Their faces weren't right. There's something wrong,' She lowers her voice but they can hear, 'come on. I think they're crazy people. Look how they look. There's a lot of crazy people around. I love you, I don't want you hurt. I must protect you.'

As the car drives off, Rags starts to laugh. Barley looks at her and joins in. They can't stop laughing for ages. They look at each other. Bystanders look on amused, or laugh just to participate, just to be friendly, or to fill in time. What a lovely couple, says an old woman wrapped in newspaper. He's wearing my trousers, confides a young man sitting on a tea chest, wearing glasses and jeans.

'What shall we do?' asks Barley, looking at Rags as they wipe their eyes.

She frowns, puts her hands on her hips, looks around, and then back at him.

'Help?' she asks.

'Why not,' he agrees.

Lost Maps of London

GEOFF NICHOLSON

William and his therapist sat in an awkward though not hostile silence for almost all the first half of the session. Sun streamed into the basement room, and the shadows cast by the window frames cut the carpeted floor into sharp bright diamonds of light. William's therapist, a slender, prematurely grey-haired woman who wore big rings and yellow silk stockings, stared out of the window at the tangled Kentish Town garden beyond, but she had the trick of letting her clients know that her attention was still in the room with them.

At long last William said, 'I think I'm changing.'

'Is that a good thing?' she asked, slowly turning her head towards him.

'Yes, I think so.'

'And in what way are you changing?'

William wriggled in the leather Charles Eames chair and thought hard before beginning to speak.

'I think I'm becoming more complex,' he said. 'More dense, more full of noise and pollution, more beset by problems of organisation and infrastructure.'

His therapist had to work hard not to show how interested she was.

'I display signs both of renewal and decay,' he continued. 'Strange sensations commute across my skin. There is vice and crime and migration. My veins throb as though with the passage of underground trains. My digestive tract is clogged. There are security alerts. I'm developing tourist attractions. I think I'm turning into Greater London.'

The therapist coughed to hide a snigger of derision, but she failed to hide it completely. William knew he had been foolish to come here to this expensive session in a part of town he never frequented to be mocked by a woman he neither knew nor trusted. He wasn't sure of the precise origin of his problem, but he suspected it had begun with a 'cute meet'.

He was sitting in a square formica booth in a snack bar in the Charing Cross Road, nursing a cappuccino in a worn white cup, pretending to read his newspaper. It was mid-morning and the place was empty apart from him and a lean, twitchy young woman in the next booth. He no longer had any inhibition about staring at people. He saw she had a narrow, smooth face, completely without makeup, but as he watched she began to apply mascara, eye-liner, eye-shadow, eyebrow pencil. Her eyes were set wide apart and looked tired and sad and innocent, but as she worked on them they became more defined, more hard-edged, more knowing. A slick of metallic blue and grey formed itself above each of her eyes, and finally she drew two long feline points leading away from the outer corners of her eyes. She worked hard, continually checking progress in a small circular hand mirror, and it took a long time. It didn't look like a labour of love exactly, but it was something she had to do. He could tell she was aware of his stare but she wasn't ready either to acknowledge or repel it.

He tried hard not to make assumptions about the people he saw in London, but sometimes he couldn't help it. There was something infinitely foreign about her, a foreign-ness that included but was not limited to nationality or race. He could not have said where in the world she came from. He was certain she was not a native Londoner, but neither did she look like a tourist or visitor or student. Perhaps she'd just moved there, just got her first job, was living in expensive squalor in some shared flat. He was wrong about all the above. He noticed there was a well-thumbed *A–Z* on the table in front of her.

At last her eyes were finished. He wondered if she was about to start on the lips, but she wasn't. She put her makeup away, finished her coffee. She was ready to go. She slipped on a pair of wraparound shades and left the café.

Nobody cleared the table she'd vacated and when he next looked in that direction he saw that the *A–Z* was still there. He went over, picked it up, took it back to his own table and thumbed through the pages. It was heavily annotated with words, doodles and asterisks, and certain routes through the city had been shaded in with different coloured magic markers. Then he turned to the first page and saw a name and address. The name was Elizabeth and the address was Cromwell Road, but there was no surname or postcode. An instinct made him check the index and he discovered there were fifteen different Cromwell Roads listed. He wondered if he was crazy enough to visit each location in an attempt to return the *A–Z*. But he needn't have worried. A moment later she returned for the lost book. He handed it over cheerfully.

'Elizabeth?' he asked.

'Yeah,' she said, in an accent that was instantly identifiable as more authentically London than his own, and which instantly changed all his assumptions about her. 'You know, like the queen,' she added.

She was going to Stanfords, the map, guide and travel bookshop in Covent Garden, and he went with her. They went downstairs to the London section. There were all kinds of treasures there; tourist maps, parking maps, motorists' maps, 3-D maps, even a 'murder map'. There were books called *Naked London*, *Lesbian London*, *Beatles' London*. There was even a guide that called itself *Complete London*.

'A book like that would have to be bigger than this shop,' he said.

'Bigger than London itself,' she added.

After an hour or more of browsing she said there was nothing there that she wanted. 'I like to make my own maps,' she said.

They went to her flat in the Cromwell Road, the one in Earls Court, not one of the fourteen others in places such as Teddington or Worcester Park or South Wimbledon. The living room was bare, brown, uncluttered, but pride of place went to a large map of London that was laid out on the floor like a rug. It was perhaps three feet by four feet, and it covered an area from Brentford in the west to the London City Airport in the east; from Harringay in the north to Streatham Common in the south. William realised that despite having lived in London for the best part of fifteen years he had never been to any of these places. Elizabeth pointed out that the map, of course, didn't show the full extent of what might be defined as London, or what certain people might describe as London, but she said it was good enough for her purposes.

'When I bought it the assistant asked me if I wanted it encapsulated. I didn't know what he was talking about.'

What he called encapsulated most people would probably have called laminated. Elizabeth's map of London came coated in a smooth, shiny, protective layer on both sides. She had been worried that this high gloss finish might be too reflective and make the map difficult to read in certain lights, but on balance it seemed like a good idea. The map would last longer, wouldn't get torn. Marks and stains, including lines and doodles made with felt tips and markers could be removed with a wipe. That was to prove very important.

She went to a desk in the corner of the room and took two marker pens, a red and a blue, and handed him the latter. Then she asked him to make a cross at every spot on the map where he had ever lived. He thought that by most people's standards he'd moved around a lot in London, especially in his early years there. That fact seemed to please her. He knelt over the map and found himself making a dozen small crosses.

There were some strange, distant scatterings, one in Greenwich, one in Seven Sisters, two in Hendon. Even at the time these had seemed like excursions away from the places where he belonged. However, there was a definite clustering around West London, half a dozen or so locations within a trapezoid that had Notting Hill, Marylebone, West Hampstead and Swiss Cottage as its corners.

William looked at the map and the crosses he had made and was somehow disappointed. He had hoped that his nomadic wanderings might have revealed a pattern, a recognisable shape, but they did not. Clearly they were in no sense random, nor was there anything accidental about them. He had made certain choices about where he lived, although not all of them were exactly free choices. Nevertheless he was surprised at how haphazard the arrangement looked.

Then she gave him the red marker and told him to mark all the places he'd ever had sex. Initially the pattern was the same. With the exception of one rough bed-sit off the Goldhawk Road he had managed to have sex in all the places he'd lived. But soon the pattern became very different indeed. There were now marks in all sorts of outlying districts, places where girlfriends had lived; places like Hackney, Crouch End, Elephant and Castle. There were occasions when he had slept with women on other people's floors after parties in Brixton and the Old Kent Road. He had a clear but disconnected memory of being at a very dull dinner party, and of slipping away with a woman called Lynn for a very rapid and intense act of intercourse in the bathroom. He was fairly sure this was in Acton and he placed a cross accordingly but its positioning was necessarily vague.

By now there appeared to be no patterning at all in the crosses. A critical eye would have seen a preference for west London and north of the river, but it was only a slight preference. Beyond that the marks now looked as though they might have been made at random.

William revealed that he had had sex with women in twenty-six separate locations around London, not twenty-six different women, he was keen to tell Elizabeth, since he wanted her to respect him. He had no idea whether this counted as a lot or a little. And he had no idea why he was counting or why he had made this map, except that she had asked him to. Then she produced an expensive camera and photographed the finished map, before taking a damp cloth and wiping away all the crosses from the surface.

'Good,' she said. 'Now we can start with a clean slate.'

One day she showed him her photograph album. It contained maps, or rather photographs of maps, maps like his own, made by her other friends and acquaintances. He saw how the city was overlaid with the patterns of where other people had lived and had sex. And he saw how these patterns resembled or differed from his own, how they sometimes intersected his own maps, sometimes seemed to compliment them, other times seemed to be have been drawn in strict opposition to his. There would be people whose maps centred intensely around Kensington or Belsize Park, others who were concentrated on South London, others who had lived and fucked all over London at all points of the compass. In one or two cases the patterns appeared to be not merely promiscuous but systematic and exhaustive. Every single borough, every district, every postal area had been the scene of sex for certain determined map makers. He wasn't sure whether he found this encouraging or not.

In the weeks that followed Elizabeth showed him her own version of London. She took him by way of the Piccadilly Line to try to locate the pissoir in the Holloway Road that Joe Orton writes about in his diaries. By his account it was 'the scene of a frenzied homosexual saturnalia' sometime in 1967. The diary said the toilet was under a bridge, but they failed to find anything that could be positively identified as Orton's old haunt.

'Twenty-eight years is a long time in the life of a cottage,' Elizabeth said philosophically.

They went to 28 Charlotte Street, the home of an eighteenth-century whipping brothel presided over by Mrs Theresa Berkeley. It was a place where, in general, customers were flogged with birches, cat o'nine tails, and even fresh nettles. But customers could give as well as receive, there were prostitutes there who could be whipped including, for two hundred guineas, Mrs Berkeley herself.

They found two doors in Charlotte Street, both marked number 28. One belonged to the offices upstairs, and the other was the door to a double fronted bookshop called Index Bookcentre. A copy of Trotsky's *In Defence of Marxism* was displayed in the window. Afterwards Elizabeth and William had a Greek meal at the Venus Kebab House a few doors away.

They walked along Waterloo Road and she recalled a passage from Flora Tristan's *Promenades dans Londres* in which she describes how in the late 1830s the entire road was filled with prostitutes, leaning out of windows, sitting on doorsteps, many of them bare-breasted, raucous and cheerful, arguing with each other and their pimps. Elizabeth took William to Waterloo Bridge where Flora Tristan had stood and watched as a great tide of females had crossed the river, heading for the brothels, the parks and theatres and 'finishes' of Central London where they would stay and be debauched till morning, when they would return used and sated.

One Sunday Elizabeth and William took the bus to Fleet Street and looked for Fleet Alley where on 23 July 1664 Samuel Pepys took a turn or two with a most pretty wench in one of the doorways. But Fleet Alley was not to be found. Similarly there was no Axe-yard in Westminster where, according to Aubrey, Ben Jonson got a terrible clap from a 'black handsome wench . . . which cost him his nose.'

They came to Gray's Inn Road to a distinguished four square red brick building now called Churston Mansions. In a previous incarnation it was called Clevelly Mansions and was the home of Katherine Mansfield and her lover Ida Constance Baker, known as L.M. Here in a three-room flat that had as its centrepiece a stone Buddha surrounded by bronze lizards, Mansfield and Baker committed acts that were for the times and in the public imagination genuinely shocking. Here too, at least one of Mansfield's male suitors threatened to shoot himself for love of her.

Elizabeth and William walked the streets of London trying to pick up on this mass of erotic energy, the afterglow of these coming togethers, these acts of intensity and desire, of love and transgression; acts of defloration and perversion; acts stemming from diverse needs, psyches, cultures.

But eventually they said to one another that perhaps they'd been too in thrall to the glitter of celebrity, to the scurrilous act and the famous name. Surely, they said, there can be no room, no kitchen, no hallway or cellar or dark corner of London that hasn't at some time or other been the scene of sexual activity, of gratification, relief and release. They felt themselves to be sexual democrats.

She said, 'There are other maps than these; death maps, crime maps, drug maps, maps of resistance and insurrection, of liberation and oppression.'

He couldn't deny it. She held him in her arms and stroked his thick black hair, let the palms of her hands smooth their way over his body.

'Imagine being blind in London,' she said. 'Imagine having to negotiate the streets, or travel on the tube, having to listen to all the noise, the traffic, the building work, the buskers and beggars. What kind of map would a blind man use? How would he use it?'

She massaged the nape of his neck and said, 'I'd like to have you tattooed. All across your back. With a map of the London Underground. Or perhaps not just a tattoo, more a form of scarification, so that the scar tissue would be raised, a little like braille, to represent the lines and the stations. And you could stand naked in the entrance halls of tube stations and blind men and women would come up to you and run their hands over you until they'd worked out their routes.'

Sunlight no longer filled the therapy room. The weather had turned and it looked like rain. William was agitated and excited, aware that his therapist's hour was coming to an end.

'Please,' he said determinedly, 'I'd like you to look at my body.'

'Aren't we getting a little ahead of ourselves?' asked the therapist.

'No, no,' said William. 'Please look.'

Before she could protest further William had stripped naked and was showing her his body, revolving on the spot so she could get a rounded view. She saw at once that there was a strange serpentine marking curled around his torso. At a first glance it appeared to be a kind of bruising but it would have been a strange kind of injury that created such a long, thin, precise bruise. She looked more closely and saw that in another way it was more like a rash, a series of dark blue spots that linked together to form a long, continuous line. But again it was the wrong shape for any kind of rash she'd ever seen.

Then William began to point out certain features of the mark, how it meandered in certain places, how at one point it formed an almost ninety degree bend. 'Much as the River Thames does at the Embankment,' he said archly.

And as the therapist looked more closely she saw that there was indeed something strangely familiar about the shape and design of the mark. William pointed to various parts of it and said, as though he were a tour guide: 'Here we see Chelsea Reach, here Battersea Reach, here the Isle of Dogs, and here the Upper and Lower Pool . . .' And before long the therapist was utterly convinced. The rash or bruise or whatever it was had formed itself in a perfect representation of the River Thames, so accurate, so detailed that you could have used it as a navigational aid.

'William,' she said softly, 'I can see you may need more sessions than we first thought.'

Rosa's Ritmo

ALIX EDWARDS

The alarm rang. A red plastic Mickey Mouse kid's alarm with giant white hands.

'God! Is that the time?' Rosa yelled, chucking the duvet off her side of the bed. Today was Rosa's special day. Her break. Her chance. And she was half asleep. Rosa slumped on to the living room sofa, grabbed the remote control and flicked the TV on.

'Good morning to you too,' she mimicked the newscaster, resenting the drizzle that persisted outside. The flat felt like a fridge. Rosa fumbled towards the airing cupboard and turned on the vital switch. Stephen hated central heating, but Rosa couldn't stomach the English cold and damp. Stephen harped on – how he'd never ever had such ridiculously high fuel bills. So what, you only live once, was Rosa's matter-of-fact response. Stephen told Rosa, seeing she'd never paid a bill in her life, or at least in the four years he'd known her, she was hardly in a position to criticise him for attempting to run her household in a normal fashion. Wasn't the Colombian refugee act wearing just a little thin, lectured Stephen. His gripes always ended, 'I belong, you don't.' Every single time.

Rosa pushed on her fluffy-dog pink slippers, shuffled into the kitchen and sprinkled four teaspoons of special offer Nescafé into a London Underground mug that Stephen said was naff. 'Stay asleep you pig,' she thought spilling scalding water on the sideboard.

Why couldn't Rosa get a grip on her surroundings when she woke up? Every morning she traded spangly tropical sunshine, banana groves, coffee plantations and the hot, spicy smell of streets booming salsa music for the heavy grey toxic disappointment of Euston Road. Rosa expected to open her eyes and see the flat as she'd found it that miserable January afternoon they gave her the keys: bare floor boards, smoke-stained walls and a nauseating acrid smell that took months to go. Instead, the inside was spruce clean, filled with matching white IKEA furniture and stacked with electrical appliances.

She sipped her coffee and laughed. Stephen was certainly turning into a miserable git – but the flat got better and better every day.

When the Latin American Women's Co-operative presented her case to the council, she was awarded a hardship allowance to buy £130 worth of furniture. Rosa knew to play grateful so she smiled at everyone and thanked them so much for all their help. But when she got back to the flat, knowing it'd still stink and stay empty for some time yet – she just sat on the floor and cried 'til she felt sick. That day she'd wanted out. She'd pictured herself arriving at Cali airport, feeling her mum's all-embracing, no questions hug, seeing Pedro's smiley face; forgetting that London had ever existed. Then she'd walked into Drummonds and met Stephen.

And now this! Rosa Gonzales live on stage in London. If only her mother and Pedro could see how well she lived with her TV and Hi-Fi and porta studio . . . they'd die! Only the mafia and born rich got a foot on that ladder at home. In London anything was possible with Dixons 0% finance and benefits and loans and people like Stephen who paid for everything.

She must remember to make Stephen take the video camera. Her mother would tell everyone back home. *Rosa Gonzales y su ritmo* by the River Thames, in London, capital of England, Europe, with her very own band on stage and on TV. Songs by Rosa Gonzales. Costumes by Rosa Gonzales. Musical direction by Rosa Gonzales. Not bad. Not bad at all for someone acting the refugee in Stephen's country. She'd really stopped mucking around and made it this time.

No! Quarter to ten already. Was that a ray of sunshine piercing through that fat grey cloud?

'Rosa,' came a grunt from the bedroom.

'I'll bring your coffee in a minute,' she snapped.

Rosa locked the bathroom door and perched on the bath stool hugging her pink angora sweater round her knees. How long before she showed? She sipped the bitter coffee. Her mother said Rosa was worse than any hurricane. As soon as she smashed her way out of one mess she hurtled headlong into all-out disaster. And she did not want to count on Stephen. Even though he was English and clean shaven and sane and took her shopping all the time – he was getting distant. Ever since she suggested bringing Pedro out of Colombia.

She opened the bathroom cupboard and dug out a silver sponge bag stuffed with caked-up stage makeup. She dabbed foundation on. Painted her lips cherry-red. Sprayed plenty of mousse in her hair. Even now it was short, black and spiky it never stayed. Shame, she thought, running her hands through her fringe. The blonde had nearly all grown out. She'd liked it blonde. She'd looked like Annie Lennox when she met Stephen, felt sophisticated, light-headed, smiley, attractive – all at the same time.

She stared at the mirror. The smoky blue eye-shadow emphasized her tiger-gold eyes. She'd planned to look dramatic and stagey in red. But she felt exotic. Elevated. Special. Today she'd wear blue. The band in black and Rosa in her aquamarine sparkly mini-dress, with mother of pearl sequins and grey stilettos and skin-coloured tights and those enormous star earrings she'd bought in the Covent Garden glass shop. She rushed out of the bathroom, rooted madly through her wardrobe. Why was she so disorganised? Stephen was right about that. She kicked the door, tipped clothes on the floor and threw them round the room.

'... don't forget your sombreros ... live on London's South Bank, Corona presents Fiesta Sabor all-dayer. See Roberto Vega, Ricardo Sanchez, Isidrio Vargas and Colombia's very own Rosa Gonzales y su ritmo live.

' – and get smashed on Tequila – '

'Yes, thank you for that, Richard,' smarmed the DJ's ultra smooth voice.

'That's me! That's me! Come on you dumb dress,' she despaired. She was on the radio. She was going to stun them all. 'Hijo de puta!' she yelled as it appeared from under a pile of leggings.

'What are you doing, Rosa?' Stephen lifted his arm to shield his face from the morning sunshine.

'What do you think? I'm going shopping – or haven't you noticed there's nothing to eat in this house!'

Stephen liked his full greasy horrible English breakfast, or brunch, as he preferred to call it.

'And you be sure to go to Tottenham Court Road and get some video film before I get back.'

'Sure Rosa,' he yawned and turned over.

Rosa wriggled and squiggled. She would get into that dress, even if it never came off again.

'You're not going shopping like that!' exclaimed Stephen. 'You look like – '

'Like what, Stephen?' snarled Rosa, incensed he'd woken up before she could escape. 'I look like a singer in a band of Latin American music,' she said, pulled her Reeboks on and slipped through the front door.

The stairwell stank. Someone had pissed in it last night. The sun shone pale wintery sunshine. Rosa galloped down the concrete passageways, through a labyrinth of identical grey council flats, past the Catholic school where she'd send Pedro when he came to England. The air was crisp today – almost clean.

She stepped into the buzz of Euston Road. It was impossible to cross without obeying the traffic lights. She hopped from one foot to another, watching the myriad traffic zoom past. The lights turned orange. Four black guys drew up in a red BMW.

'Wow!' she exclaimed, as one of them hung out of the window, his Rolex temptingly near her hand.

'Wanna come with us?' they asked, gigging up and down to techno blaring from massive car speakers.

'No, but you can come see me!' she yelled as the lights changed.

She looked good. Men were staring at her. She took off her coat, did a twirl for the Saturday shoppers and bolted down Judd Street.

Rosa had met Gloria four years ago in Safeway. As housing worker for Latin American Women's Co-operatives, Rosa owed her everything she had. Gloria was like her mum; liked to make people happy, whereas Stephen wanted to think he owned her.

She bumped into a large woman wearing a magenta tracksuit, stuffing spinach and bean sprouts into her trolley.

'When are you going to get glasses, Rosa? You're so vain,'

she cried picking out totally white mushrooms from a green tray.

Gloria was the fussiest eater Rosa'd ever met. She'd subjected Rosa to Mildred's, Neal's Yard and Cranks; put her off pork for life. Gloria also drank Johnnie Walker Black Label with gusto, jogged for miles to find Players cigarettes and avoided coffee.

'I suppose you want to come upstairs,' she drawled in her raspy Marlon Brando voice. Gloria lived in a swanky concrete flat above the Brunswick Centre. 'You know Rosa, coffee's shit for your brain – but you're in luck, muchacha, one of my clients brought me some fresh from la Republica Dominicana last week. So today's your big day, muchacha,' she chewed on her cigarette.

'Yes!' sighed Rosa.

'Well, aren't you excited?' Her penetrating gaze pierced through Rosa's sequins. Just like her mother!

'Very,' she hesitated, smiling a cherry pout.

'Why don't you put silver gel in your hair. Go on Rosa. It'll match yer dress,' came a squeaky voice from behind the living room door.

'Shut up and get on with your homework, brat,' said Gloria, kicking it shut. 'You certainly got dressed early, Rosa!' she sniggered.

'Yeah, I feel lucky,' murmured Rosa, wondering how she'd ever get out of this dress if her stomach grew another millimetre.

'So are you going to tell me what's up or are you going to sit here all day!'

'Get out of this room. Now, Maribel!' she shouted at the cowering teenager, who'd sneaked in to watch *The Chart Show.* 'Children are so revolting,' Gloria pulled a face. 'Why can't they stay babies?'

Rosa watched Maribel's skinny legs disappear behind the

door. 'Remember how I told you how I was in the band back home and the ass-hole of a bass-player screwed me and – ' Rosa whispered.

'You got pregnant and they kicked you out. So – this is your band, this time, Rosa. People can't behave like that in this country. You're the boss.'

'I thought this time I'd really got it sussed. I really thought by next spring I'd bring Pedro over to London and that would be it,' she sighed.

'You wanna go to Rosa's show or what?' yelled Gloria at the slowly turning door-handle.

'Well, I woke up this morning and,' Rosa sniffed. 'I think Stephen's a jerk and a pig and I hate him and I don't want him living in my flat – and I know he hates Pedro and he doesn't want him in this country and he keeps saying things about me being an immigrant.'

'So – throw him out. The flat's in your name. I told you before, Rosa – English men are just as macho and stupid as the rest of them. Colombian nationality has nothing to do with it. If it's male, it's an ass-hole, Rosa,' Gloria sighed, heaving her broad shoulders.

'I was going to. Really, Gloria. I kept telling myself, now I got the band and everything I could get rid of Stephen, go on the dole, work part-time or just stay at home and look after Pedro – '

'Or drop Pedro at the Calthorpe Centre and have a career,' suggested Gloria.

'But I can't get rid of him now,' Rosa wailed. ' – I think I'm pregnant.'

'What's wrong with that?' said Gloria. 'You always say you'd like Pedro to have a little brother. And you don't need Stephen. 'You're slightly stressed out. Stage fright. Concentrate on the show. Someone from a record company could show up. They may even want to sign you. I'll be there this afternoon but come over tomorrow anyway. We can talk properly then.' She peered at the door. Maribel went to her father's on Sundays.

Rosa grabbed her Safeway bags, kissed Gloria goodbye and smiled at Maribel.

'Wait!' yelled Maribel. 'Take this home. It's for your hair.' She handed her a tube of Shock-Waves party gel. 'It'll look great. Go with yer dress and everythin''. Maribel's London accent sounded strange around her mother's Dominican drawl.

'Ven,' rasped Gloria, putting a stout hand on Rosa's shoulder. 'Maybe it's you who's changed, not Stephen.' She gave Rosa a giant hug. 'Put Stephen behind you. It's time to find yourself.'

Rosa headed for Southampton Row. Catch a 68. A man stood outside Russell Square tube selling outmoded post-cards. She bought ten for 50p. Rosa always sent her mother the touristy ones and wrote 'I'm fine'.

Another scrape, her mother would sigh. If Rosa would at least persuade Stephen to marry her so that both children could have a father, she'd moan, shaking her head, clasping her crucifix to her breast. Music was a curse.

True enough, thought Rosa, avoiding a maniac courier. Last time, she'd not only ended up pregnant . . . Rosa'd got in with the wrong crowd and had to leave Cali before things got hot. When Rosa thought of the girls Gloria visited in Holloway prison, she felt grateful. At least she'd cleared customs with nothing to hide. And now she had her own band, without having to be a mule for anyone! People at the bus stop stared at her glittering dress. She put her jacket back on. Gloria was right. Whatever happened, today was still her day. Not even Stephen could wreck it.

'Do you know what the time is?' yelled Stephen as she threw the shopping on the kitchen table. 'I've had the whole bloody band phoning up for you. Your sound check's in fifteen minutes. Get your stuff, I'm going for the car.'

Rosa went into the bedroom and got out a photograph of her mother holding Pedro, with his brown curls and smiley olive face. She folded it carefully and shoved it down the front of her dress.

'I can't understand what you see in that dreadful dyke woman,' griped Stephen, as he put her gear in the boot.

'Just 'cos she hates men.'

'. . . and you've been smoking those bloody awful cigarettes . . . I give up, Rosa. You've met everyone I know and still refuse to have a proper English friend. What's the point of leaving your own country if you don't make the slightest attempt to integrate?'

'I speak English,' she retorted, ejecting his M People tape, slamming La Sonora Poncena into the deck.

Stephen leant over and magicked white roses off the back seat. 'Good luck,' he sighed, thrusting them into her lap.

The band moved through the crowd towards her. 'You're late,' said Sergio, menacingly waving his guiro.

'Come on, let's finish the soundcheck,' said Victor, grabbing Rosa's wrist, dragging her towards the stage. 'Now say something down the bloody mike. Is the height okay? Now remember. Don't leap around when you sing. Especially with those dumb shoes,' he added, eyeing her stilettos with disgust. 'I thought you were wearing your Reeboks.'

'I changed my mind.'

'Well, just don't break your neck.' He ticked his list. 'We've got a room out back. Maria and Ana are waiting for you. And how are you er – Stephen,' he asked, smiling his snakiest smile. Victor understood everything. Victor was from Cali.

'God, you bloody late,' screamed Maria, spitting gum on to the floor.

'Can't smoke in this dump,' snapped Ana, leading them outside. 'So – what's Stephen bought you this time?'

'Clothes,' she said defensively. 'Oh – I forgot. I need to go speak with one of the organisers.' She disentangled her arm.

Rosa could see Stephen on the main terrace, milling round the stalls looking gooky, lost, out of place and very English. She remembered teaching Stephen to dance salsa and felt sad. She ran after Victor and caught his arm. 'I want to be alone for a bit. Okay?'

Rosa thought she saw someone walking towards Stephen. A woman. A blonde, English woman in her late thirties.

'Nervous are you?' asked Victor, passing Rosa a silver flask of aguadiente.

Rosa hid behind the stage. She didn't want to meet anyone from the other bands.

When Rosa came to London, Gloria had rung them all. 'Salsa's in, muchacha,' she'd said. But no one wanted Rosa in their band.

'I can play trumpet and congas,' she'd protested, although she really wanted to sing.

'We rehearse in the afternoon,' insisted Roberto Vega. 'No, we can't change our schedule! Anyway, if you're the shit-hot musician you claim to be, why you need a day-job?'

'Sorry, we're an all male band,' said Isidrio Vargas and hung up the phone.

'We're Venezuelan actually,' agonised Pedro López. 'Your – er – Colombian image is not right for us at the moment.'

'Hell – you're that bird that got knocked up by Frankie Mones! Sorry love. You'd look great dancing right out front – boy – you'd zap'em up,' Ricardo Sánchez grinned, peering down her shirt. 'But we're not looking problems. Maybe later.'

Rosa stared into the Thames. Golden glints caught the ripples as a barge drifted past. If anyone was still after her, they'd see her tonight.

'Come on Rosa. Get on the stage,' hissed Ana, dragging her up the black crêpe covered steps.

Rosa looked up at the setting sun, stamped four and sang. She looked into the audience and saw Stephen arguing with the blonde woman. Her singing became fiery. Victor looked at the band, puzzled. How could she feel possessive about a jerk like that?

How dare Stephen speak to anyone that wasn't her – Rosa spun round furiously – especially a bland-looking English bitch in Marks and Spencers clothes. She leapt off-stage, strolled though the audience singing 'Ay! Dolores – ' until she came face to face with Stephen, then danced all the way back.

'So this is why the Child Benefit Agency couldn't find you. Been dancing the bloody cha-cha-cha – ,' yelled the woman. 'Don't say you haven't told her, poor foreign bitch.'

'This is my wife, Rosa,' Stephen coughed. 'We're separated. Have been for some time.'

'I only go off stage twice,' said Rosa, breathlessly, clamped her hand over her mike and skipped away.

'What you doing out there – signing autographs?' sneered Ana. 'There's a journalist hanging around – you stay up here and smile – or I break your neck.' Rosa poked Ana in the ribs and began the next number.

Screw Stephen. Screw all those pathetic male bands and their pitiful excuses. Screw music is a curse, she thought, swaying like a lunatic. She stared into the audience and saw Gloria slugging Black Label. Maribel pointed at her hair and gave a thumbs up sign. The timbales sounded. This was it. The end.

'Great!' Victor patted her on the back.

'More, more, more. We want more. More! More . . .' screamed the audience, stamping their feet.

'Shit hot babe!' shouted Ricardo Sánchez, standing in the sidings shaking his head.

'Damn!' screamed Rosa. 'He didn't do the video. Stephen didn't make the video!' She shook Victor. 'That stupid English woman. Why did she show up today, Victor? The puta! I'm gonna smash her head in!' she yelled, strode back on stage and gave it her all.

' " . . . an impassioned performance," *The Standard* . . . "Rosa Gonzales fired the audience off their feet," . . . "The power of ritmo . . ." it says. You did it this time, muchacha!' said Gloria, collapsed on her couch, reading out reviews through a haze of smoke. 'So how's Stephen?'

'He's history,' laughed Rosa. 'But the baby's growing,' she patted her stomach.

The doorbell rang. 'I knew you'd be here, I got something for you, Rosa,' he said, pulling a video out of his bag. 'My wife taped it.' 'See, Gloria – she gets mad and then she don't listen.' Victor winked, slamming the door behind him.

Rosa held the video in her hands. Just wait 'til mum saw this!

Coming Down South

ALAN DAY

When I still lived up north, Dad were known as something of an intellectual. He used to read newspaper from front t'back wi'out going straight t' sports pages. Little things like that impressed Eckersley folk. Even made Mr Patel in t'paper shop sit up and take notice, and he were from Barnsley. Dad had spent the whole of his life in Eckersley, a miner to his fingertips. In his later years he'd become personification of Eckersley pit itself: he were abandoned and full of dust.

One stormy July day, Ma had gone out to get a sheep's head to tide us over, but she'd never returned to t'family home. Come late September this terrible tragedy really started to hit home to our Dad. He'd just gone to throw more coal on t'fire only to find coal-scuttle damn near empty. He knew then that something was horribly wrong.

'She's left thee, Dad,' I said to him, as kindly as I knew how.

'Left me what?' he replied, his old eyes looking vaguely around t'room.

It were about that time when Aunt Maud moved in and some semblance of order were restored. We made her welcome and pointed her int' direction of coal-shed. Not a moment too soon as it happened. That back room were starting to get pretty chilly of an evening, I can tell thee.

Aunt Maud was a short woman with trim moustache, long nose and frizzy grey hair. She were often mistaken for a French poodle that had learnt to stand on its hind legs. But, fair do's, she were a dab hand in t'kitchen, put in a sixteen-hour day, and only complained under her breath so as not to disturb our new-found peace and quiet.

No, I have to admit it, it were me that had to go and throw t'spanner in t'works. I were to move down south to work in London. When I broke t'news, Aunt Maud just burst into tears and Dad had shook his wise old head gravely at me. His face were too caked and crusty wit' grime to turn pale, but I could tell he weren't best pleased. He pointed the well chewed end of his old briar pipe in my direction.

'We'll have words later lad, so think on,' were all he could bring himself to say at that moment. All this fuss over going down to London, eh. It were as if I'd applied to join M.C. bloody C. Nevertheless, my mind were made up, and I steeled myself for t'showdown with Dad in t'evening.

I found him sitting on the indigo, elephant-patterned sofa with the matching tobacco stains. I stood silently and watched, as with unerring accuracy, he spat a glob of day-glo yellow phlegm into the fire. He sat back, a look of grim satisfaction on his face, to watch it hiss and sizzle away over the red-hot coals. He motioned for me to sit down right next to him. Something that he hadn't done since my schooldays. His eyes flickered uneasily in his gaunt features as he thrust his head right up close to mine, the lamp on his miner's helmet catching me a nasty blow on the temple.

'What I'm about to tell thee now is not for t'ears of t'womenfolk,' he said in a quiet, rasping tone. As it happened 'womenfolk', in the peculiar shape of Aunt Maud, were out back repointing t'brickwork on t'outside lav.

Dad's face were contorted into an ugly grimace, as if someone had just offered him a fat-free black pudding.

'It's this London business, Brian lad,' he went on, seemingly struggling to find the words.

'London yer see . . . well, London is all pubic hair and keg beer.' His voice began to rise and his eyes rolled alarmingly. 'Ay, and 'appen as not, both in t'same bloody glass.'

Well, as you can imagine, those last words had an instant effect on me. A strange mixture of anticipation and revulsion welled up inside me. Being only twenty-eight, I was still wet behind t'ears, as Ma used to say. It was certainly beginning to look as though going down to London were set to be a real eye-opener.

And so it were, I mean was, to prove. It was a different world, and no mistake. Madmen roam the streets of London at will, some of them smartly dressed. Taxis would just as soon run you down as stop to pick you up. Mind you, one thing I will say, it was certainly possible to get a fair pint of ale down here, for the price of a four-course meal. I found this out quite early, in the company of my new friend Tony Hughes and his girlfriend Hattie.

Tony was an expert and mine of information on UFOs and all related subjects. And it was while sitting in the public bar of the Albion that I was told things that would boggle your mind. It transpired that not only had Tony actually seen a UFO, close up like, he'd met bloody driver as well. I'd just got a round of drinks in and prepared myself to hear all the amazing details.

Before getting properly settled, I held my glass of bitter up to the light and studied it closely. 'What the bloody 'ell are you doing now,' Tony yelled, causing me to spill about a quid's-worth of it on the table.

I felt my face start to redden, and mumbled something

about hygiene standards in pubs. I didn't want to go into details with ladies present. Suffice to say, I had my reasons. As we waited for Tony to calm down, I managed to mop up most o' t'beer with me old cap. Tony could go on a bit once he got started on his pet subject. The gist of the first quarter of an hour or so was that the UFO-Watchers Network now believed that these alien craft were due to target the south of England for their landings.

'This is where it's all going to be happening, Bri,' he beamed, the light of the true believer shining in his eyes. He then got on to a really interesting bit, a first-hand account of a UFO landing.

'Anyway, after the vehicle had landed, the whirring sound stopped and everything went deathly quiet. Then, ever so slowly, a panel slid back noiselessly to reveal this humanoid creature.'

Hattie broke the spell that had held us enthralled.

'Did it have any clothes on?' she asked enthusiastically. Hattie went to art classes and was interested in fashion and that sort of thing. It seemed a fair question to me, but Tony just emitted an exasperated cry and clasped his hands over his ears.

It seemed as though it was left to me to fill the embarrassed silence that followed.

'Bound to have, Hattie. It wouldn't come to t'door starkers. Give a right bad impression to anyone watching, would that.'

For some reason, Tony seemed even less pleased with my explanation than with Hattie's question. But he's an excitable sort of chap, so we just waited for his face to turn back from purple to red to normal, and then he seemed ready to go on. First, he had a furtive look around the room.

'Well, if you must bloody know, there was something

unusual in the humanoid's clothing. There was this strange multi-coloured glow emanating from its . . . well . . . nether region.'

Tony leant back in his chair and pointed surreptitiously downwards to somewhere below his trouser waistband. Hattie nearly choked on a peanut flavour crisp. I was pretty impressed by this revelation myself. Any life-form that can get its flies to light up like Blackpool Illuminations gets my vote as a Higher Intelligence, no danger.

As it turned out, this was the high spot of the whole episode. The doors closed again and it was off, quicker than a rep up a motorway. Miserable bugger didn't even wave goodbye, apparently. If it had thrown its rubbish out on to the grass before going, it would have seemed like any other typical tourist to me.

Of course, I didn't get to hear about the Great Conspiracy until the next Monday. Tony and I were in the Albion making short work of two of their home-cooked meals. Home-cooked, down here, means that they're defrosted on site and get two minutes in the microwave. Tony was busy chasing several half-frozen peas round his plate with a fork, and wishing he'd had the baked beans, same as me. The Albion's beans at least stick to your fork, or anything else they come into contact with for that matter. In fact, I've still got a couple of the little sods stuck to my tie from last week. Can't shift them at any price.

Any road, Tony had gone into full-rant mode, as they say down here, about how UFOs were the subject of a world-wide conspiracy of silence. I nodded as I ate just to show interest, like you do.

'There's always a lot of them around in times of war, you know,' he was saying. 'Take the Asian theatre in the Second World War. Known as 'Foo-fighters' they were then. Used to fly alongside fighter planes all the time.'

I kept nodding.

'And in Vietnam. In 1966 at Nha Trang base a UFO vehicle descended slowly in full view of lots of servicemen. The base generator failed and blacked out the whole place. Aircraft engines, bulldozers and trucks all went dead for the four minutes that it hovered there. But I bet you've never heard about it, eh?'

'No, makes you think,' I said, without really thinking.

Just then, Hattie rushed up to our table in a state of some agitation and excitement.

'Have you seen today's *Standard*?' she asked shrilly, plonking the newspaper down on the table, folded to an inside page. Tony picked it up and began to read it with a growing intensity.

'What's all the fuss, Hattie?' I asked, unable to get a look at the page myself.

'It's a UFO landing in England, somewhere up north I think.'

Tony threw the paper down on to the table, obviously irritated.

'Up north, up north!' he snarled. 'All the information we had suggested that it would be down here. Bloody typical! And there was this silly old duffer, got his picture here, who opened his bedroom window and threw a lump of coal at it.'

My eyes were now riveted on the two pictures on the page in question. One was very much like the Eckersley High Street that I remember. The other depicted the face of a proud man in a miner's helmet, his narrowed eyes gleaming defiance. It were Dad. It even had his name written underneath: Joseph Hardcastle.

'When he threw the coal, does it say he hit the UFO,' I asked.

Hattie and Tony both looked at me strangely, saying

nothing. I glanced at the headline – ECKERSLEY MAN SENDS SAUCER PACKING – and read on. Or I tried to read on, but my eyes were beginning to mist over. I'd got to the bit where Dad were giving his own account of events.

'I told 'em straight – "Bugger off, we don't want any." – Any road, I left my mark on yon fancy tram contraption. Caught it right on t'bloody windscreen. He'll not be back round 'ere in a hu . . .'

I could read no more. I let newspaper slip out of my fingers and brushed away the tear that had begun to trickle down my cheek. I looked up at Tony and Hattie.

'He did hit it, see. I knew he bloody would.'

The Apotheosis of Lea Bridge Road

IAIN SINCLAIR

'My father used to call me his "little lamb without a spot".'
Alfred Hitchcock

In backwards through the open window you came. Bald head crowned in a soft green nimbus. No previous aspirations towards Virginia creeper. Cardinal red in your day. Knew its place, kept to the suburbs. Who says it doesn't pay to have a lousy memory? Forgetfulness is better than sex ever was. Better than Edgar Wallace. You can be whoever you want to be.

Grass could do with a bit of a crop. You wouldn't fancy the job. Gardens were just for visiting. This is no garden, no one selling tickets. Mob of piss scrawny pigeons kicking up dust on a chalk path. You'd swear that was a white parrot, a freak, up there in the branches. Lovely wet light off of the gravel ponds. Remember now? Slim brown tarts in pyjama bottoms and bangles. Pointing at the bird. Laughing. Can't make sense of it myself.

Indoors, settled, you'd have to admit, you're growing fond of it – the crematorium muzak. As if you'd fallen down through a river membrane, damaged the inner ear. The usual irritants are filtered out, a cotton wool bung dipped in olive oil. No background, no depth of field. You're encouraged to listen to what is being said. That's a laugh, after all those years training yourself to do the reverse; bring marginal effects up against the mike to erase the wife's unceasing monologue. Lips move, nothing is said.

Quiet down, you old cunt. Nothing to be quiet *with*, that's the bleeder. You're here as much as anywhere else, but is it *you*? Was it ever? No meat. The piquant (and mildly arousing) tang of formaldehyde. No teeth. No bone.

A tidy gaff, give it its due, notably pleasant dining room. Wood panels, the business. Enjoy the ambience without fretting over the bill. Without suffering a pang of hunger. Or having to stuff your face to justify the wad you're laying out.

Nice table in the window, guv? Belfast linen, fresh chopsticks in the packet. Colour of a dog's dentures. Chinese fans pinned up, spread open like beheaded doves. Angel outfits for the ungodly. Enough class for an advert. Haven't been to the pictures in years.

See how the bright clear water floats independent of the jug, honouring its shape. You'd have to die twice to appreciate the way light behaves, how it moves and trembles, the weight of it.

Outsiders peeping over the hedge, cheeky buggers! No need to summon Charlie Chan. They're on the upper deck of a yellow bus. A *yellow* bus? Get your breath back, old son. Sit it out till you're fit to go looking for the shop with the carpets. It's never too late. Not for the Lea Bridge Road.

Grieving and celebrating: the warmth of the day, the first of summer; the walker moves out early, dew on the grass, across London Fields, moulting avenues of Edwardian planes. Mare Street. He is dazzled by the brilliance of the Town Hall steps (washed in dirty money, European slush funds). Narrow Way: TV rental booths (busy with bad light), caves of Non League schmutter. The baroque infirmities of Lower Clapton Road. He is positively disengaged, he lets it all drift. He has no claim on what he sees: the London Orphan Asylum, a temple of absence. Voices that will not draw his red notebook from its carrier bag. His target was quite specific: the Lea Bridge Road. A journey dedicated to the memory of his father – who had believed, and frequently asserted, that the road contained all the ingredients necessary to the good life. LBR was a zone of transition, a walkway between life and death. A shining path. Literally so. It blazed with cargo cult trophies, gimmicks, novelties, labour-saving devices (that, taking hours to set up, self-destructed at first use in a satisfying thunderflash). Out there on the LBR was his late father's holy grail, the shrine of the ultimate cut-price carpet. A knockdown Axminster that could be fitted, floor and lid, to his torpedo coffin. A Turkey fake in whose intricate curlicues he could lose himself, stories within stories. Two long years now in St Pat's, Leytonstone, his old man: in the earth, under a page of stone – unvisited. Just how he liked it. By request. Left in peace. Brought off the street with more dignity than those who make it, half-alive, to Whipps Cross Hospital. What was he *doing* that day, in the heat, hatless, loaded down, staggering from window to window? What was he after? What were the last words?

The walker gnaws on a gristle of guilt. There's a junk market down a passageway, open – it has to be chanced. Most of the stalls are sheeted, a tea urn the only area of activity. Gash videos, disconcertingly like oversize books, cover a table; otherwise, this stuff is indistinguishable from the rubbish you'd dredge from the foreshore, downriver of the Thames barrier. Hearing aids stolen from the pockets of the drowned. A child's blazer split to accommodate the muscular shoulders of a dwarf.

Without enthusiasm, he sifts a few hundred paperbacks.

They've been crammed into red plastic trays by a non-reading sadist who is punishing himself for moving out of deleted EPs. To select a single unit from the conglomerate requires a perverse dedication. The book-objects are flavourless, drained of their original bombast. Deactivated. A drawer filled with dud batteries. One volume alone seduces the hand, a black cloth number with the gilt worn from its spine. *Less than Dust*. Joseph Stamper. *The Memoirs of a Tramp*. Worth 40p of anybody's money.

Grecian statues and squashed cockroaches! Sold! The walker has to have it. *My bread and butter had become live-cockroach sandwiches*!

The carrier bag accepts its ballast. Encouraged, the walker escapes: a 'guidebook to the abyss', nostalgia for the assumed liberties of the road. He is buoyant, and so soon, the journey scarcely begun; he hasn't achieved his projected starting point and already he's wearing a splash-headline placard – SUCKER!

From a vantage point at the churchyard gate, the soft-bearded vagrant targets him, hand out: 'I need a cup of tea.' The pound coin is given, gladly; they clasp wrists like Republican comrades. Benedictions, sentimentalities. The breath on the schnorrer ripe enough to drop a cloud of midges. Add the toll to the price of the book and it's still a bargain. A fine old man, one of the resources of the city, a living fossil; put some bone in his cheeks, manure in his boots, he'd be a dead ringer for the Queen's consort. Proof positive: there is no such thing as 'absolute poverty', except of the imagination.

Charlie Chan's inscrutable smile. No loss of face (you wish you could say the same!). First punters for his dining room. They must be talking in tongues, can't understand a bleedin' word they say. Let out, that's your guess. From the nuthatch.

Clean feeders, though. Not a dribble into the napkin. The Chink gave them a choice of tables and they went straight for the pillar in the middle of the room. Make sure the loony has her back to the mirror. She grins, the old bird, they're playing her tune. Admit it, you always liked a good show yourself, up west, the Crazy Gang. But the dark was better. A double-bill for preference. A thriller. Anything with trains, Boche quacks, hypodermics, bandaged blondes. Keep it straight: a doxy with spunk, a bloke who could handle his pipe.

You'll turn it around, old son. Never had a takeaway in your entire life. Proud to say it. Back towards the smoke, that's favourite. The boy. He must be older than you are now.

> **FESTIVAL OF GRIDLOCK**
>
> A Festival at the Hindu temple closed Whipps Cross Road, Leytonstone, to traffic on Sunday as police struggled to cope with a flood of up to 15,000 worshippers.
>
> Furious neighbours received no advance warning of the event and were overwhelmed by visitors from as far afield as Plymouth and the Midlands.
>
> Said Tommy O'Toole, manager of the Hitchcock: 'My philosophy is that everybody in all walks of life, of all races and religions, should try and get on.
>
> 'But the organisers of this festival told none of us it was happening and had a total disregard for everybody else's feelings and needs.'
>
> Hotel guests from abroad were unable to get to Whipps Cross Road.

The American Car Wash: a yellow oilskin mannequin, incapable of sweating on the hottest day, twitches a robotic arm in Bates' Motel welcome. A greeter with a hollow brain. His glove hands are filled with mayonnaise. Airfix skin. Misapplied blackberry lip gloss. A *Texas Chainsaw* hairpiece held in place by a denim cap. Flesh-eating grin. Eyes that breed their own shadows.

VACUUM & WINDOWS. FOAM & WASH. DONE IN MINUTES.

No genitals. No underwear. A guardian of the shower units who successfully deters potential customers. Keep moving, son.

Synagogue in a blitz of headache brickwork. Malign rumours: paedophile ground nettled in obscurity at the rear of the building. Disposal of child corpses. Tower block abuse. Sleeping pills, cheap booze. Confessions that no sane person can transcribe. The worst of the worst: a loop of anguish to infect poor soil. A clay poultice that refuses to drain.

Open grassland, plucky with dog turds, declines towards a sluggish river. OTV: a pyramid of ex-rental sets. Multi-screen playback of oncoming traffic. Reclaimed sewage gardens on the far shore. A dosshouse for wild nature.

The Lee Valley ('e' and 'a' interchangeable) is a prophylactic sponge soaking up grant aid. Cleansing itself, it staunches the flow of migrants. A new bridge. A raft of pamphlets suggesting walks for motorists. The Lee Valley Ice Centre is a blue hanger shipped in from the Arctic. ICE HOCKEY SUNDAY FACEOFF. 7.00pm. LEE VALLEY LIONS.

I liked London. There's such a lot of brick, such a lot of solidified mortar, all in one place. I could shut my eyes and see uncomputable millions of men of uncountable generations all scurrying out from London, grubbing in the earth, digging out clay and sand and stone, putting it on their backs, scurrying back to London, scurrying about till they found some spot where there was no baked clay or lime-mixed sand or chisel-chipped stone, and hurriedly dumping their burden down with a satisfied grunt ere some other scurriers saw the vacant spot and dumped their burdens there.

A white bicycle flat on the path, squashed into itself; a diagram to signal a specially designated track. Instead, it warns – like the outline of a remembered fatality. An invocation of disaster to temper privileged access.

The Riding Centre. Rude scrunch of horses cropping alongside a pylon mound. HORSE MANURE. FOR SALE. £1.00 PER SACK (50P FILL YOUR OWN BAG).

Horse imagery is frequently exploited to announce a zone of upward mobility, jodhpur sex – which no longer has to be face to face. Use a tackle block to raise yourself. Give your career a patina of self-confidence by acquiring the perfume of equestrianism (like MFH Jimmy Hill). Ice-skating is for Essex girls (which explains the alignment of the rink). Water sports (post-inoculation) are for socio-economic losers with attitude.

The walker can't afford leisure. He's professionally unemployed. He knows what the hobbyists will never discover, the secret meadow behind all this stuff, the sheds and enclosures. Lammas land. A green place that lifts you out of the city. Ambrosial air. Screened from the effluence of the canal, the carcinoma-provoking messages that surge down the pylon rail.

Memorials are built by subscription to ensure that we forget. Were you part of this? 7th Battalion. The Essex Regiment (T). 3rd East Anglian Field Ambulance. RAMC (T). Who gave their lives in the Great War, 1914–1918.

We are the dead.
To you with failing hands
We throw the torch;
Be yours to hold it high.

Good to be walking again, a trick to perform in your sleep. No splints. Go anywhere you've been before. The Terriers. Inns of Court and City Yeomanry. Signal Squadron. 'The Home of the Devil's Own.'

Move aside, grandad. He looks like you used to look. Knackered. Spark out. Pissed. Pissed off. Dog meat melting into the cracked sets. Give him air, you cunts.

See the whole shebang reflected in the window. Like your Gamages of old. High Holborn. You *can* go back to it. Airguns, targets, tackle. THE INTERESTING SHOP. New and Used. Knives. X-Bows. Radio. Photographic Equipment. Watches. Model Trains. Curios. Lighters. Tool's (sic). Part Exchange Welcome. No extra charge for rogue apostrophes. (Lea Bridge Road: a geophysical anomaly causing the unconvinced apostrophe to behave like a greasy butcher's hook.)

Kit for a bedroom mercenary. This *Boy's Own* checklist: Ox-Hushpower Magnum Air Guns, X-bars, Telescopic 4×40mm sights, 'Fox' recoiless (sic) Self-Assembly Air Rifles. 'Interesting' is the euphemism for deadly, death-delivering, mean. All those things you loved, saved for, got. They killed you. A sleek crow perched in the foam of an apple-tree. An antique BSA that had lost its pop. The boy fired. Bird so much bigger when it flaps bloody on the path. He left his old man to dispatch it. Muck on the spade. 'Must have flown into a wire, dad.'

As the walker climbs, the diesel fug rising with him, the LBR becomes a three-dimensional copy of *Exchange & Mart*, a stroll-through consumer catalogue; a window-shopping experience. Everything you never needed and then some. All the major specialists in obscurity.

CAR GRAPHICS MADE TO ORDER. MAGNETIC VEHICLE SIGNS. The inverted V of the billboard outside the newsagent: AUTO TRADER. The craft of the sandwichman is off the agenda. Exit left, Joseph Stamper.

Slowly you parade along, lolling and rolling from one side to the other at every step as a paddle-boat in a swell. Going along a main street in the gutter at one side, crossing at the end of the street, and coming back along the gutter at the other side. Traffic whizzing by you within an inch; despised and ignored for the most part by the pedestrians, it is the most dead-alive business man has ever devised, like to that of the dull-eyed bullock yoked to an ancient pumping windlass.

Furtive, cuffing salt sweat from his eyes, the walker takes note of the collage of tout's cards. A lurker. A punter without a pot to piss in. A freak without a legitimate fetish. He's clocked (as he imagines it) by decent strollers, purposed citizens. Scratch scratch. Difficult to write. Impossible to interpret. A bibliography of urban ephemerals. The left-handed scrawl of frostbite. The heady delusions of bad bear meat.

PONDERS END SAUNA MASSAGE. SOUTH AMERICAN. SEXI TONI (ALL SERVICES). FLUFFY, HALF-PERSIAN. BUSTY CARIBBEAN. NIKOLE – DISCREET MASSAGE. 38″ MASSAGE BY BLACK GIRLS (QUIET LOCAL). SWEET KITTENS GIVEN AWAY.

Black limos purring; three of them in convoy. Black enough to burn your eyes out. Flat roof flower-gardens. They slide effortlessly uphill. A single cab weaving as it tracks them. Foot to the floor can't match the motorless (panther-powered) transit of the meat wagons. Air-conditioned: the ride of a lifetime.

OVERALLS: WE ARE THE CHEAPEST. NEW & RECONDITIONED BOILER SUITS. END OF LINE BOILER SUITS £10.50. CHEF'S TROUSERS £8. NURSES DRESS £10.

Emmanuel Church (CHRIST IS SPOKEN HERE).

Time for a coffee. The Roma. Noticed in passing and

now rediscovered. The Captain's Table blocks the rite of passage with a grinning plaster chef (kitted out, at a discount, by the overall shop). Beard: a clump of pubic clippings painted with glue. Moustache like rust on a file. The chef's hand masks his nipple in a masonic gesture, leading the unwary gaze to a lidded silver platter (big enough to contain the parboiled head of Sir Edward Heath). An invitation to be spurned – unless you fancy being reincarnated as a bowl of vichyssoise soup.

In the cool of the café, there's a handbell to summon the catering operative. RING FOR SERVICE. But how hard? It's the mid-morning lull, between shifts, complimentary copy of the *Sun* folded away, bowls removed. The formica shines in scarlet streaks. A damp band catches the elbow – like the trapezoid area of a windscreen smeared by a single blade. The crumblies, at a crouch, are beginning to manifest themselves, to appear at their reserved tables without ever passing through the door. They eke out a communal cuppa while they stare at the street.

The walker finds the courage to lift the bell, the faintest of tinkles. Immediately he has to take the decision between two sizes of coffee. He risks the large, the porcelain spittoon. Feels obliged (in his notebook) to pay tribute to the singular method by which the coffee is prepared. A squirt of water, a generous measure of milk. Steam hosed into the mixture. Only *then*, the brew hissing and spitting, is powdered coffee spread across the surface; a sinking pyramid (like the chocolate flourish in Frith Street cappuccino). It's left to the customer to do his own stirring. Or to swallow the tarry lump and take the diluted milk straight. Very acceptable, actually. The final third as cold as yesterday's gravy.

A bacon roll: confess it. A slap of brown sauce (Daddy's

Own?). Butter running, the tongue-crisp poking out of the inflated bap.

You'll never find him now, the boy. He goes his own way. Door to door in a borrowed tie: one of those splashy affairs that pre-empt a good coronary. Car maintenance kits to palsied pensioners. Bum bags to darkies in discount stores. Got a nerve, give him that. Keep it up another six months and they'll take him on the firm.

NEW & USED WHEELCHAIRS AND SCOOTERS. Know what? Without breaking wind, you can cause the scarlet golf carts to shunt backwards and forwards, seemingly at their own volition. An act of disinterested consciousness: imagine it. The shopman sprints out, all his electricals rocking like moored cruisers hit by a tidal wave. He smiles, revenge in his eyes. Looks up and down the road. Suspects a *Candid Camera* set-up. Determined to appear game at all costs.

LEYTON LEISURE LAGOON, THE FAST TANNING CENTRE. Lea Bridge Road: all centres and no circumference. Metaphors that really fancy themselves. Like those ladders propping up the tall thin shop. DREW, CLARK & CO. By Appointment to Her Majesty the Queen, Manufacturers of Ladders. (Make it easy on the midnight prowlers, solicitors of crested cigarettes. God bless you, ma'am.) Ladders like strips of blank film looped over a bottomless bin.

After the shooting of Georgie Cornell (fat bullet, fatter target), this is where Ron hid out, above a barber's shop. Still there. Not the shop: Ron. The exchange of consciousness, murderer and murderee, printed on a screen. Powder burns on the ceiling. Bottles on the bamboo bar. Plaster falling like spray into the net-filtered light. Dark glasses. Ron's eyes hurt. He's short of company. A secret half the faces in East London are forced to share. Fear of blindness.

Spit turns to acid. The pub's name, the Beggar, sticking to his cuffs. Tainted by association.

Cornell's first soul splinters on impact. His second soul takes flight, tendrils of sunshock. His name-soul is cursed by repetition. It struggles to define itself above the gossip of clippers. Liquid soap and linoleum. Bent cigarettes smoking in the cat's dish. Plastic-shrouded furniture. Food sent in on a tray. The convalescence of killers.

The Bakers Arms, a significant bus stop. A destination respected throughout the length and breadth of East London. Postpone the finish by checking a charity shop. SENSE (Eyes & Ears of Deaf-Blind People). The walker shoves his way into an unfumigated wardrobe: imprinted carpet slippers, suits from stiffs, brogues rivetted in braille. Shelves of books packed too tight to breathe. The unpaid stacker, who is searching for an author (and also for something to do), has no formal training to guide her hand. Books are sorted according to size and colour. The rationale goes like this: top shelf for hardbacks, second shelf for paperbacks, third shelf for Mills & Boon, and the rest, the unsorted juvenilia, in boxes on the floor.

'It's too easy being miserable. Anyone can get stuck into a good book. *Who* was it you wanted again, dear?'

'Lena Kennedy. Some people can definitely use words. She can. And she's from round here. Gets it right every time.'

'Good then are they?'

'I'm telling you, you could *be* there.'

'We are, dear, some of us. Bleedin' stuck 'ere. That's the trouble.'

COMPETITIVE INSURANCE/DENTURE REPAIRS (QUICK SERVICE). ORTHOPEDIC BED CENTRE. ROYAL DOLPHIN. The Traditional Sunday Lunch: Spaghetti Bolognese, Avocado

Vinegrette (sic), Fried Squid, Chicken Helenic with Salad, Deserts from Trolley, Coffee and Mints. £9.50 + 10 per cent service.

The human terraces reassert their grip. Strips of dusty grass. The vehicle procession has almost made it: escape. Zephyrs of warm diesel spun from the Whipps Cross roundabout. Residential care for the old ones. Turf that's well worth forgetting. VICTORIAN FIREPLACES MADE TO ORDER. LOBSTERS. NEW SEASON COOKED EELS.

Greenery you can ignore. Over-exposed travelling shots. The fag end of Epping Forest. The walker is pleased with himself. He can turn for home. Groves sacred to all religions, extremes of asceticism and perversion. He remembers the reproduction of a forensic photograph. A transvestite in black underwear who miscalculated a breeze block suspension. 'These deaths are accidental; and not to be confused with suicide.' An over-reaction to the first (tame) breath of the forest.

Sunshafts of waterlight backing through an open door, a curtain of ivy. Cool as an icehouse in here. He carries his drink across to the Hitchcock shrine, a wall of production stills. A blonde in a choke of birds. Photocopied interviews.

'My secret? Put an ordinary man in an extraordinary situation and you have full audience participation.'

Cigar smoke. Cold Pils. Let the photographs form their own stories. Voyeurism. Acts of programmatic violence. Spools of malign energy, unravelling, at both ends of the LBR: tight as a ligature.

A coven of old folk infiltrate the bar, blinking out of the harsh sunlight. They are blustering, unsure of their status, talking loud enough to shame the ghosts of the place. Grey hair, reprieved suits: it was hardly worth the return from the graveyard. But they are lightheaded with it, don't need the drink, the outing was enough; a preview of their fellow dead. St Pat's: a mica beach, brilliant with angels. One jewelled droplet of semen hanging from a granite lip. He'll never find the old man. Wouldn't look, when he had the chance, into those cold blue eyes. Wouldn't place his hand over the open mouth. You'd never want it, now or then.

Patterns that would unhinge you, colours that put the rainbow in its place. At long last, the carpet shop! You've searched for it all your life. What next? Bugger the expense. A carpet woven just for you, your story. A shape like a bird's head, a parrot. Grandad kept one of them for years. Evil fucker, temper like a woman. Spiteful. The empty cage lasted longer than the old man, rusting away in the garage. You're rid of the lot of us. You should be crowing, my son. Follow me down. We're all in it, no choice. Pick any thread and trace it to the finish.

Ice

KIRSTY SEYMOUR-URE

Francis rises as usual before dawn but today, despite the darkness that looks as if it will never lift, despite the bitter cold and the ice in his basin, he is joyful, the blood singing in his veins, he is warmed just by thinking about the day to come. It's his free day, a whole day's holiday, today more special than ever because it is the day his true love will be his. *O my heart, my Olivia, O my love.* He dresses quickly by candlelight, shivering with cold and anticipation too, warm woollen leggings, his best britches over the top and his best boots with fur trimming. He makes his way quietly down the stairs, the big house still sleeping but some of the servants starting to stir, and stops by the outer door at the back, taking a lantern; although it's his free day and there's nothing he need do he goes out of habit to the stableyard to see his horses. Which are not really his horses of course but it is he who has chief care of them, knows all their little likes and dislikes – which one's sweet for bran mash, which one won't go well on a rainy day – better than the master does; not for nothing has he worked practically his whole life at this house, worked his way from stablehand to head groom to equerry. Yes, he has earned his place here, his place in the master's favour, and who knows what it might lead to one day. *One fine day . . .*

Out into the cold yard with his lantern, the sky still dark

as anything and the cobbles skiddy underfoot with ice: in the harness room little Jim the stable lad sleeps curled up on a pile of horse blankets with a thicker pile pulled over the top of him. Francis shines the lantern in his face – Wake you lazy bag o' bones you. Should have been up a half hour ago! – The boy groans and stirs – O, sir, let me sleep a while longer, let me sleep a while. – Francis pushes his boot into the blankets and prods him – Up, boy, it's my free day, have you forgotten? It's Mr Charles you'll have to answer to today, so better look lively.

– Mmm, mmm. – And Jim stirs finally, pokes his little thin arms out into the freezing air, gasping and groaning fit to bust. Grinning, for he reminds Francis of himself not so many years ago, he leaves the boy be and goes out to greet his horses, eight of them and all beauties, and observing that a stealthy glow is creeping into the sky at last he wraps himself in a blanket and sits himself down in the straw in the stall of his favourite, Bonnie, to wait. Wait and think.

He thoughts turn at once to his love, his Olivia, and to what he shall say to her later this day, she having agreed to walk out with him to the river. He feels sure, almost sure, she suspects his intentions, and he is sure almost sure to the tips of his toes that she feels the same way about him. For how can she not? Lovely Olivia, like himself an orphan, though unlike him never left to fend for herself, she having the luck to possess noble relations ready to take in an orphan child however disgraced her poor mother, however bankrupt in more ways than one her scoundrel father. A monied uncle, what luck, what fortune, but still Francis counts himself to possess all the riches in the world just by feeling her attention bestowed upon him, and he hopes her love. And he knows he too is lucky, perhaps even more so than she. For he was plucked from the flames.

Scarcely alive, scarcely even born, he was snatched up

and carried away, leaving behind his dead mother's body in its bed of fire, passed from hand to hand swaddled in a rough blanket, and somehow saved from the inferno. They tell him all of London burned that night and nothing to be done. *But I was saved.*

Saved from the Great Fire, by such chance, he reckons his life is bound to be a lucky one, that's the reasoning he's always followed and it has paid off so far, everything turning out well for him, taken in here age twelve or maybe even less, working at a great London house for a kind master with kind folk. Never looking back. And Miss Olivia, *how my heart sings with her name*, coming to live here at the same age as him, child of the master's fallen brother, half daughter of the house, half servant, and such liberties that gives her! Playing together as children she and Francis, she with the taint of her parents upon her always and he with no parents, no history at all save the strange fact of his survival, he could be the son of an earl or the offspring of a streetsweeper, no one can say. Thus they're awarded an intimate equality of sorts, and the master content to leave them to associate in their own way although they're long since grown, so that Olivia even, Francis sincerely believes, has come to regard him in the same way he regards her. – *Can this be my imagination? I must needs be careful, so much, my very life, at stake.* – For, he must own, his imagination has more than once run away with him, ever the optimist that he is. But he's honest and hardworking and his prospects are good and he cannot think what more a lass could want.

She has helped him with his letters, for in truth his early schooling was not what it might have been and what little he did learn at the charity school soon passed clean out of his head, for what did the likes of him want with book-learning and such? Often now during the winter evenings he reads with Olivia, their heads close together in the firelight, *Paradise Lost* which grips him with fervour, and Mr Dryden's poetry that speaks to him of the Plague and the Fire. But it is the political talk that spurs him most, what with the master being so involved, and with the changes in the wind he likes to think that one day he, too, might venture into the public field with his master's backing. And so he applies himself to learning from his sweet Olivia, that he may be lacking in none of the skills necessary to his advancement, already he can read comfortably and he can write, enough, one day perhaps to write his story. *For I am certain-sure as I sit here now that one day I shall have a story, I can't have been snatched from the fire for nothing, no reason.* No, there'll be sense in it somewhere, of that he has no doubt.

And so. The sun is come up, the yard slippery-white with hoar and frozen snow: another day he thinks the master will prefer to walk than risk the horses' legs with his fine carriage and four skittering along the perilous streets. Such a winter this is turning out to be, Francis can't ever recall such a perishing cold that gets into your bones and ices you right up from the inside. And here's another thing: the year of his birth, how long ago, that was a year of strange harshnesses too, the Great Plague that carried off so much of the city, and then the Fire, merry London blazing to death, and then that very winter the Thames was full of ice. He doesn't remember it any more than he does the fire and yet as with the fire he sees it clear as if he was there, the Thames full of ice. All that in one year, and his birth too: now: *I say I was saved for a reason.* And part of his excitement today is because this bitter winter has frozen the river again, and he is to go there. It has been iced over this past month and he has driven the horses past but not yet been close, set foot. The city was abuzz at first, but it is come to seem quite normal now, the society folk holding dances on the surface at night, bonfires and fireworks and all, it is become the frozen playground for half the city. And today he is to take Olivia there and there on the pure ice he will ask her to be his. The glow of her face. The touch of her lips. *O my Olivia, my heart.*

It is quite light now and his feet and fingers numb with sitting too long and too still, he always was a one for dreaming idle hours away, if ever there were idle hours to spare. Jim has fed the horses long ago and the old groom, Charles, is starting to rub down the riding horses. Francis stands up stretching and walks stiffly to the kitchens, where Cook, seeing his frosted state, shrieks – Mercy lad! what are you thinking of, you'll catch your death! – and thrusts into his senseless hands a big bowl of porridge steaming and warm. He eats it gratefully and washes it down with a mug of ale, smiling at Cook who makes him shy when she says – Ah now your free day and you'll be off with Miss Olivia won't you, now you take care mind, don't you let no harm come to that good girl. – and then he sets off round to the front of the house where he has fixed to meet Olivia.

And almost forgets. Turning he runs slipping and sliding back across the yard, up the back stairs to his room, last week a ship from the Indies came in and he, hearing of her arrival on his half-day, got down to the wharf just as she was docking. For not more than a few pence he purchased some silk ribbons, some cinnamon and cloves, a bag of fine oranges and a small tame monkey with its teeth pulled. All for Olivia of course, he thought she would be taken with the monkey but it died that very first night, of the cold he thought, of pining for its own warm land, and he couldn't help feeling glad as its sad little toothless face was beginning to trouble him. So now he stows in his pockets the fruit and spices and silks, scented and glowing like his heart that's beating so hard and so happy and he fairly skips to the front gate.

She is not there but Francis is early and he does not doubt her, settling himself to wait on the other side of the street where he can watch the house, a big house of strong red brick that would not have burned even if it had been in the path of the fire, although the fire did not spread this far west, and now in the city new brick houses are rising like this one in place of the old timber frames. The light is so bright with the low winter sun glancing off all the snowy surfaces it seems the very air is on fire, another good omen he thinks, stamping his feet to warm them. A carriage comes down the wide street, very slow, passing between him and the house, the horses held in tight and their breath in big feathery plumes showing the effort of their pent-up strength, the coachman's eyes narrowed in concentration, Francis nodding at him in comradely approval . . . When the coach has passed, Olivia is there outside the house, just closing the door, she comes carefully down the steps holding up her skirts with one hand and clutching the rail with the other and Francis watches her feet in their black boots so as to delay the moment of seeing her face, five careful paces to the gate he hears the crunch crunch of her boots on the hard frosted ground, sees the shine of her red cloak, and finally he raises his eyes and there she is. His heart leaping and bounding away with his spirits up to the blazing sky, the light so pure it pierces him to the core, *O my life, my Olivia.*

There she is.

Though he sees her almost every day, each time she is more beautiful, her rosy cheeks, her blue eyes, her curly dark hair escaping from her bonnet, more beautiful than he has a right to expect and for the first time he feels a shadow cast over his happiness. How can she love him, orphan stable boy, and she the daughter or as good as of his master? Whatever his prospects? But then he recalls that there is nothing to stop him becoming a courtier even and remembers that she too is orphaned and in some ways less fortunate than he.

– Francis, it's such a beautiful day! – Olivia exclaims for greeting and they set off with one accord towards the river, not a long way off, maybe a half hour's walk, but they step out slowly on account of the icy surface underfoot. Once Olivia slips and would fall but that she catches hold of Francis's sleeve and he steadies her, and after this it seems quite natural to be walking with her on his arm as if they were an old married couple. *If she knew how my heart was thrashing . . . and perhaps she does.*

They walk down through Piccadilly where the fashionable carriages are making their slippery way and through the Park, the sun higher now and warming their faces, the black frost on the trees beginning to drip and the puddles returning to slushy water. He is tongue-tied in his reckless joy but Olivia chatters on, stopping once to turn to him – So quiet Francis! nothing amiss I hope? – O, no – says he – nothing amiss when I'm with you, it's just I'm thinking of something that makes me very contented. – Her face lights up and at her next words he feels a deep warmth spread through him. – O Francis I too have a special reason to be happy today! – her laughter bearing him heavenwards, he feels so light he is barely anchored to the ground. – Something I'll tell you later and I know you'll be pleased. – the glow deep in her eyes drawing him in so he can hardly concentrate on her words.

She is telling him about the harpsichord concert she attended last night with the master and his wife, her uncle and aunt, music by a Mr Purcell who she says is tremendously popular and Francis believes he has heard tell of him though the composer's first name escapes him. – O Francis – she cries – I wish you could have been there! – and stops suddenly, a queer expression on her face, and once again he senses the shadow and he wonders if she senses it too. But no matter, the important is to love, everything else will follow, and he listens hazily as she speaks now of the grand new cathedral she was taken to see which is being built in the city rising – how slowly! – in stone from the ashes. It is to have a great dome that will make it the envy of cities all across Europe, Olivia tells him, and he is ill-equipped to disagree, especially with her little gloved hand tucked under his arm. How she places her trust in him! *All will yet be well.* Nothing can go wrong for him, not on this day of all days with the ice and the frost flashing like fire, he is too lucky for that.

They come to the river and stop in their tracks with the wonder of it, Olivia's hands fly to her mouth as she gasps with delight. The Thames is frozen indeed and is become a frostbound pleasure garden. The snow has been cleared from vast areas and although it is yet early in the day all of society seems to be out on the ice, some skating, some sliding on sledges and trays, some simply chatting and strolling as if this was Covent Garden itself! There are one or two young men on horseback and a couple of pony-drawn sleds skimming colourfully over the ice. And there are potato- and chestnut-sellers too and little groups of people gathered about the braziers warming themselves. It is all colour and sparkle and light, the bright shine of the ice, the great white light of the sky, and the sun turning everything to fire. They move in a dazzle down on to the ice, Olivia and he, she turning to smile at him and Francis, his heart bursting with love, smiling back at her gravely, on this the most important day of his life. In his pockets the oranges and spices and silks wait, giving off warmth and sweet scent, giving him courage.

On the ice all is transformed, magical. All differences seem cast aside, ladies rubbing shoulders with chambermaids, dukes with urchins, and although he knows it is fantasy all is for an unending moment nothing less than fantastical. They walk on the ice somewhat dazed with the splendour and Francis begins to think of speaking, how should he start, what words should he use, although this is something that has occupied his every thought for the past month, it will not come easily to him. Further delay as they pause to buy roast chestnuts, splitting the blackened skins to extricate the sweet nuts that burn in their mouths, Olivia sucking in cold air through pursed lips that he yearns to kiss. They watch in the distance boys driving their pony-sleds in a mad race up from under the bridge, Francis worrying lest one of them should fall, the ice hard as stone, something should certainly break, a pony's fragile leg, a boy's thin skull . . . And she catches his hand, *O my life my Olivia*, and he feels the world to be already in his grasp, and she turns up her shining face to him – Francis I can't wait any longer I must tell you . . . – and he knows somehow that this will be something he does not want her to say but how can he prevent it, how can he forbid her to speak? *My love, O my heart.*

– Francis – she says her eyes far away – Francis I want you to be the first to know as I am fondest of you in all the world, – the words a terrible mockery as she continues – I am betrothed! – and in a dark silent place he hears her go on to speak of last evening at the concert by Mr Purcell, the golden harpsichord music, the young gentleman at her side, the friend of her uncle, friend and not servant, and still Francis cannot wrench his burning eyes away from her face, his heart become numb no longer bursting but frozen and chill as if winter was suddenly within him – and so Francis will you be happy for me! – she finally cries. It is Henry his name, Mr Henry Purcell, he remembers it now and she whirls on the ice away from him, away.

Is it for this I was snatched from the flames? Spared for this raw this hideous pain, nothing but this? She spins away on the ice, her red cloak billowing, her eyes flashing fire, he knows the depths of her joy and what is it he is to do now? His glorious prospects all turning to ashes, what now does he care that he may rise to prince's equerry, may be put forward to parliament, may distinguish himself as a king's lieutenant? All futile. Stablehand he may as well be. She spins, she whirls, her red cloak flying.

And then he sees her fall – *Olivia my heart!* – and suddenly the world comes in on them, shouts and commotion, a raggedy crowd racing in their direction and there is a runaway sled, two shaggy ponies bearing down on them, on Olivia. She, fallen on the ice, struggling to rise, her boots slipping not finding a grip as the sled veers closer, her happiness turned in a second to fear she screams his name, Francis! she screams out his name as if it is the last word she will ever utter and *am I the last thought in her head?* she screams his name, Francis! and all this in an instant as he leaps and dives and throws himself on top of her, rolling them both out of the path of the careering animals, the deathly sharp wheels passing an inch from their faces, the sound searing through them of steel slicing ice.

And he holds her.

She trembles in his arms, they are lying on the frozen surface of the river together. Ice. Snow in their eyes. *O my heart. Olivia.* He whispers he doesn't know what into her ear his lips grazing her face. It is like this he will hold her, her young gentleman whoever he may be, her betrothed *it is like this in his arms and I nevermore.* They lie in their icy bed together the first time the last, no more than a skin of thin ice between them and catastrophe. – You saved my life. – and Francis knows of course that it was for this he was spared but he can take no comfort, he cannot see how his heart will ever thaw. *If I had died in the fire.* Juice from the crushed oranges seeping into the snow, but it is not blood, the smell of it sweet. Cinnamon and cloves, silk for her hair, the dying monkey's stutter. Holding her he thinks of the miracle, the fire, the Thames freezing over and he seems to hear a vast creaking and booming far below where surely there is running water still, and the sound is the ice beginning to crack. Holding her he imagines the start of the thaw, the ice splitting asunder, he falls or imagines he falls, through a fissure, deep water suddenly there to take him embrace him to hold him safe as he falls through its dark silky depths and her face glowing with another man's joy – Francis! – looking down at him through layers of ice, *my love, O my heart.*

Lost and Found

ALAN TUPPEN

After the burglary, it seemed natural to look in Portobello Road. Even a clapped-out Transit van would make the mainly downhill trip from Hampstead in less than an hour, so Godley considered a week ample for the journey from mantle to stall. So many of his treasures had come from the Portobello Road market in the first place that it gave him a grim amusement to prowl up and down the lines of stalls, searching among the cracked china and scratched tinplate for the nuggets of value that sometimes lay hidden there. It occurred to him with a jolt that maybe such stalls were the natural habitat of some items, which would make forays into the homes of new owners until they were again liberated by the eternal underworld, growing more and more tatty with each cycle, so that eventually they became unsaleable, and were either discarded as useless or taken home by the stallholder.

More out of routine than hope, Godley had started at the southern, expensive end, where items of real desirability nestled in shops rather than on stalls. But he found nothing he recognised, and by the time he had reached the Electric Cinema and the antiques were giving way to fruit and vegetables he was feeling peckish, so bought a bunch of bananas and sat on the cinema steps to eat them. A dishevelled man lurched out of the supermarket across the road clutching a half bottle of cheap whisky, and began to pick his way across, waving it uncertainly at the shoppers. Godley decided it was time to move, so got up and dumped his skins in a bin, leaving the man swaying in the middle of the road, mouthing unintelligibly.

The provisions stalls gave way to clothing, and as the road passed under the Westway flyover, the first junk stalls appeared, next to the gypsy caravan where he had once, in a moment of weakness, had his palm read. He remembered nothing of the reading now, only the woman's expensive jewellery and how too late he had remembered the saying about fools and their money. He had felt it was part of a learning process, that everyone should be taken for a ride at least once in their life, in order to learn humility. It was the same lesson gunfighters had to learn or die. No matter how sharp you thought you were, there was always someone sharper. Unfortunately, some people couldn't take it philosophically, and tended to get angry and aggressive, so there was always a heavy outside the caravan.

Now it seemed the gypsy had competition, for under the flyover makeshift cubicles had been erected, using sheets and threadbare carpets slung over poles, where anaemic girls and earnest young men with wispy red beards gave readings by tarot, or I Ching, or a host of other esoteric techniques. For all Godley knew, somewhere a luckless chicken could be having its entrails examined for portents.

But all this was a diversion, and Godley continued up past the second-hand television shops and stalls full of rusty tools, broken bicycle parts and obsolete domestic equipment.

It was on a barrow in front of the blank, featureless wall of the convent that he saw the box. His heart leapt when he saw it and he glanced anxiously at the stallholder in case he had given away his excitement, as this was the item above all others he was hoping to find, but the man was busy trying to show a lank-haired girl how to work the cream maker she had picked up.

'... but you've got to use silver top milk, none of this semi-skimmed stuff, or it won't work.'

The box was smallish, about half the size of a cigarette box, with a domed lid and four small feet. It had come down from his great-grandfather who, he had been told, had got it from a French prisoner of war who had fought in Russia as a young man. It was supposed to be a reliquary. The family was sceptical, but Godley thought it just possible, as in the centre of the lid was a shallow recess that could have held a medallion or a picture of some sort. There were marks that could be where whatever had been there had been levered out long ago, and in its place, a rough cross had been cut. The wood was dark and close-grained with smoky markings, and someone had suggested it could be olive wood, but to Godley that seemed unlikely if it really was Russian. Either way, it was old and empty and had been treasured by his family ever since his ancestor had obtained it. He could see it had a couple of new, deep scratches, presumably from when it had been thrown into a bag with the rest of the haul, but somehow it didn't seem to matter. They would be polished and become another part of the box's long history.

Godley tried to look nonchalant, flicking through a stack of dog-eared paperbacks and scratched 45s. He fingered a thirties bakelite clock that might actually be worth having, and his heart stopped when a woman picked up his box for a moment, but then laid it aside to look at the pile of magazines underneath. He had better move quickly.

'How much is the clock?' he asked the stallholder in a flat voice. The man came over. Pale eyes watered under the pulled-down peak of a tartan cap. His florid, open-pored face spoke of alcohol and tobacco.

'Firty quid.'

'Does it work?'

'Dunno mate.'

Godley was worried. If the man wanted that much for the clock, how much would he ask for the infinitely more valuable box, but the question had to be asked.

'And the box?'

'Fifty the box.'

Godley was encouraged.

'Seems a lot for that,' he ventured.

'I'm selling it for me mate, that's how much he said, but yeah, it does seem a lot. Tell you what, he's having a kip in the van. You can ask him. Yellow Tranny, round the corner. Ask for George. The clock's his an' all.'

Godley considered whether he should just pay the asking price, but then thought no, why should he have to pay over the odds to get his own property back, and walked to the corner to look for the van, all the time keeping an eye on the stall in case someone else should pick up his box. The van was unmistakable. Once Telecom yellow, the bruised and battered vehicle had been touched up in a thousand shades among the blisters of rust and hand painted ochre primer. A figure was apparently sleeping in the driver's seat. Beer cans and half empty fried chicken boxes covered the passenger seat beside him. Godley hesitated, then tapped on the glass. The man opened one eye, looked at Godley for a second, opened the other, then wound down the window. The reek of smoke and beer flowed out.

'Are you George?' Godley asked.

'Who wants to know?' the man wheezed.

'I've come from the stall, round the corner,' Godley

explained. 'I wanted to ask you about the box, and how much it is.'

'I told him fifty notes, or has he forgot?' And then, 'You in the trade?'

'No,' Godley replied, 'I just like it.'

'Ah. Well, I thought at first it might be a tea caddy, but it's got no lining, then I saw the cross on top, so I s'pose it must be for something religious, like keeping the wafers in, p'raps.'

'Well,' Godley ventured, 'I thought fifty pounds was a bit dear, especially since it's quite badly scratched.'

The man snorted. 'That's why it's only fifty quid.'

Would you do a deal if I had the clock as well, say sixty pounds for the two, because I don't even know if the clock works?'

George looked down at his hands and picked at his ragged nails for a moment, then looked up.

'Make it sixty-five.'

'All right.'

Godley was well pleased, but strove not to show it. George opened the cab door, leaned out alarmingly and bellowed. 'Eddie!'

'Shortly the stall holder appeared at the corner. 'Yes mate?'

George bellowed again. 'Let this geezer have the box and the clock. Okay? He can pay me here.'

Godley took out his wallet and handed over the money. George quickly scanned it, deftly folded it and slipped it into his trouser pocket, then without a word wound the window back up and sank back into the seat, eyes shut.

Godley hurried back to the stall to find his purchases already in a plastic bag, waiting for him. He couldn't wait to get home and restore the box to its rightful place, and headed towards his car, parked somewhere the other side of Ladbroke Grove, wondering as he walked what the nuns would have made of the box, which he had found right outside their walls, if they had only known. It was ironic it had been just there.

Afterwards, looking back, he could remember passing the Caribbean restaurant, the heavy reggae beat pouring out of the open door, as much a garnish as the hot pepper sauce on the tables, when suddenly he was spreadeagled against the wall in an alley, one youth holding him, another with a knife to his throat, blond bristles and hard blue eyes inches from his face. When the youth spoke he could smell the stale lager on his breath, and the words were commands, not requests. 'Wallet. Watch. And what's in the bag?'

It was torn from Godley's hand before he could answer, but his brain cried, 'No, no, not again, please.'

The blond youth looked into the bag, reached in and opened the box, then with an obscenity flung bag and contents away from him. 'Crap. Come on Jag.'

Calmly the two walked away and disappeared among the people in the street. Dazed and scared, Godley rubbed his bruised wrists and staggered over to where the bag lay, up against the wall. Looking inside, he saw glass from the shattered clock face everywhere. One of the little feet on the box looked broken, but at least he still had it, that was the main thing. He still had his car keys too, and running back to the car, shoved the bag under the seat, cutting his finger on a splinter of glass sticking through the plastic. He locked the doors and got his *A–Z* out of the glove box to find the nearest police station.

He was shown into a waiting room by a young constable, and while he waited for someone to come and take down the details of the attack, he looked in the bag again. He wasn't going to let it out of his sight for a minute. The clock would surely be a write off. Even if the glass could be replaced, the bakelite case was badly chipped and cracked, and he doubted it could be repaired so that the damage wouldn't show. He took out the box and looked it over. The foot he had thought broken was on a kind of short stalk, and along the front of the box, along a couple of parallel lines he had assumed were carving detail, the wood seemed to be coming away. He picked at it with his thumbnail, but it wasn't loose, it was a solid piece. He wiggled the foot and it moved a little, so he hooked his nail around it and pulled. Gradually he managed to lever the piece out until he could get a grip with his fingers. It had been stuck fast by years of polish and dirt until thrown against the wall of the alley, but when he pulled it out, he found a shallow drawer lined with paper illuminated with the most exquisitely written cyrillic lettering in glowing red, blue and gold, and in the centre of the drawer, held in place by a sliver of gold, was a twist of hair. He could read no Russian, but at once he knew his great-grandfather had been right. The box really was a reliquary, and it had never been empty. This holy thing had been there among his family all the time, and a sense of wonder filled him.

A detective sergeant came in. 'Would you like to tell us what happened, sir?'

But Godley was on his feet, smiling. 'It's all right officer, it doesn't matter now.'

About the authors

Tim Connery has a dog with a propensity to chew official documents. This is his first publication. He has also been shortlisted for the 1995 Ian St James Awards.

Alan Day is wont to misprint his own age as fifty. He too is previously unpublished. 'Coming Down South' is joint winner of the Jack Trevor Story Memorial Prize.

Alix Edwards works in publishing, marketing children's reference books. This is her first published story.

Elspeth Edwards is now engaged in some tedious research, visiting both Paris and Nice for her novel of suspense. She hopes to include Preston Sturges somewhere in the book.

Crispin Green was born in Lambeth and raised in Montreal. He has a daughter aged two and a cat and lives in south London. A winner in the main Competition, 'Trigger' is also joint winner of the Jack Trevor Story Memorial Prize.

Sheena Joughin is working on a collection of stories about the characters of 'A Mackinstosh Sky'. She also writes poems and occasional reviews for *Crafts* and the *T.L.S.* She lives in London.

Francis King is the author of more than twenty novels, as well as short stories, poetry, biography, and an autobiography, *Yesterday Came Suddenly* (Constable).

Hari Kunzru does research for a TV company and writes on technology and culture for *Wired* magazine.

Deborah Levy is a poet, novelist and playwright. Her publications include poetry, *An Amorous Discourse in the Suburbs of Hell*, and short stories, *Ophelia and the Great Lake*. She has published three novels *Beautiful Mutants*, *Swallowing Geography* and *The Unloved*.

A winner in the previous London Short Story Competition, **Alison Love** was also shortlisted for the Ian St James Competition in 1994.

Simon Miles has written for *The European*, *The Guardian* and other national newspapers. He currently runs a live arts cabaret club in the West End.

Marion Molteno is the author of a collection of short stories, *A Language in Common* (Women's Press), and a novel, *A Shield of Coolest Air* (Shola Books), winner of the 1993 John Thomas Prize.

Lauretta Ngcobo has recently returned to her native South Africa, after living in London for more than twenty-five years. Her most recent novel is *And They Didn't Die* (Virago).

Geoff Nicholson has now lived in London longer than he's ever lived anywhere else. His latest novel is called *Footsucker*.

John Riethmüller works as a freelance copy editor. He also writes songs and is a member of the Pink Singers.

Kirsty Seymour-Ure has been writing 'ever since I can

remember', and works as a freelance editor. She was a winner in the first London Short Story Competition.

Deirdre Shanahan's stories have been published in magazines in both England and the United States, and she has written plays for stage and radio.

Iain Sinclair has lived in London since 1965. Between 1970 and 1979, he ran Albion Village Press. His most recent novel is *Radon Daughters* (Cape).

Atima Srivastava was born in Bombay and now lives in north London, dividing her time between writing and video editing. Her novel *Transmission* is published by Serpent's Tail.

Alan Tuppen currently works in a garden centre. He has been writing 'on and off since the late 1960s'. This is his first published story.

Mark Walder works as a freelance writer. He has written extensively for the gay press, specialising in the arts and travel; this is his first published piece of fiction.